SCOTCH ON THE ROCKS

OR

"THE CAMANACHD CUP"

SCOTCH ON THE ROCKS

OR

"THE CAMANACHD CUP"

*Adapted from original Stage Play and
Screenplay of the same name*

ROY McCORMICK

© Roy McCormick, 2013

Published by Roy McCormick

NOTE: This work is entirely fictional, and any resemblances to persons living or dead, are purely coincidental.

The rights of Roy McCormick to be identified as the author of this work have been asserted in accordance with the Copyright, Designs and Patents Act 1988.

A CIP catalogue record for this book is available from the British Library.

ISBN 978-0-9576322-0-2

Book cover design and layout by Clare Brayshaw

Prepared and printed by:

York Publishing Services Ltd
64 Hallfield Road
Layerthorpe
York YO31 7ZQ

Tel: 01904 431213

Website: www.yps-publishing.co.uk

PLAYS BY THE SAME AUTHOR

FULL LENGTH: SCOTCH ON THE ROCKS
BLACKMAIL IN BENIDORM
CULTURE CRAZY

ONE ACTS: THE CHIEF GUIDE
THE CAMANACHD CUP
A CHRISTMAS CRACKER
MIX-UP IN MARBELLA
THE PUNCH PARTY
ROYAL RELATIONS
THE LOVE OF THE FATHER

SCREENPLAY: SCOTCH ON THE ROCKS

ABOUT THE AUTHOR

Roy McCormick is a former Whisky Industry executive who has written 10 Plays which have been performed throughout Scotland. This book is adapted from his Stage Play, and he has also completed a Screenplay version.

He is an Award Winning Actor, Producer and Playwright and has acted in Hollywood USA. He lives in Glasgow with his wife and has a son in Boston, USA and a daughter in Wales.

CONTENTS

Chapter 1

LONDON

There was an eerie silence over London. It was approaching 4am, and even the usual late night sitting in the House of Commons was finished. All at Westminster had gone home for the night. Big Ben struck the hour, and the pigeons in Parliament Square reacted as if on cue, as they were swept up into the air through a gust of swirling wind, their fluttering wings disturbing the pre-dawn peace. They disappeared into the dark night sky and as was their habit, came to rest on the roof of Westminster Abbey. All was quiet once more.

Suddenly, a red MG sports car broke the silence. It was also breaking the speed limit as it endeavoured to beat the lights at Westminster Bridge. Its driver, Penelope Whitehouse, was obviously in a hurry. She didn't care if she disturbed a few pigeons. As long as she didn't disturb the Metropolitan Police as she went through the lights. Probably Her Majesty's finest were not at their most alert in these early hours of the morning.

She turned into Whitehall and came to a halt quite abruptly, outside one of the Government Buildings, not far from Downing Street. She had barely time to check her watch when a young man dressed in black jacket, striped trousers and wearing a bowler hat, came rushing out of The Home Office building, carrying a briefcase and a holdall. He got in the car.

"Sorry I'm late" she said. "No problem" he replied, placing his holdall in the small space behind the two seats. "I've just arrived myself."

"We have nine hours to get there" said Penny wistfully.

"I'm beginning to think we should have left last night after all."

She put her foot down on the accelerator, and sped off through the still empty streets of Central London.

"You forget, I had to attend that meeting with the Minister last night" her passenger reminded her, as if he could have done without it. "It didn't finish till 10 o'clock."

"Of course" she replied somewhat apologetically.

"I forgot about that. It's just... I don't think we are going to make it in time."

As she spoke, she went through another amber light and swerved out to pass an early morning Cleansing Department lorry in Trafalgar Square. She just missed a cursing refuse collector, and caused her companion to speculate, "If you drive like that, it won't be for the want of trying."

He watched her aggressive driving technique for a moment, and added "You're not related to Jackie Stewart by any chance?" referring to the iconic former Scottish Formula One Racing Driver.

"We were given so little notice. I mean, it was such a sudden death" she reflected.

"Death does come quite suddenly, to those concerned" he replied, trying to make light of it. Anyhow, she was barely listening as her thoughts were elsewhere.

"And the funeral was arranged so quickly."

"At least we can share the driving" he suggested as he already fancied the idea of driving such a sporty open-topped car. Perhaps he thought it would be safer, in any case he wasn't a very good passenger, and this was going to be a long drive. They proceeded on their way through the almost empty streets, making for the Motorway to Scotland. It would be two hours before the sun would rise.

Penny had only met Roderick Ponsonby a couple of times before. After graduating with a Marketing Degree at London University, she had started as a Management Trainee with Marks & Spencer. Following a couple of minor promotions, she became a Deputy Store Manager in Milton Keynes, before recently taking up her present position as Public Relations Manager, for one of the World's leading Scotch Whisky Distillers.

Although based in their World Marketing Headquarters in Piccadilly, she had yet to visit their distilleries in the Highlands of Scotland. The sudden death of the Chief Guide at the Glendivot Distillery provided her with the ideal opportunity to go North, attend the funeral, meet the staff, appoint a successor, and rejuvenate the Marketing efforts at the location. She was charged with the task of planning and organising the development of the Brands Worldwide.

Glendivot was the Company's signature single malt, and the Distillery was almost one hundred years old. Sales had been expanding steadily since the Second World War.

They had started to encourage visitors to come and see the distillation process, have a 'Dram' and hopefully purchase the 'Cratur' while they were at it. They certainly hoped the visitors would talk to their friends about their tour, and the hospitality they received. They already had achieved some success and now employed several guides to show people round.

Penny had spent her first few weeks doing research into the Company, its products and markets, and had come to the conclusion that, if she played her cards right, she might be able to apply for some financial assistance from the Department of Tourism. She found that The Government had set a new increased budget for the development of Tourism in the United Kingdom.

In the early 1970s, it had in its wisdom, recognised that hundreds of thousands of the British public were going to sunnier climes abroad on Continental package tours. Unless something was done about it, more and more of their hard earned cash would continue to go into the French and Spanish economies. It was time to attract tourists to our own Country, and we had to utilise what assets we had.

Penny had surmised that, since Scotland didn't have the weather, at least the Tourist Board could boast of its world renowned whisky industry. Why not get on the bandwagon and apply for the Government Grants that were available? To succeed, she had to firstly persuade the appropriate Government Department that it was a sound investment.

Her Company had agreed to set up a commercially viable Visitor Centre at its main Distillery at the picturesque village of Glendivot in Speyside. This charming community was known as the 'Whisky Capital' of the Highlands. Rome may have been built on seven hills, but Glendivot they say, was built on seven stills.

The Company already had a modest Reception Centre, with a few artefacts and some old sepia photographs of early employees at the start of the 20th Century. Penny wanted to expand this into an attractive Museum with an accompanying up-market shop. There, they would sell the full range of the Company products including their internationally known Single Malts, and their range of Blended Whiskies. These sales could be augmented by a variety of high quality Scottish goods such as tartans, kilts and associated clothing, as well as the bespoke items required by the lucrative hunting, shooting and fishing brigade.

This could probably be achieved within the Company's own budget, but it would take time. She wanted to forge ahead of the competition by developing an Audio Visual Theatre presentation, illustrating the history, development and importance of 'Uisge beatha, the Water of Life.'

Together with a new Restaurant, it would require financial assistance through The Government's 'Development of Tourism' initiative. She was hopeful that the new Government would be more sympathetic to the development of the whisky industry. After all, the new Prime Minister was known to like his "dram". She was also ambitious enough to want her Company to become the leading Visitor attraction in the Highlands. That is where her passenger, Roderick Ponsonby came in.

He was a handsome athletic man of thirty years of age. His mother came from a wealthy Banking family who lived in Bromley. She had died shortly after he was born, and his father had never returned home after the War. As a result, he was brought up by a rich maiden aunt in Kent. This probably accounted for his rather quaint old fashioned ways.

His aunt reared him in a rather strict traditional manner, which was more common in the 1930s than the fast changing post war era. Despite his narrow upbringing, and lack of a father figure at home, he did win a scholarship to Cambridge where he studied modern languages. University life was quite a culture shock, and he suddenly found that he had been living up till then, in somewhat of a cocoon.

Clearly he had been limited, living within the straightjacket of his aunt's influence. While he still enjoyed reading Tolstoy and Hemmingway from her extensive library, going with her to orchestral concerts in the Royal Albert Hall and attending plays by Noel Coward, Chekhov and Ibsen, he nevertheless took full advantage of the broader social side of University life.

However, he had not yet found the right girl, but he was willing to persevere in his quest, and enjoy the experience he had previously been denied. Privately, his maiden aunt thought that he was 'Making a meal' of this aspect of his life. He made sure he enjoyed every course and he displayed a good appetite for it. He also found success representing the University on the hockey pitch and had even been an Olympic trialist.

After taking his Degree, he applied for the Civil Service. There, he worked in several Ministries, where he found the traditional culture well suited to his nature. He was a natural conservative, where his comfort zone was adhering to the well established procedures and rituals for which the hierarchy of the Civil Service was famous. Indeed, his habits were so entrenched, that he probably needed a good woman to sort him out!

He had been making steady, if not spectacular progress, up the hierarchical structure of the Civil Service, hoping ultimately to achieve a position in the Foreign Office. He was however, impatient to progress faster. Having now reached thirty years of age, he was beginning to think that if he did not make a breakthrough soon, he would have to go into politics. 'The things a man must stoop to, to get on in this world,' he often thought to himself.

To his surprise, his nomination to become Conservative candidate for the constituency of Maidstone, Kent, was accepted. Perhaps it was due to the fact the Mayor was a cousin of his aunt. Whatever the reason, he decided to go for it, and again, a little to his surprise, he was successful with a modest majority in the recent General Election, which saw the Tories return to power under Edward Heath.

He could not believe his luck when he was soon appointed Under Secretary of State for Tourism due to a relatively minor expenses scandal involving the previous incumbent. It appeared that he had been fast-tracked for promotion already. He was given the authority to approve financial grants for certain Tourism initiatives. There was no way he would have made such rapid progress had he remained with the Civil Service.

Penny had decided on a three-pronged attack on Roderick Ponsonby. First, she had to manipulate a one-to-one meeting with him. That was hopefully the easy part. Secondly, she had to work her wicked way with him, and persuade him to come North with her to see her proposed initiatives for himself. Finally, she had to persuade him to provide the finance to allow her Company to expand its Visitor Centre ahead of the competition.

She had obtained an invitation to a Cocktail Reception held for people in the trade, at the Dorchester Hotel, in Park Lane, and hosted by the Department of Tourism.

Now Penny was in her mid twenties, and not being unattractive herself, had invested in a most alluring cocktail dress in the pale blue hue of Cambridge University. At least that would provide a conversation starter. Its length would reveal that she had a particularly shapely pair of legs. She knew exactly how men's minds worked, even if they were Members of Parliament.

At that time, she had only met him once before, when he spoke at a Management Seminar on 'The Importance of Tourism to the UK Economy.' She had shaken his hand, but would have to forgive him if he didn't remember her, as she was only one of 250 delegates on that occasion.

Her research had established that he could be of value to her, as he had his hands on the purse strings, and being a typical woman, she was determined that he opened the purse for her.

As the Taxpayer-paid cocktails flowed, and the level of conversation increased, she finally caught sight of her prey, standing near the room's large Louis XV marble fireplace. However, it wasn't the replica fireplace which caught her attention. It wasn't even Roderick Ponsonby! Not to put too fine a point on it, it was the rather buxom, rosy cheeked, effervescent woman who was talking to him, who caught her eye.

The lady in question was clearly holding Ponsonby's attention, and her body language suggested that they had known each other for a long time. In fact, their conversation was so animated that she concluded that this was not the time to interrupt.

While continuing to make polite conversation with others in her group, she kept her eye on the couple at the marble fireplace, and waited for her opportunity. She had to be patient for the pair continued their lively conversation for some time. Penny hoped the same lady was not also asking him for Government money. Despite the distractions of the cocktail party, she gradually became aware that she recognised the lady in question. But where had she seen her before? What was the connection?

She wrestled with this conundrum for some time as she tried to make polite conversation with her colleagues in the milling throng, as they all endeavoured to communicate with one another, without losing their dignity by spilling their champagne or canapés. It was not easy for her to carry out an intelligent conversation while her mind was on other things.

She was sure she recognised the extrovert lady who appeared to have such a hold over the Under Secretary for Tourism, but the connection eluded her, as her thoughts were constantly interrupted by various people who joined in her group's conversation.

Suddenly the talkative lady who had been holding the Under Secretary's attention for so long, had broken off her conversation, left him, and appeared to be heading in Penny's direction! The expression on her face suggested that she recognised Penny, even through the throng. If so, then Penny's problem was about to be solved one way or another.

"Penny my darling! Fancy meeting you here! How lovely to see you, after all these years!" greeted the ebullient buxom lady, with the loud floral print dress that did nothing for her figure. Whereupon, she enveloped Penny in a bear-hug of which a Japanese Sumo wrestler would have been proud. Penny just managed to keep her champagne glass under control, but half of her canapé fell to the well-carpeted floor. Fortunately, there was no damage to her new dress.

Still, she could not make the connection, but obviously this breath of fresh air was a long lost friend. She was in the process of narrowing it down to her school or University days, when her loquacious friend put her out of her misery.

"How is my little Yum Yum?" It only took Penny a moment to link her friend's question to her Buckinghamshire School Production of Gilbert and Sullivan's "The Mikado."

"Beryl Beveridge! How are you?" she blurted out, just before her embarrassment was exposed. Beryl was known at school as "Beryl the Peril" for obvious reasons. She was a year ahead of Penny at Great Missenden College, and was appropriately cast as the venomous 'Katisha' in G & S's Operetta. Penny had been equally well cast as the delightfully attractive 'Yum Yum', the principal soprano, in the same production.

Beryl had always been larger than life in more ways than one. Even as a teenager, she was well endowed, not only with two large attributes in front, but also with an over enthusiastic personality that was all-consuming, and made her the life and soul of the party. Obviously after observing her commanding the conversation with the Under Secretary for Tourism, Penny was in no doubt that she had not lost this talent.

After a few reminiscences about their experience in 'The Mikado,' and the school hockey team, in which the burly Beryl, weighing in at about 12 stones, was a formidable goalkeeper, Penny could see that she was now at least 3 stones heavier. She had therefore given up both hockey and her first love of horse riding. Penny did not know which came first, and who was the more relieved, Beryl or the horse! However, she suspected it must have been the horse!

By the time these pleasantries had been completed, Penny had ushered her old school friend sufficiently away from her party, to ascertain that Beryl was now running her own small travel agent's business in Pinner, hence her presence at this function. Having clarified that matter, she then informed her old friend of why she was there, and her desire to meet the Under Secretary of State. How to obtain an introduction had been troubling her all along.

"You obviously know him well" suggested Penny, perhaps implying that she was a little surprised that even a Junior Government Minister was prepared to spend so much time with a relatively modest independent travel agent.

"Oh Rod?" exclaimed Beryl, rather dismissively. "God yes! He is my cousin! I haven't seen him for donkeys. Not since my sister's wedding. We were just getting up-to-date with our families, and he didn't know I was now in the travel business."

Penny could not believe her luck. Here was an old friend, she hadn't seen for years, who had a direct connection with the very man she was trying to corner! She explained her situation, and the reason she was anxious to take Beryl's cousin up North to her Distillery. Fortunately Beryl had always been a positive optimist, and could not have been more helpful. An introduction would be no problem.

Better still, they were able to chat about old times, until the most opportune moment of the evening arrived. This was when they saw that Rod Ponsonby had just parted company with an influential, but rather pompous and boring old boy from the British Council. Rod was making his way towards the substantial buffet that was provided, courtesy of the poor old British Taxpayer once more. Penny's first objective had been achieved with surprising ease.

While a little bit of Beryl went a long way, even after all these years, Penny was prepared to put up with her company a little longer, at least until she obtained her introduction. Beryl did not let her down. She introduced Penny as her long lost friend, who wanted him to do her a favour! She even went further by insisting that she would take it personally if he refused, and it was more than his life was worth if he let her down!

As far as Rod Ponsonby was concerned, he did not require any threats, or even persuasion, for one look at the elegant and attractive young lady in the Cambridge blue dress, was enough. It would be an unexpected pleasure for him to do her a favour. Beryl's up-and-at-them manner rather threw Penny. She much preferred the more subtle approach, stalking her prey until there was no escape.

However, her friend's approach had the desired effect, because in a very short time, he agreed to go to Scotland with Penny, to assess her plans for the development of her Visitor Centre, and to consider whether they merited Government financial support.

What he did not tell her however, was that for the last 3 years or so, he had been planning to travel to Scotland in search of his long lost father, and ascertain whether he was still alive! He had never returned home after the Second World War. The proposal to accompany such a charming young lady as Penny, soon put an end to his procrastination.

Penny had good reason to go home satisfied with the outcome of the evening. She could hardly believe how easy it had been! It only took one more meeting to work out the details, and agree dates for the trip.

It was then that he indicated that he might combine business with pleasure, by taking a few days holiday at the same time. This actually suited Penny very well, because she could not afford to spend all her time with him at the Distillery. She knew she would require several days to complete the other business she planned at the Distillery.

Chapter 2
JOURNEY NORTH

Roderick Ponsonby was one of the youngest, and last of the Members of Parliament to wear the traditional black jacket and striped trousers. If truth be known, he had simply decided to wear out his 'Civil Service Uniform.' This fashion was fast disappearing by the early 1970s, and Penny thought, the sooner the better. She did not know what her work colleagues in Scotland would make of this young man, coming up to the Highlands dressed like that.

She consoled herself with a wry smile, as she mused that maybe they will think he is an undertaker! Well, they *were* going to a funeral after all! At least he had removed his bowler hat for the journey, and she wondered if he would survive the open-topped car journey. At the speed she was driving, so did he!

Her first objective was to get past Spaghetti Junction at Birmingham and on to the M6 North before the early morning rush hour. This they managed with ease. Her second objective was to use the journey to soften him up by establishing a friendly business relationship with him.

Despite his rather stuffy first impression, she used her considerable inter-personal skills to establish some kind of rapport, as the journey progressed. She became aware that he appeared to be taking considerable interest in her sporty little car, and began to get the impression he was itching to drive it.

They stopped for a break at the Keele Service Station, and she noted how much he appreciated her offer to let him drive. His reaction was that of a little boy with a new toy, and after a few miles, he could not resist the temptation to drive as fast as she had been doing. However, she was impressed by his driving skills, and soon complimented him, by letting him know.

Meanwhile, she steered a cautious diplomatic course, trying to convince him of her ideas for attracting tourists to visit the Distillery. She played a great deal on the fact that Scotch Whisky was a major exporter and essential to the Country's economy and balance of payments. She explained that she had already made arrangements to recruit multi-lingual guides to show the foreigners round, and that her plans for an audio-visual cinema would include headsets with commentaries in different languages. In some ways, she was ahead of her time. She was therefore offering employment opportunities to the local community and potential growth for the tourist industry.

However, she was careful to avoid boring him, and interspersed her brainwashing with some more refreshing social conversation, a technique that she had perfected at Finishing School. She also made full use of the low-slung seats in the sports car to show off her legs! By the time they reached the Scottish border, she was a long way to achieving her second objective!

As if ordained, the clouds which had been threatening for some time, suddenly turned very dark, and before they knew it, they felt the first drops of rain.

"Just like the thing" said Penny.

"Welcome to Bonnie Scotland!"

"We had better pull in here, and get the hood up" suggested Ponsonby, as he saw the Gretna Green Service Station loom up ahead of them, not a minute too soon.

When they drew to a halt, the whole car park seemed awash with activity, as people rushed to and from cars, hastily putting up umbrellas, and trying to avoid a soaking in the deluge that had now descended upon them.

"This is unbelievable" cried Penny. "I do not believe this is happening" as she struggled to release the hood.

"You get back in the car, and leave this to me" called Ponsonby as he displayed commendable chivalry, and a degree of authority. He then started wrestling with the stubborn contraption. He had taken on more than he bargained for.

"When did you last have this hood up?" he enquired.

"I couldn't tell you. I have no idea. I always drive with it down." 'And your foot down as well' thought Ponsonby to himself, after having experienced her fast driving. By this time it was a full blown thunderstorm, and the interior of the car was drenched with water.

Her wet skirt was clinging to her shapely thighs, and Ponsonby felt a rare moment of excitement, as she dried herself down with a small towel, which she kept in her glove compartment, for emergencies. She was an expert at subtly seducing men in a most natural way.

She had to shout to be heard above the noise of the spattering rain. He managed to cover her with the hood, but he continued to have problems fixing it securely. He was becoming thoroughly soaked, but despite his discomfort, he ultimately managed to attach it in place.

As he squeezed into the confined space of the two-seater, and sat on the wet seat he gave out an involuntary oath! Whereupon, she observed, "Look at you. You are soaking wet, I hope you are not beginning to regret this."

With true English stoicism, he countered, "Now what makes you think that? I've always wanted to do this," as he borrowed her towel, and tried to stop the rain from running down his neck. Penny noted that he did have a sense of humour after all. She checked her watch, adjusted her skirt, and moved on.

It soon became obvious that they could not complete the remaining 300 miles with Ponsonby soaked literally from top to bottom! Not even his Daks black jacket and Liberty's top quality striped trousers could repel such a downpour.

While the cockpit of the car was small and potentially intimate, she had to be practical too. "You are wet through" she said, stating the obvious.

"To the skin" he replied with feeling.

"You can't carry on like that for the rest of the journey. There's nothing for it. You will have to change." She paused, and thought. "Do you have any spare clothes?"

"In the bag" he replied.

"Right... I think this is just a passing shower. Look, there is some blue sky up ahead. We will stop as soon as it is over...and we can get rid of your clothes."

"But, they cost me a lot of money" he joked, before protesting rather mischievously, "Besides, I hardly know you." 'At least he hadn't yet lost his sense of humour,' thought Penny.

A few miles farther on, after he had tried to dry his hands and face with the towel which Penny passed to him, she took a slip road off the M74 on to a quiet country road in the Borders between Ecclefechan and Lockerbie. She stopped the car a hundred yards past a lane leading up to a rather remote farm. There was no sign of life, other than a few belted Galloway cows chewing the cud in the field.

Rod was thankful for the opportunity to divest himself of his wet and uncomfortable clothes. He obviously could not do this within the confines of the two-seater, and let's face it, it was a bit premature to strip off in front of a young lady he hardly knew.

He therefore jumped out the car, took out his holdall, and had a quick look around. There was no traffic to be seen, and the only sign of life, apart from the cows munching away, was a small flock of starlings frolicking in the trees. He went to the rear of the car and proceeded to strip off to his vest and underpants. Before he had time to open the holdall, a policeman riding a bicycle, came down the lane from the farm and turned into the road in full view of the hapless Ponsonby.

The policeman's surprise was such that he almost fell off his bicycle. It was matched by that of Ponsonby who got the fright of his life, panicked, grabbed his wet clothes and holdall, and jumped back in the car in his underwear, beside a startled Penny. "Now wait a minute" she exclaimed, as he knelt on his seat, stuffing the clothes and holdall into the small luggage compartment behind them.

In the confined space, he was almost on top of her. "No, it's not what you think" he tried to reassure her, as his backside brushed her face.

"I know what I'm thinking. It's what you are thinking that worries me" she replied.

"There's a policeman out there" he stammered.

"Thank God for that" she said, with some relief. Nevertheless, she could not help admiring his strong athletic physique, especially in such close proximity. Somehow he looked more muscular, masculine and attractive in his underwear, than he was in his black jacket and striped trousers.

By this time, the policeman had reached the car, alighted from his bike, took his time to park it with great care, and slowly, as policemen do for maximum effect, bent down and put his head through the window, which Penny had conveniently wound down.

"Well well, what have we here then? A striptease show?" he enquired in time honoured fashion. Ponsonby turned round and sat down trying to cover his...embarrassment.

"It's not what you think Officer" he pleaded. His aunt had taught him to always call a policeman 'Officer' to make them feel important.

"Now where have I heard that before?" replied the sergeant, for that is what he was. Clearly he was a man of experience in these matters.

"I'm wet. I mean, I *was* wet...was caught in that thunderstorm." Ponsonby appealed to the officer's good sense. Unfortunately, by this time the sun was out.

"Thunderstorm? What thunderstorm?" enquired the sergeant, quite oblivious to the recent downpour.

Penny thought to herself, 'Only in Scotland would they think it had been a light shower.' She didn't know that the sergeant had spent the last half hour blissfully enjoying a morning coffee indoors, with the farmer.

"The thunderstorm we just went through at Gretna" replied Ponsonby.

"You don't say" continued the man in uniform, not at all convinced.

"I do. I mean.......my clothes" Ponsonby pointed behind him.

"Yes, your clothes. That is what I was wondering. Where are they?" he asked, knowing full well, the answer.

"They are in the back. See. They are soaking." explained Ponsonby, appealing to his sense of reason.

"Soaking you say" continued his inquisitor milking the situation.

By this time, Penny felt she had to come to her companion's rescue. "It's all right Officer. He was just going to change into dry clothes."

"Kinky" replied the Officer. "So he's a cross-dresser too?"

"*Dry* clothes! Not *my* clothes!" she appealed.

"You know we are not accustomed to men going around in their underwear in this part of the World" explained the man in blue as he considered the situation.

"No of course not" Ponsonby grovelled. "Here in Scotland, we are more civilised."

"Yes, of course" agreed Ponsonby.

The Officer made full use of the pregnant pause, rubbing his chin, before delivering his verdict.

"All right. I'll let you off this time." he said rather patronisingly. He made for his bicycle, then turned and warned the Under Scretary of State. "But don't you wet yourself again!" and off he went, making sure they could not see the smile on his face. Her Majesty's Government Minister had been made to feel very small by the country policeman.

Ponsonby struggled to retrieve his holdall, got out the car and started to rummage for suitable dry clothes. As he did so, it started to rain again, so he gathered his bag and clothes and returned to the car having made no progress.

"Not again" exclaimed Penny as he entered the car and shut the door.

"It's raining again," he replied as she started the engine and put on the windscreen wipers. He proceeded to endeavour to put on another shirt and a pair of trousers while she reversed at speed, to the lane, and accelerated back in the direction of the Motorway.

All these manoeuvres involved a fair amount of swaying to and fro, resulting in Ponsonby losing his balance, hitting his head on the roof and the driver's mirror and his backside on the gearstick and bumping into Penny's face, and almost landing on her lap. Having only met her travelling companion for the first time a few days ago, she had to smile to herself. It was indeed an intimate little sports car.

Chapter 3

GLENDIVOT

That morning, while Penny and Ponsonby were travelling North through the rain, it was a bright clear day in the village of Glendivot, nestling in Speyside, in the Highlands of Scotland. It was far enough North beyond the Grampian mountains, and near the Moray Firth, to be in a relatively dry area of the Country.

The village had a population of about 1,500, yet it boasted more whisky distilleries per head than any other area in the world. It was a sleepy little community where the farmers and the whisky distillers lived in harmony and interdependence.

The farmers would sell the barley of their fields to the distillers, who added water, and converted it into whisky. They then happily resold it back to the farmers, who equally happily consumed it, and converted it into urine.

There were three churches serving the needs of different denominations, so they catered for everyone. A pleasant salmon-filled river flowed through the village, and it even boasted the ancient Balroonie Castle which had survived remarkably well for centuries, considering its proximity to the bloody Culloden battlefield some 30 miles away. No doubt the Duke of Cumberland or General

Wade had used Balroonie Castle as a barracks for their troops while fighting the Jacobite Rebellion.

The locals called the area 'God's Country,' and with much justification. Glendivot even had its own golf course, bowling green and shinty team, so it was really quite civilised.

It wasn't too surprising that the locals occasionally found the interference of outsiders rather irritating. Hence 'Outsiders' were treated as such for many years. They used to say that if it took a good malt whisky 8 years to mature, then an incomer should expect it to take as long to become accepted.

For generations the population had lived an almost idyllic existence, reaping a healthy livelihood from the land, and rearing sheep and cattle for the local markets. This was enhanced by the employment opportunities offered by the whisky industry which had enjoyed exceptional growth since the late 19th Century. At one time there were up to seven working distilleries in and around the town, and dozens more within a twenty mile radius.

This little Nirvana's economy was augmented by the landed gentry and wealthy 'foreigners' from England, and even farther afield, who came regularly for the grouse and pheasant shooting seasons. Many locals also made a good living from the salmon fishing fraternity. All this was good, repeat and almost guaranteed business.

The prudent ones lived quite royally and they even boasted Royal neighbours with Balmoral not far away, over the hills in Deeside. A few however, fell foul of 'The

Cratur.' (Locals that is, for I can't speak for the Royals.)

Most Distillery Managers in the area lived in Company houses, and the Glendivot Manager, Angus McDougall, lived with his wife Mary and her widowed mother Mrs. Grant, in Balroonie House, just across the road from the Distillery.

It was an imposing solid granite mansion of about eight rooms, rather typical of traditional Scottish Presbyterian Ministers' manses. It was large enough to be used as a 'Bed and Breakfast' and with some investment, could be expanded into a small private hotel, as it also had a large garden.

In fact, Mary had obtained approval to make changes to the house, but these had to be put on hold when her father died the previous year, and her mother had to vacate the Manse, and move in with her. Mary had already increased the size of her lounge, by removing part of the hallway wall.

While this had the advantage of providing more room for what she intended as the main guests' lounge, it had the temporary disadvantage of exposing them to the downstairs cloakroom/cum toilet she had in the hallway. This, she intended to relocate upstairs. This would make room for her plan to install a small neat reception desk, and combine it with the adjacent cupboard, to provide some limited office space.

At 7.30am that morning, the alarm at Angus's side of the bed rang in the big front bedroom upstairs. He had been totally immersed in one of his favourite dreams, from which he often awoke, just as they were becoming exciting.

On this occasion, he was a powerful Roman Senator, dressed in his mandatory toga, reclining on his couch in his opulent villa overlooking the Bay of Naples. He was surrounded by a bevy of beauties who would do justice to a Cecil B de Mille Hollywood film epic. Needless to say some of these nubile creatures were performing exotic, and even erotic dances before him, to his great satisfaction.

Meanwhile other equally alluring and shapely maidens, were attending to his every, or almost every wish, as they fawned over him, posing provocatively, offering him tureens of food and fruit, and goblets of fine wines, and goodness knows what else. Naturally, they were barely and seductively attired in diaphanous robes which left little to his imagination.

It was one of those dreams he had enjoyed over the years, but he could never quite understand how he was consistently frustrated, by arousing from his slumber, just as the titillating excitement was about to reach its climax.

More often than not, it was his long suffering, yet faithful wife Mary, who woke him from his heavenly dreams, and very quickly, brought him back down to earth with a thump!

On this particular morning, he was perspiring profusely as he gradually regained consciousness, and, with his eyes still half-shut, he grappled unsuccessfully with the noisy alarm, until it fell on the floor, still ringing. He then tried to go back to sleep, and return to the fun and games going on at his Roman villa.

Mary, her head once more in curlers, and wearing a mask over her eyes, appeared from under the blankets. "Angus...That's the alarm...Angus!" she called, trying to arouse him. It wasn't the first time she failed to do that!

She rose and opened the curtains, and then went to his side of the bed, to pick up and put off the alarm, which had continued ringing. Wondering what she ever saw in him, she shook him and enquired, "Angus. Do you no' hear the alarm?"

He turned over and moved to her side of the bed. She raised her voice, "A'm sayin', d'ye no' hear the alarm?" and put on her moccasin slippers and chintz dressing gown.

He turned over reluctantly, picked up the now silent alarm, put it to his ear, and hearing nothing, put it to his other ear before shaking it, and listening again.

"Nothing" he replied sleepily. "Not a sound."

"I give in. Come on, get up out that bed and get a move on. Remember, you've got Airchie McNair's funeral to go to the day." She then went down the stairs.

Angus slowly rose and lifted from under the covers, two cold hot water bottles, a couple of his wife's curlers, and an empty banana skin. He then reluctantly rose from the bed, stretched and scratched himself, and moving to the window, surveyed the pastoral scene outside.

He was just in time to observe two pretty girls riding their bicycles to work. He recognised them, for they worked in the bottling hall at his Distillery. On seeing him in his pyjamas and catching his eye, they collided with each other and fell off their bikes. He closed his eyes as if he was enduring their pain, and turned away to put on his clothes.

A few minutes later, he had dressed, washed and shaved, and was in the kitchen reading the morning paper, while Mary prepared the breakfast. Mrs Grant, Mary's mother came into the kitchen, wearing carpet slippers, a dressing gown and a net on her hair. She looked like death warmed up.

'Here comes trouble,' thought Angus. He was still getting used to his mother-in-law living with him.

Mrs Grant looked in the mirror, and didn't like what she saw, before exclaiming, "Getting up this early is not good for me."

'And for us' thought Angus under his breath. Normally, he would be off to work before she rose from her bed in the morning.

"You'll be fine," his wife tried to assure her mother.

Mrs Grant opened a kitchen cabinet, revealing an array of medicine bottles and packets that would have done justice to a chemist shop. She hesitated a moment. "Now which ones are they?" she mused. Ultimately she chose two. "I can never remember which is for my cholesterol and which is for my blood pressure." Angus felt his blood pressure rising.

"Come and have your breakfast" invited her daughter.

"Do you really think I should go to this funeral Mary?" she asked.

"I mean, ladies didn't used to go to funerals.....except their own."

'Now there's a thought,' thought Angus.

"Of course you should" replied Mary. "After all, you were very fond of Archie McNair."

Meanwhile, half a mile away, the Main Street in Glendivot was bustling with school children going to school. Most parents didn't have to do 'School runs' in this part of the World. The shops were opening and numerous people were going to their work. Considering its population, it was always a bustling village at that time of the morning.

Bulk tankers were departing with their loads of whisky for the bottling halls in the central belt of Scotland, while other lorries carted loads of staves or completed barrels to and from the various cooperages in the area. All this, combined with the early morning farmers' traffic of trucks and tractors, with their loads of wheat and barley, meant there was always a buzz about the place.

They were also used to the tourists' cars and buses which descended daily on the village and the distilleries. However, today the traffic seemed heavier than usual. Perhaps this was something to do with the 'Big' funeral due to take place later in the day.

Lizzy McPhee was a rather plain local girl in her twenties. She had a ruddy complexion and tended not to wear make-up. Her father was the Grieve at the nearest farm. Now Lizzy was regarded as not terribly bright, but she was a willing, likeable girl, if a little overweight. Mary had given her a job at Balroonie House as a housemaid for the anticipated business she hoped to generate with her new Boarding House.

So far the job was not all that taxing, but the poor girl had difficulty with job interviews, so Mary employed her on a modest wage in the hope that she might come in handy, and justify her wage, if her proposed 'Bed and Breakfast' venture took off.

Lizzy had joined the local amateur Dramatic Club, and to her surprise, found that she had some acting ability. She always knew that she could 'Act the goat' at school, but even she was surprised to be given her first speaking part the previous year. She stole the show with a few surprising comedy touches, some of which were intentional.

As a result of this, she had been given a big break when the normal leading lady of the club was taking maternity leave. Lizzy landed the part of Mary Queen of Scots in a period play that was going to be performed within the next three weeks. None of the other actresses fancied having their heads chopped off.

She came out the local grocer's shop, carrying a pint of milk, and strode purposefully towards Balroonie House. Suddenly she recognised her boyfriend Hughie McLeod across the street. He was her first and only boyfriend, so he was not too bright either. However, he gave her a feeling of self confidence that had been lacking all her life.

Hughie worked at the Distillery and was also in the play. They had arranged to have some extra rehearsals on their own to learn their words, so that they wouldn't let down the other brighter members of the cast. Hughie crossed over to speak to her.

"Hi there Lizzy. Are you not late for work?"

"Too right I am" she replied, hardly stopping. "Oh, by the way, the costumes have arrived. So don't forget to come up to Balroonie House to try them on."

"When?" he asked.

"If you come about 1 o'clock, they'll all be away at the funeral. We'll have the place to ourselves" she said with a hint of excited anticipation.

"I can't wait" he replied with a grin.

And off they went in their separate ways.

Chapter 4

"ALL WE LIKE SHEEP, HAVE GONE ASTRAY"
HANDEL'S MESSIAH

Penny and Ponsonby continued the race against time in their journey North. It took them through romantic and historic places like Blair Atholl, with its beautiful white Castle, the home of the Duke of Atholl and Scotland's only private army, and Killiecrankie, where John Claverhouse, known as 'Bonnie Dundee,' was killed fighting for the Restoration of the Stuart dynasty.

As they journeyed through the Drumochter Pass, and then on to Dalwhinnie, Newtonmore and Kingussie, they could not fail to be impressed with the well preserved Ruthven Barracks where Cumberland's army was billeted before and after the Battle of Culloden, the last battle to take place on British soil.

They remarked on the historical significance of the area and were conscious that every village had its War Memorial to those Highlanders who gave their lives in the service of their Country. Clearly, the local population had sacrificed much to preserve their way of life. Rod Ponsonby seemed to take a particular interest in the Memorials to the Highlanders.

In due course they reached the winter skiing resort of Aviemore and crossed the winding and fast flowing River Spey at Grantown on Spey. They were strangers to this part of the world, and having crossed into Speyside, they were now officially in 'God's Country,' at least according to the local population.

Unfortunately, as they tried to absorb the breathtaking scenery, in their haste, they missed the turning for Aberlour, and finished up on an ever-narrowing B road, leading to the Haughs of Cromdale. "I hate to say it, but I think we are on the wrong road" observed Ponsonby, as he surveyed the road map he had found in the passenger door pocket.

"Damn" exclaimed Penny, blaming herself for the mistake. She slowed down to a speed that was still dangerous for such country roads. "What do we do now?" she asked. While he contemplated, they approached a crossroad, so she took her foot off the accelerator, and brought the car to a halt.

Ponsonby got out, with map in hand, and was relieved to see a signpost at the crossing. 'At least they are civilised up here,' he thought to himself. In fact the signpost had signs for Knockandhu, Tomnavoulin, and Tomintoul as well as Glenlivet, Glenfiddich, Glenfarclas, Glendivot, Glenbroom and Glendarroch pointing in all four directions. The names rolled off the tongue in such a way that he could be excused for thinking he was in a kind of 'Brigadoon.'

The Under Secretary of State was pondering his dilemma when, in the peaceful tranquillity of this

Highland paradise, he became aware of a faint bleating noise, gradually becoming louder. The peaceful heather and gorse scented air, was such a contrast to the odours and clamour of the London traffic, with which he was so familiar, that it took him some time to appreciate the source of the noise.

As the sound increased, it was accompanied by the occasional barking of dogs. Only then he realised that the commotion was caused by an approaching flock of sheep. He looked round, to ascertain from which direction they were coming. Even at the crossroads, it was still a pretty narrow road. As the babble increased, he heard their hooves on the tarmac and the occasional call from what he presumed to be the shepherd. He soon became aware that he may be in danger of being overrun, in some form of stampede.

Suddenly, they appeared round a bend behind him. Not until that moment had Ponsonby realised just how fast a flock of sheep can move, particularly when being hounded by demented working sheepdogs, in a confined space, from which there was no escape! He didn't have time to decide what to do, as he was almost immediately surrounded by the ewes and rams, bumping and boring in what appeared to him, to be in all directions. For a brief moment, the whole scene reminded him of the January Sales in the big Oxford Street stores!

Sheep are reputed to be stupid animals, but in his situation, they didn't look half as stupid as he felt, as he immediately lost his footing, and his map. The sheep dogs, apparently sensing that they had come upon the crossroads, went berserk in their attempts to keep their charges under control, and avoid them splitting up and going in all four directions.

Penny, sitting in the car observing this scene, gasped in horror as her precious Ponsonby disappeared, re-appeared and disappeared again under a hail of hooves and a cloud of dust. After the soaking at Gretna, the threatened arrest, and now this, she saw her chances of impressing the Secretary of State disappearing as fast as he did. She shuddered to think what state he would be in if, and when he survived.

Sheep have no mercy in such situations. Even football crowds rushing out of stadiums before the days of all-seated stadiums, would endeavour to stand aside, and perhaps even help a colleague who had fallen in a stampede. Sheep don't think like that. For them, it's a case of the survival of the fittest.

A young lad, looking a bit out of his depth in this situation, was yelling instructions, and had been trying desperately to keep the sheep under control. Even in his dire straits, it crossed Ponsonby's mind that this youngster, in his enthusiasm, had probably been responsible for the ensuing chaos.

It seemed an eternity before the last stragglers had passed, the cloud of dust cleared, and Ponsonby reappeared, looking sheepish, as if he had been dragged through a hedge backwards. He had been 'fleeced' by conmen while he was at University, but this brought a whole new meaning to the word. He struggled to his feet, thoroughly dishevelled and filthy, looking quite stunned and feeling sore all over. He grovelled around to retrieve the remnants of the map.

He was somewhat relieved to see an old red-faced shepherd come into view as the dust settled. The old boy was clearly out of breath, and had been unable to keep up with his flock. Ponsonby noticed he was wearing two large old-fashioned hearing aids.

"Excuse me!" shouted Ponsonby dusting himself down. "I say, excuse me!"

"Are you speaking to me lad?" replied the shepherd, watching with some anxiety, the youngster and the dogs trying to control his flock. Ponsonby, still in a state of confusion replied "No. I mean, yes. As a matter of fact, I am."

"Diane? That's a funny name for a man" said the shepherd, adjusting his hearing aids. "Can I help you?"

"Well yes, I am afraid we are a bit lost." The old boy hesitated.

"Frost? No, no frost. Not at this time of the year. Mind you, it was a bit snell at 6 o'clock this morning."

"No. You don't understand...."

"You'll have to speak up. I'm a bit deaf" continued the shepherd above the noise of the sheep, and pointing to his hearing aids.

Ponsonby raised his voice. "We are lost! We are not sure which road to take. We are trying to get to a funeral in Glendivot!."

"Glenlivet?" replied the old man with a glint in his eye. "Ah now, that is a fine whisky so it is. I always keep a bottle in my barn......"

By this time Ponsonby was becoming impatient. "Glendivot! Can you tell me which road takes us to Glendivot?"

"No" responded the shepherd to Ponsonby's chagrin. "No road will tak' ye laddie.... you'll have te use yer car! It'll tak' ye."

"Which way?" asked Ponsonby trying to control his temper.

"Ye just tak' that road there" pointed the local man. "No' there...there. On through Glenfyvie, straight on by the Haughs o' Cromdale, up ower the Carse o' Glen Rhinnies, and then ower the brig o' Glenbroom....and ye canna miss it."

'I'm not so sure' thought Ponsonby.

"Thank you. Thank you very much" replied Ponsonby ever the gentleman, looking at his watch.

He returned to the car, and mercifully noted that by this time, the sheep were well on their way, in the other direction.

"We've got about an hour. It's that way" he pointed, noticing blood seeping from a wound in his hand.

Penny rammed her foot on the accelerator as if she was starting Le Mans, and in her impatience, took the road to Glenlivet, instead of Glendivot. The old shepherd watched in disbelief, as they vanished in another cloud of dust.

"Mercy me, they've taken the wrong road! They've gone to Glenlivet!"

He mused to himself, "Still, they will get a fine dram there!"

Chapter 5
THE FUNERAL

The front door of Balroonie House opened and Angus came out looking a little harassed. He was followed by Mrs. Grant who was assisted by Mary, his wife, both dressed in sombre black. Lizzy stood at the door glad to see them off.

Suddenly, Angus stopped, searched his pockets, and turned.

"I've forgotten my keys. I'll be back in a minute." He returned to the house, as Mary and her mother waited by the car in the driveway.

"He'd forget his own funeral if that was possible" said his long suffering wife.

"He has a memory like a hen" agreed her mother. They rarely disagreed when it came to criticising Angus. After a pause, she continued, "Do hens have memories?" thinking out loud.

"I mean, they're not like elephants, are they?"

Rather than continue with this fruitless conversation, Mary chose to pass the time of day by waving to two ladies she recognised, who passed their driveway, obviously on their way to the funeral.

Angus returned with the keys, and they got in the car. As he put his feet on the pedals, he realised he was still wearing his slippers. He could not pluck up the courage to explain his embarrassment, so he simply left them in the car, and returned to the house, leaving the two ladies wondering what on earth he was up to.

On his return a few minutes later, wearing his best shoes, he explained that he had a sudden call of nature, and he drove out the driveway, accompanied by the disapproving mutterings of the two ladies in the back seat.

Glendivot Parish Church lay in a secluded little dell at the far end of the Main Street. It stood in its own grounds, surrounded by quite a large well-filled cemetery. It was a sanctuary with which both Mary and her mother were very familiar.

Mrs Grant's husband had been the Parish Minister for over 30 years and she knew every corner of the Church and its grounds, and a fair number of its residents for that matter!

Her husband had been buried there only the previous year, and she had visited and tended his grave regularly and religiously every week since. She now never entered the Church without taking the slight detour required to pass his grave and 'Have a wee word with him.' Angus always insisted, that she spent her life keeping him in his place, and she continued to do so even now!

While his mother-in-law was keeping her husband in his place, Angus met up with various people he knew. One was his old crony Dr. Hector McPherson, who had until a few years ago been the local GP. Unfortunately he had fallen foul of the demon drink, and being a buddy of the local Distillery Manager had probably not helped. Angus invited him to join their party for the service.

The Churchyard was crowded with mourners arriving, and it was clear that Archie McNair had been a very respected man in the Community. 'Funeral going' was very popular in Speyside, if that is the right word, but this was exceptional. The Church was full to overflowing, and fortunately, seats had been reserved for them near the front, due to the importance of Angus's position as Distillery Manager, and more significantly, the fact that Mrs Grant was the former Minister's widow.

They took their seats, and as is usual at funerals, proceeded to look around to see who was, and who was not there.

"I see Violet and Rose Hannah are here again" observed Mrs Grant, referring to what she nick-named 'The Ugly Sisters' from Glenbroom.

They ran the local hotel in the neighbouring village, and their brother Thomas, managed the rival Glenbroom Distillery. "They never miss a thing" whispered Mary.

"Especially funerals" retorted her mother. "They specialise in funerals. That's what keeps them so cheery" persisted Mrs Grant, noting that they looked as if someone had stolen their biscuit.

The coffin was placed on a bier at the front of the chancel and the new minister, the Rev. Carmichael McCutcheon, entered, and with due solemnity, commenced the proceedings.

"Dear friends, welcome. We are gathered here today, in the presence of God, to celebrate...." For a moment he forgot where he was, because in Glendivot, they don't 'Celebrate' a funeral. They 'Mourn.'

He was not in his previous Parish in Ayrshire, where they tended to celebrate the life, rather than mourn the death of the incumbent. He corrected himself. "I mean...to mourn...the passing of Archie McNair, formerly the Chief Guide at the Glendivot Distillery...and dearly beloved by all........"

Upon which there came the audible response from Violet Hannah, "Aye, beloved by some mair than others" as she observed a row of rather attractive younger ladies in the congregation.

While the funeral service progressed, Penny and Ponsonby continued on their nightmare journey. Even Penny, who was experienced enough to cope with most embarrassing situations, was hard pushed to retrieve this situation from Ponsonby, whose English stiff upper lip was being sorely tested. His only consolation was to notice how her skirt had edged up her thighs since the start of their arduous journey. Never in a thousand years did she anticipate the situations he had landed in already, when she obtained his agreement to come North with her, at the cocktail party in the Dorchester Hotel! What is more, they hadn't even reached their destination yet!

The clothes into which he had changed just North of Gretna, were quite unsuitable for the due respect expected at a Highland funeral. Not only that, but they had suffered in the stampede, and were now covered in dirty and smelly traces of wool, from their encounter with a hundred or more stampeding sheep. She hadn't the nerve to ask if he had any other clothing, and consoled herself with the likelihood that, despite her best endeavours, they were not going to make it in time for the Funeral anyway.

This likelihood became a certainty when, on entering the next village, still too fast, she had to jam on her brakes, and nearly put Ponsonby through the windscreen, upon which he smashed his head. At least she drew up six inches from a whacking great trailer lorry which was slowly manoeuvring its way out of the narrow local distillery entrance. It was trailing a very large valuable copper still. The lorry driver, on hearing the screech of breaks, stopped immediately, descended from his cabin and approached them, only after checking that his trailer and cargo were intact.

"Are ye tryin' te catch a train?" he enquired. Ponsonby whose humour had now been sorely tested, thought it was a stupid question, since Lord Beeching had closed nearly all the railways in this part of the Country over 10 years ago. "Ye cut that fine" continued the driver.

This was no place to pick a fight. "Sorry," apologised Penny. "Is this Glendivot?" she continued.

"No madam, this is not Glendivot. This is Glenlivet," he replied disdainfully.

"Oh, I thought we were in Glendivot," persisted Penny.

"No madam, Glendivot is 10 miles down the road." Penny turned to Ponsonby, "We are too late now anyway."

Seizing his opportunity, the driver enquired, "Would you like to come in, and see round Glenlivet? We've got a fine new Visitor Centre, the best in the area, and the whisky is second to none!" he said, rubbing salt in the wound.

"No thanks, we've got a funeral to attend," thankful that she had a legitimate excuse. She drove off to the parting cry of the driver, "Oh well, enjoy yourselves!" as if it was a dance they were attending.

The funeral party had by this time reached the graveside for the committal. The Minister distributed the cords. He gave Angus his at the head of the coffin, and Hector McPherson was allocated a cord for the other end.

Unfortunately, despite the solemnity of the occasion, Angus got a little carried away, and he let down the head of the coffin too quickly, suffering it to hit the ground with a thump.

The Minister grimaced and Angus felt a pain in his head.

Mary looked to the heavens in embarrassment. She could not help noticing an unusually large number of seagulls hovering overhead. She thought it was funny because they usually only came this far inland if there was a storm brewing, and today was a lovely day....so far.

"For as much as the Lord giveth, so he taketh away. We herewith commit the body of our dear departed Archie McNair, to the ground, earth to earth, ashes to ashes...... Good Lord!" the Minister exclaimed, as a particularly large seagull swooped down and deposited its excrement spot on the coffin's nameplate, to the horror of the closest mourners, and the surprise of the Minister.

The Rev McCutcheon was not to be upstaged by a seagull, so with hardly any hesitation, he continued, "Dust to dust....In the sure and certain hope," somewhat contradicting himself, "Of the resurrection, and the life everlasting. May he rest in peace."

But it was not to be, for as the cord handlers dropped their cords into the grave, the seagull's mate dive-bombed and dropped its load onto Archie's coffin and flew away squawking, as if in triumph. By this time, the graveside mourners were replacing their hats on their heads with more than usual haste.

Chapter 6

CAUGHT IN THE ACT

Back at Balroonie House, Lizzy was in full flow. She was dressed in her "Mary Queen of Scots" costume and with script in hand, was giving it her all, as she acted.

"With what conspiracy doth my cousin, the noble Queen Elizabeth accuse me now?

For I fear, it is my head she is after.

And yet, as each day doth pass, she sitteth more uneasily upon her throne..."

Almost immediately, the toilet cistern flushed in the adjoining cloakroom, and Hughie McLeod emerged with a battered script in his hand. He was in full regalia, dressed as Lord Darnley, with a particularly large floppy hat and outsized feather in it. His ill-fitting emerald green tights did not do justice to his long spindly legs.

"That toilet seat is shaky! You'll need to get that sorted," he observed.

"Och, why did ye have te interrupt my big speech? I've lost my place noo" Lizzy complained, ignoring him.

"Ye've lost the lock on that door as well. That could be embarrassing."

"We are no' replacing that at this stage, for Mrs. McDougall is having the cloakroom replaced.

She just needs to find the money. Now, where was I?" she asked as she fumbled with her script.

Hughie adjusted his tights. "Ah dinna ken how they got on wearing these claithes in Lord Darnley's time" adding, "He wouldna need te be goin' te the loo in a hurry!" Lizzy continued his theme, "Well I'm in a hurry te learn this play. Tell me, what comes after, 'She sitteth more uneasily upon her throne'?"

Hughie, found it reassuring to learn that Queen Elizabeth The First had shared his problem, observed, "Just like me in there" as he pointed to the toilet.

"Just get on with it" insisted an impatient Lizzy.

He consulted his well worn script. At least it indicated that he had been doing his homework assiduously.

"Wait now. Where is it?" He paused. "Don't tell me I used that page!"

He returned to the toilet and found the missing page on the floor.

"That was a relief!"

"Well now that you've relieved yoursel', maybe we can get on" said Lizzy. "Where were we?"

"Ah yes." He searched his script and carried on, "She is entangled in a web……"

Lizzy resumed her acting.

"She is entangled in a web of intrigue and rumour.

I do not know what I would do without my dear Lady in waiting…"

"You be the Lady in Waiting" she urged Hughie.

"What news do you have for me this day?"

There was a pause. "Well? I'm waiting!"

Hughie braced himself for his Oscar Winning performance, as he used a high pitched falsetto voice, as the Lady in Waiting.

"It is rumoured Your Majesty, that she doth contemplate coming to Fotheringay." Lizzy in all her majesty, continued,

"Foresooth, she has never communicated directly with me before."

At that, the telephone rang.

"Guidsakes!" said Hughie. "That's no' her, is it?"

"Dinna be silly" scoffed Lizzy as she went to answer the phone.

"Hello. Balroonie House... Who's speaking please?... Who?" She covered the phone with her hand. "You are not going to believe this."

Returning to the phone, she enquired, "Could you say your name again please?" After a pause she put her hand over the phone again.

"You'll never guess.... It's a Mr. Knox!"

"No' *thee* John Knox?" joked Hughie.

"Ah bet he disnae ken he's speakin' te Mary Queen o' Scots!" Lizzy sniggered, before regaining her composure with difficulty.

"Yes Mr. Knox..... From Littlewoods.....Mrs McDougall?.... No, she's no' in... No, she's oot....at the funeral....They're all there....auld Archie McNair....I see.... I'll tell her you are sending her a letter.....Important?..... No, I'll no' forget.... I'll let her know right away....Cheerio" and with that, she put the phone down.

"Whit wis that all about?" asked Hughie.

"Ah dinna ken," replied a bemused Lizzy "It was a Mr. Knox from Littlewoods, telling us he's sending a letter to Mrs McDougall. We've to look out for it, for he doesnae trust the Post."

"That's funny. Are they no' the mail order people?" suggested Hughie.

"Ohrrr I wish they were. I'd love one!" purred Lizzy, "Aboot six feet tall...and just like Sean Connery!"

"Am I no' guid enough?" Hughie asked, somewhat disappointed.

"Of course ye are! My big handsome hunk of Aberdeen Angus Beef!" and with that, she threw her arms round his neck, and kissed him.

A few moments later, Hughie suggested they had better get on with the play or Lizzy would 'get her head to play with.' As she agreed that she didn't want to be 'For the chopping block' she enquired, "Where were we?"

"Fotheringay Castle" replied Hughie, resuming his acting.

"It is rumoured, Your Majesty, that she doth contemplate coming to Fotheringay Castle."

And with that, the doorbell rang.

"My Goad! She cannae be here already," panicked Hughie. Whereupon Lizzy stripped off her Royal costume and revealed her maid's outfit underneath. She rushed to the window, and gave out a despairing yell, "Guidsakes man. It *is* her!"

"Queen Elizabeth? I ken we're near Balmoral...but this is ridiculous!" exclaimed her boyfriend, half joking.

"Naw, it's Mrs McDougall, and her mother, Mrs Grant, they're back from the funeral!"

"Already?" Hughie reacted like a frightened rabbit, and checked his watch. "I'll need te get back te work!"

"It's great how time flies when ye're enjoyin' yerself" suggested the maid mischievously.

"Well there is no way they'll see me dressed like this. I'm off."

Hughie's first thought was obviously self preservation.

"Wait!" shouted Lizzy. "Here, take my clothes."

"Notbloomin'likely" replied Hughie, misunderstanding her.

"I don't mean wear them. Take these, and put them in the kitchen."

At that, there was a loud knock on the door, and the doorbell rang again.

"Ye'll have to go oot the back door" she continued.

"Dressed like this?" complained Hughie. "No' on yer Nellie!"

By this time Mary McDougall's patience was wearing thin. "Are you there Lizzy?" she shouted, as she banged on the front door.

At this point, Lizzy lifted a feather duster and a can of furniture spray, and ushered him towards the back door.

Unfortunately, as she turned to answer the front door, Hughie in a state of uncontrolled panic, carried, dropped and picked up parts of Lizzy's Mary Queen of Scots' costume. In making for the kitchen, he mistakenly opened the cupboard door next to the cloakroom/toilet he had been in a few minutes earlier... and went in. Lizzy then opened the front door.

Immediately, Hughie realised his mistake, and reappeared saying "Help ma Boab! Wrong door!" He then saw the ladies entering. It was a few yards to reach the kitchen door, and he would have bound to be seen. So he immediately turned on his heels, and disappeared into the cupboard once more, costumes and all!

Mary McDougall strode in, followed at a funereal pace, by Mrs Grant. "If I had known you were going to be that long Lizzy, I would have taken my key. Where have you been?"

Lizzy had to think on her feet. "I, I was up the stairs... dusting." Mary took one look at the telephone, and, using her woman's intuition, lifted the phone, put it to her ear and declared, "You have been on this phone again! It's still warm with your ear! I'll warm your ears for you, tellin' lies like that." she threatened. "No, no I can explain," pleaded Lizzy.

"It will be that boyfriend of yours, Hughie McLeod, you've been on to again" continued Mary in full flow. "No wonder the phone bills are mounting." By then, Mary had taken off her coat and hat, and was about to put them in the cupboard, when Lizzy almost grabbed them from her, "I'll take these, thank you," and hung them in the cupboard, above a scared, crouching Hughie.

"Wis it a guid funeral then?" she enquired, changing the subject.

"Och aye, it was. As far as funerals go" replied Mrs Grant, taking her coat and hat off, and giving them to Lizzy.

"There must have been hundreds there. Poor auld Archie McNair, one day he wis there, and noo, he's nae mair." By this time Lizzy had put Mrs Grant's clothes in the cupboard above a complaining Hughie.

Mary had started to tidy the cushions as housewives do, when her mother persisted, "And him still in his fifties too. He was only a lad."

"It's all relative mother" observed her daughter.

"Well it's no' good for my rheumatics, going to funerals at my age" complained her mother, as she lifted the rear of her dress to warm her backside at the fire.

Mary was removing her shoes and started to rub her toes. "There, there now, he got a good day for it anyway."

"Ay, the sun always shines on the righteous." stated Mrs Grant, quoting her late husband.

"What a fine man he was so he was. Did you ever see him in his kilt? A true Scotsman, if ever there was one." Mary and Lizzy couldn't avoid exchanging looks.

"Well, if you say so mother, we'll take your word for it."

Chapter 7

ARRIVAL

Penny and Ponsonby eventually arrived in Glendivot, after their marathon and eventful journey. One was tired and the other was untidy, dirty and sore. She felt sorry for him, and he admired her stamina.

They had already stopped off at various hotels in the area, which catered for the huntin' shootin' and fishin' brigade, but they were all full of tourists, and others who were there to attend the funeral. Each succeeding hotel appeared to be less appealing than the previous one.

It had all been very frustrating. By this time, they would both have gladly accepted a bed of any kind, preferably in separate rooms, for they were still relative strangers. She hadn't even addressed him by his Christian name yet.

For once she drove slowly, up the Main Street until she came to the little square at the top of the hill. Next to the clock tower, they found 'The Commercial Hotel.' This was a dowdy uninspiring place, frequented only by the odd commercial traveller. They would have to be odd if they wanted to stay there.

Other clients were long distance lorry drivers and the local farmers and workmen who came in for a pint or three after work, to watch the football on TV, have a natter, or play pool. It obviously needed a coat of paint, a good window cleaner and a thorough dusting.

Penny drew up outside, as it didn't appear to have a car park. "You are surely not thinking of staying here?" queried Ponsonby despairingly.

"We have no choice. If it wasn't for this damn funeral we would have found a room by now, no bother" replied Penny.

"And all those tourists!" added her companion.

"You can thank our Distillery for that Mr. Ponsonby," retorted Penny defensively.

They were now both very tired, and Ponsonby became conciliatory. "Sorry. Perhaps you should call me Rod."

"Will that help us get a room?" she asked. He was taken by surprise. "I would have thought you would have wanted separate rooms?" In the great game of romantic chess, his Bishop had responded to her Pawn's first advance.

They had now reached the small dingy, cluttered Reception desk. An equally untidy, aged and decrepit looking man ultimately appeared in response to their second ringing of the bell. He needed a wash, a shave and a haircut, and he looked like a refugee from Eastern Europe, still with the clothes he wore when arriving after the War. More likely, he had probably inherited the hotel, and drunk the proceeds for the last fifty years. One thing he did not have, was a Degree in Hotel Management.

"What do you want?" he grunted.

"We were wondering about a room...rooms," queried Ponsonby, feeling quite smart compared with the hotelier.

Up until then, he had felt thoroughly embarrassed by his own appearance.

"You'll get none here. A'm fully booked. They're a' here fur the funeral" replied the apology for a Receptionist, trying to remember when he could last claim to be fully booked.

"This is ridiculous." Penny was clearly now at her wits end, and the journey had obviously taken its toll.

"Oh, wait a minute" responded the dirty old man, for that was exactly what he was. "I forgot, there is one single room left. The woman left this morning....in a hurry."

'I wonder why' thought Penny, as she turned to Rod. "Look, you take it for now, and I will go to Balroonie House and see if Mr. McDougall can help us."

Ponsonby saw no alternative, and he simply had to have a shower or a bath, and if possible, a sleep. He also reckoned he would have to find a shop that would sell him some gents' clothes. He signed the grubby Register and took the key, as Penny said she would come back for him later. He climbed the narrow staircase and she left for Balroonie House.

Chapter 8

THE PLOT THICKENS

After putting her shoes back on, Mary passed the cocktail cabinet, and saw two letters.

"What is this?" she enquired. Lizzy stopped dusting and replied "It's the post. That is what I was going to tell you...."

Before she could go any further, Mrs Grant, in a world of her own, exclaimed, "It's an omen! Mark my words. Everything happens in threes. There's my Alasdair died last year, Archie McNair this year. It will be my turn next year. You wait and see....ouch!" She stepped quickly from the fireside as she felt the rear of her dress red hot.

As Mary opened the first letter, she reassured her mother that she would live to be a hundred, and that she was sure to receive a telegram from the Queen in due course. Whereupon Lizzy suggested that she could deliver it personally while she is up at Balmoral!

"Not with my rheumatics. See these aches and pains I get...Mary! Are you all right? You look as if you've seen a ghost."

"It's this letter." Mary went white as a sheet.

"Is it from a Mr. Knox?" asked Lizzy.

"No. It's from the Company. It's addressed to Angus."

"Don't tell me he's got the sack!" exclaimed Mrs Grant. "Mind you, it wouldn't surprise me."

"No" replied her daughter.

"They have appointed a new Public Relations Manager. He's coming from London for the funeral, and he wants to see Angus after it!"

She paused to consider the ramifications. "Did you see any strange looking men at the funeral mother?"

Lizzy dropped her duster and offered to put the kettle on. She then disappeared to the kitchen, with an anxious glance as she passed the cupboard where Hughie was still ensconced, "I knew something would happen. I could feel it in my bones" announced Mrs. Grant gloomily.

Mary shouted to Lizzy in the kitchen, to bring her mother's pills, and forgot about the second letter. She started to tidy up the room, moaning about the imminent arrival of the new Public Relations Manager. She picked up the feather duster and furniture polish, together with a Hoover, that Lizzy was supposed to have used while they were at the funeral.

She was about to put them in the cupboard where Hughie was hiding, when Lizzy rushed in with the old lady's pills, and insisted "I'll take these."

To Mary's surprise she had them in the cupboard on top of Hughie before Mary could get near it. Lizzy returned to the kitchen before any questions were asked.

Mary then lifted the newspaper which was open at page 3. "Look at this" she said, "I might have known. Angus has been at it again." Her mother, on seeing the topless beauty in the paper, was not slow to react.

"Sex mad! We have all gone sex mad!"

"You speak for yourself mother" replied Mary.

"What is the matter with him? Have ye been starving him?" asked the old lady.

"He gets three good meals a day" Mary explained. Whereupon her mother gave her a disdainful look, "I am *not* referring to food!"

Her daughter was shocked, as Lizzy re-entered with a tray with cups and saucers on it. Mary went to open the curtains which had been kept shut as a mark of respect for Archie.

"Well, we can let some daylight in, now that Archie has been laid to rest." She looked out the window "Where on earth can he be?" she wondered.

"Is he no' in his grave?" asked Lizzy.

"No Archie.....Angus!" replied Mrs McDougall somewhat exasperated. Lizzy made a tactical retreat to collect some sugar and milk from the kitchen.

Mrs Grant had been ruminating to herself "Did ye see Archie's auld teacher at the funeral the day Mary? Old Mrs... Mrs Mac... what do ye' call her again? Och, my memory is no' what it used to be."

"Mrs McLelland?" suggested Mary.

"No, not her."

"Mrs McLaughlin then. Lauchlin McLaughlan's widow?" said Mary, trying to be helpful.

By this time, she had decided to adorn herself with some jewellery for the expected arrival of the Public Relations Manager. She had taken a set of pearls out of a box that she kept for special occasions, and had been having some difficulty fastening them.

"No, no' Mrs McLaughlin" answered her mother impatiently. Lizzy returned with the sugar and milk.

"Here Lizzy, can you put these on for me?" Mary asked, as she gave her the pearls, turned her back and lifted her hair. She gave her mother's problem some further consideration. "Was it Mrs McDonald then?"

"Ay, That's it. Auld Donald McDonald from Dundonald's wife, replied her mother, somewhat relieved. "Mind, they've got a son...called Donald."

After a pause, Mrs Grant continued "I thought Mrs McDonald was dead! I thought she died years ago."

By now, Lizzy was trying to put the pearls on her own neck.

"No mother, you must be getting mixed up. It was *Duncan* McDonald's wife Davina, who died." No sooner had she said this, she paused, and wondered what had happened to her pearls.

She turned round to observe Lizzy, wearing the necklace and admiring herself in the mirror.

"Not you! Me! Stupid girl. Leave them to me." Whereupon Lizzy returned the pearls post haste, and ran for her life.

"She will be the death of me that girl" declared Mary, looking for sympathy that was not forthcoming.

Mrs Grant was in a world of her own. "Mind you, she looked half dead herself" she reflected.

"Who? Lizzy?" asked a surprised Mary, as she ultimately fastened the necklace round her own neck.

"No! I'm talking about the McDonald woman!"

"She wasnae there mother! She is dead as I told you.... years ago!"

Mary felt the red mist rising.

"You only told me a minute ago!" argued her mother.

"I give up. I am talking about Duncan McDonald's wife Davina."

"But I'm not talking about Duncan McDonald's wife Davina! I'm talking about Donald McDonald's wife... Donaldina! She looked at death's door I'm telling you!" By now the old lady was shouting.

Mary tried to calm her. "She did look awful upset right enough. They say her daughter fell for Archie years ago."

"What was *her* name?" asked her mother, turning the full circle.

"Don't let's start that again" replied her daughter, determined to avoid falling into the trap.

"I thought she was going to fall into Archie's grave" said the old lady, staring into the fire, and warming her hands.

"It would have given poor old Archie the fright of his life!"

"Hardly mother" her daughter tried to reassure her.

"Mind you, it wouldn't have been the first time a woman got on top of Archie!" stated her mother somewhat disapprovingly.

Lizzy then returned with the teapot and started pouring for them.

Mary moved to the window again. "It must be difficult for older people to go to funerals. They must be thinking it will be their turn next." She looked out anxiously. As if on cue, Mrs Grant added dolefully, "I wonder when it will be my turn."

"It's about time!" declared Mary positively, having seen her husband and his mate Hector McPherson, making rather unsteady progress up the driveway. She moved swiftly from the window.

"I beg your pardon?" replied a startled Mrs Grant.

"Not you mother. It's Angus!...and he's got Hector McPherson with him! I can see they have been enjoying themselves." "How dare they!" said her mother cynically.

Mary had run her mother home from the funeral as the poor old lady found it necessary to answer a sudden call of nature. Meanwhile her husband had joined Hector in the pub for 'A quick one' with some of the cronies they met at the funeral. It was the custom to have one final toast to the deceased at Highland funerals. Accordingly, they had 'One for the Road' as they called it, for whatever journey Archie McNair was now embarked upon. This was only one of the reasons funerals in the Highlands were popular social occasions, ranking not far behind weddings and christenings for convivial reunions with old friends they thought were dead, or hadn't seen in years.

On this occasion, Archie, having been in the Whisky business, had the foresight to leave a gallon bottle of Glendivot Single Malt for all his friends and colleagues, to celebrate his memory. He was going out an even more popular man than he came in.

Mary opened the front door. Angus, was standing outside with his arm round Hector.

"See, Magic! It opened without me touchin' it!" he announced, and Mary slammed it shut in their faces. "I could swear they have been drinking!" she exclaimed.

"Are you no' going to let them in?" asked Lizzy.

"They have no respect for the dead" replied Mary.

There was a loud banging on the door, and demands from Angus to be allowed into his own home. "How are we going to cope with the new Public Relations Manager with him in that state?" she pondered.

"Och, he'll no' be in that state." observed Lizzy, referring to the P R Manager.

"He'll be stone cold sober."

"Not the Public Relations Manager stupid girl. A'm talkin' aboot Angus!"

The door opened slowly, and the two slightly inebriated pals sat down on the doorstep and started to take their shoes off with great difficulty.

"If the Doctor is coming in, I'd better get rid of these" said Lizzy, wisely taking the whisky decanter and the gin bottle off the trolley and placing them out of sight, in the cocktail cabinet. There were times when the maid did rise above her station.

The two men then proceeded to have a long debate about who should enter first.

"Will ye make up your minds for goodness sake!" said Mary getting exasperated. "Mother will catch her death of cold!" Finally, they both entered together and became stuck in the doorway.

"And close the door!" shouted her mother. "There's a gale of wind outside!" She had always complained about the draft since Mary had taken away the hallway wall.

"It's no' as bad as the bag of wind inside" retorted her son-in-law. Mrs Grant ignored the remark, or didn't hear it.

Mary closed the door and Lizzy, ever alert, took the shoes from them, and placed them in Hughie's cupboard. Hughie was now beginning to feel claustrophobic, and could not avoid sneezing as she closed the door. Lizzy, quick as a flash, had her handkerchief at her nose.

"Are you catching a cold Lizzy?" enquired Mary, to which Lizzy replied "No, I'm fine."

She was now starting to wonder how on earth she was going to extricate her boyfriend in his Lord Darnley outfit, without the others discovering. He had already overstayed his lunch hour and she was already in Mary's 'Bad books.' After all, she had not sought permission to rehearse the Play with Hughie. They had only intended taking a few minutes to try on the costumes, and in their excitement, had got carried away.

Mary then noticed the second letter, picked it up, and sat down to have her tea. Lizzy offered the men tea, but they declined, saying they had had enough to drink, so she disappeared into the kitchen.

"Was that no' a s-s-s-sad d-d-day the d-day?" suggested Hector McPherson.

One of his afflictions was that he suffered from a dreadful stammer. This had become a factor in his early demise as the local GP. Not only did he suffer from a weakness for the local product, he also had to cope with this speech impediment.

Unfortunately the poor man not only verbally stammered with his patients, but his affliction spread to his writing of prescriptions. Now Doctors' handwriting is notoriously bad at the best of times, but when the brain signals of a stammerer are conveyed to the hands, prescriptions for medicines became twice the length they should be. Simple ones like 'pipapipaparacetamol' or 'cocococococodamol,' could be interpreted by the local pharmacist without too much damage, but it became a pretty serious problem deciphering some of the more unusual prescriptions.

So, after some men, suffering from prostate problems, started being dispensed antenatal drugs for pregnant women, the local Health Authority had to step in, and persuade him to take early retirement.

"Ay, and it's a sad state you pair are in, coming in like that" said Mary. "Have ye nae respect for the dead?" At this, her husband took exception.
"Just a minute. It was me that made him the Chief Guide at the Distillery."

Mrs Grant was still in reflective mood. "What a fine man he was. Not since my Alasdair died, has there been a finer man in Glendivot, than Archie McNair."
Ach awa', ye d-d-dinna k-k-k-ken the h-half o' it" disagreed Hector.
"Ssssh" whispered Angus. "Dinna spoil the illusion."
"Illusion? What illusion?" asked Mary, quick as a flash.

"Yer mither doesn't know it, but the same auld Airchie was quite a lad...ye ken" replied her husband, touching his nose with his forefinger.

"What do you mean?" asked Mary, none the wiser.

Angus beckoned her closer and whispered, "He spent maist o' his money on...whisky, gambling...and wild wild women!"

"No!" exclaimed Mary clearly taken aback.

"Ay!" interjected Hector, shaking his head. "B-b-but..... he s-s-s-squandered the rest!"

Mrs Grant had settled down in her favourite fireside chair, and was replacing the batteries in her hearing aids. Hector was not the only one with afflictions. Observing her performance, Angus suggested quietly, that she would bring tears to a laughing hyena.

"C-C-Careful. She'll hear you" warned Hector.

"Nonsense" replied Angus, raising his voice. "She's as deaf as a dodo. You should ken that. You gave her the hearing aids."

Suddenly, she came to life, and exclaimed, "I've been thinking!....That Mrs McDonald....at the funeral. Do you mind Mary? When I said that I thought she was going to fall into Archie's grave....."

"That would be grave" interrupted Angus.

"Maybe she was going to take one of her epelectric fits!" observed the old lady.

"Aye, it was the shock that did it...." Angus paused for effect.

"When I let my cord doon too quickly, Airchie's heid hit the bottom before his feet." They all looked at him as he summed it up "You could say he went in... heid first!"

"It fair gave her a start" agreed Mrs Grant.

"It may have given her a s-s-start, but it sure f-f-f-finished off p-poor old Airchie" Hector added, not to be outdone. "At least we gave him a send-off he'll no' forget!" concluded Angus with a chuckle.

Mary was mortified at her husband's failure to carry out properly, what should have been a straightforward task. In his defence, Angus pleaded that "It was the first time I ever let down Archie McNair in his life..... "And it will be the last time, come to think of it....for he is deid!" he added pensively.

Mary had other things on her mind, and now decided to open the second letter.

"Ah! I think this is the letter I've been waiting for."

"Have you won the pools?" her husband asked sarcastically.

"You know fine, I *never* do the pools" she replied dismissing the idea.

Her hearing restored, Mrs. Grant joined in "That is gambling! Mind Mary, how your father preached against gambling, in the Kirk."

"Oh but we never gamble....in the Kirk!" Angus tried to reassure her, before adding, "It's usually up at the Gordon Arms we gamble!"

"One of the seven deadly sins" pontificated the old matriarch. Hector, determined to have the last word, nodded sagely. "He should know....for he was an expert on sin!"

Mary was elated. It was indeed the letter she had been anticipating. It was a reply from the Department of Tourism.

She had written to them to enquire about financial assistance for developing her house into a small private hotel. The knocking down of the hallway wall and relocating the toilet were only the start. Her father's death, and her mother coming to live with her, led her to revise her plans. She was now becoming a little more ambitious, and had developed thoughts of an extension, a conservatory and en-suite facilities in all the bedrooms. However, she had found this a more expensive operation than she anticipated, and until her father's estate had been settled, she had decided to try her luck with the Department of Tourism.

Angus felt it was time to offer Hector a drink.

"Will ye have one Hector?" he asked his boozing pal, while searching for the whisky decanter, which he normally kept on top of the cocktail cabinet.

"I'll no' say no" replied his crony.

"Have ye no' had enough for one day?" objected Mary, reminding them of their visit to the pub. She was supported by her mother, who turned on Hector saying, "Ye mean ye cannae say no" before adding, "The only time he ever refuses a drink is when he disnae hear the offer!"

"Are ye s-sure ye can s-spare it?" enquired Hector, oblivious to their remarks, and fully confident of the reply. Angus, who had been looking increasingly anxious as he searched for the missing decanter, finally opened the cocktail cabinet to display an array of whisky bottles, and there was the decanter.

"Nae problem" he said with relief, there's plenty mair where this came from."

"Well, I'll have one...if you insist" replied Hector grudgingly.

"He is *not* insisting" insisted Mary.

Mrs Grant returned to the subject of the letter. "What have you been asking for anyway?" she asked her daughter. Hector thought she was addressing him, and immediately responded, stretching out his hand "The dram Angus is p-p-pouring!"

Mary took a large form from the envelope, "I've been waiting for this for ages." Whereupon Hector added without hesitation "So have I." as he sniffed the bouquet, swallowed a large mouthful, and licked his lips with satisfaction. Angus offered a glass to his wife. She refused, prompting him to say, "Well we'll no' let it go to waste" and downed the lot!

Hector took two glasses from Angus and offered one to Mrs Grant, "Will you b-be indulging Mrs Grant? M-m-medicinal ye ken. It's g-g-g-good for the rheumatics!"

"Medicinal, my foot!" she responded.

"Whit's wrang with yer f-f-foot? Is it the g-ghout again?" he enquired almost sympathetically.

"Ye ken fine, I only have it at bedtime!" replied the obstinate old matriarch.

"At your age? You should be so lucky." She gave him a look.

"Oh the ghout? Oh weel, we c-cannae be letting it go to waste then."

He then poured her glass into his, and swallowed another large mouthful, savouring the sensation.

Mrs Grant had had enough. "Forty years I have lived in the manse, and now I am reduced to living in this... alcoholics suppository!"

"It will take me days to finish this" said Mary, completely absorbed in the large questionnaire that accompanied the letter. "It will no' take me d-d-days te f-f-f-finish this" said Hector drinking from the glass again.

Lizzy returned from the kitchen. "We have to have a toilet in every room" said Mary, referring to the form.

"That could be embarrassing" responded her mother.

"They must think we're incontinent" Angus asserted.

"Naw. They k-ken f-fine...we're in Scotland." Hector observed with authority, before feeling an urge coming on. "Oh here, that reminds me, I'll have to use you toilet."

He picked up the decanter in one hand and with the glass in the other, made unsteadily for the cupboard in which Hughie was almost suffocating. Lizzy stopped him as he tried to work out which hand he could free to open the door. "Not that door Doctor. Try this one."

She opened the cloakroom door and ushered him in. "At least you've got a toilet here for a start" said the Doctor.

"Ay, but it won't be there much longer" retorted Mary as she surveyed the contents of the official form.

"That's a good idea Hector, I'll use the one upstairs" said Angus rising.

Hector entered the toilet, and Lizzy shut the door, and shouted after him "Remember! The door doesnae lock!"

Before Angus reached the foot of the stairs, the cloakroom door opened again, and Hector popped his head round it. "Whit will I dae?" he asked. Without hesitation Mrs Grant told him in no uncertain terms, "You should ken whit to do by this time!" She had no sympathy.

Mary was more helpful. "You can just sing, like the rest of us!" Hector nodded, closed the door, and Hughie began to sing.

"Not you. Be quiet!" said Lizzy in a loud whisper to her boyfriend in the cupboard next door. Suddenly there was silence, until Hector started singing '*I belong to Glasgow.*'

Chapter 9

THE AVON LADY

Penny had left Ponsonby at the Commercial Hotel, and drove cautiously past the Distillery, looking for Balroonie House. She could not avoid noticing two or three small groups of bored looking visitors, being shown round, by some Guides who looked well past their sell-by date.

Obviously, the Company had decided to offer these Guiding positions to some old retainers, whom they.... retained...to show visitors round. They had obviously been born and bred in Speyside, and the farthest afield any of them had been, was probably Edinburgh. Being naturally reserved and diffident, and of an uncertain vintage, they neither had the charisma nor the energy to entertain their guests, or make their tour interesting.

They were no doubt the salt of the earth, and had been most willing trustworthy and loyal employees. Indeed, they were given the role of Tour Guide as a form of reward for their long and faithful service. Nevertheless, they were not ideally suited to attracting, connecting with, or entertaining the "Foreigners" from England, plus the brash Americans, the deferential Japanese, the inquisitive Europeans or the shy Chinese, who could hardly be expected to understand their thick Doric accents. Penny took a mental note to address this problem. She found the house without too much difficulty, and parked the car in the driveway.

Inside, Lizzy cleared away the glasses that were empty, and took them to the kitchen. Hector was singing away merrily on the toilet, when Penny rang the doorbell. "Mercy me, that must be him" cried Mary.

"Who?" asked her mother.

"The new Public Relations Manager" she replied.

"And I haven't even told Angus about him yet. He is in no fit state to handle this."

Mrs Grant was not used to receiving senior managers from Head Office at Balroonie House. She immediately took fright and dropped her pills from the bottle she had only just opened. "Oh my Goad!" she cried, "Keep calm!" as she bent down onto her hands and knees to try and retrieve her pills, which were rolling around the floor. At which point, Mary complained that Lizzy had disappeared again, and was never there when she was required. The poor girl couldn't win.

The door bell rang a second time. "I'm coming, I'm coming" shouted Mary, as she couldn't make up her mind whether to help her mother on the floor, or answer the door. Meanwhile, a quite oblivious Hector was now singing in the toilet, '*A wee doch and doris, just a wee yin that's all!*' Despite her mother crawling about the carpet on all fours, Mary finally decided to answer the door.

"Is this Mr. McDougall's residence?" Penelope enquired. Mary nodded. Mrs Grant, looked up from behind the couch, and on seeing Penny's smart red jacket and brief case, declared "It's the Avon lady!" She thereupon disappeared again behind the couch on all fours, trying to retrieve her pills and grumbling to herself.

"Are you the housekeeper?" Penny addressed Mary, not noticing the old dear on the floor.

"You could say that." replied Mary, not for one moment thinking the lady in red, was the P R Manager.

"Is Mr. McDougall in?" continued Penny.

"Well it depends." Mary stalled, wondering who she was. "Who are you?"

"I'm Penelope Whitehouse, I am the Company's new Public Relations Manager!"

At this, Mary dropped her glasses and the questionnaire. Her mother, on trying to rise from the floor, hit her head on a casual table at the side of the couch, sending it flying with its contents, and again dropped the pills she had been gathering. Simultaneously, Hector flushed the cistern!

"May I come in?" asked Penny, trying to ignore the distractions. Somewhat flustered, Mary blurted out

"Eh yes...yes please do... We weren't exactly expecting you."

"Yes we were" contradicted her mother, who was now crawling around Penny's feet, in pursuit of her pills once more.

"Weren't you?" replied Penny a little surprised, while looking inquisitively at the old lady on her knees at her feet. She then got the fright of her life when Hector banged the toilet door at her back, demanding to be let out, as he was now trying to open the door.

"Well" said Mary, thinking fast. "Not until we got your letter." At this point, a harassed looking Lizzy came in with a bucket of logs. Without looking, she explained "I was oot the back. I didnae hear the bell."

All of a sudden, she saw the imposing Penelope, and in her rush to place the bucket at the fireplace, fell head over heels over Mrs Grant, who was still grovelling around, trying to find the last of her pills on the floor. The old lady gave out an uncharacteristic oath, of which her deceased husband would not have approved, and Penny joined Mary in coming to her aid.

Despite her ailments, Mrs Grant was a wiry old soul. They assisted her to her feet, and after a few complaints about her aches and pains, they helped her to her favourite chair by the fireplace, where she gradually recovered her composure.

Penny could not avoid noticing the impressive original painting of the founder of the Company. He was in full Highland Regalia, dressed as a Major in the Gordon Highlanders. They were proud of his contribution to Wellington's victory over Napoleon at the Battle of Waterloo. The ornately framed painting had pride of place above the mantelpiece.

"What a magnificent painting" she exclaimed. "I presume this is the founder?" Mary nodded, "That's right."

"We all have a lot to thank him for" said Penny, thinking of the many employment opportunities the Company had offered the local community over the years.

"Ay...ye're not the first young lady to say that" replied Mary, rather disdainfully. The remark appeared to go over Penny's head.

"They say he had nine children" she continued. "He must have been awfully fond of children."

"It was more their mothers he was fond of!" interjected Mrs Grant. Mary added "He was fonder of the drink, than the children!" Warming to the critical theme, Mrs Grant summed him up perfectly. "An old scoundrel he was!"

Mary now realised she had not formally introduced her mother. "This is my mother." Penny shook Mrs Grant's hand, saying "Then *you must be* Mrs McDougall?"

"No. I'm Mrs Grant" replied the older lady.

"I am Mrs McDougall" explained Mary, and Penny apologised on realising her mistake.

As they sat down, Hector started banging the toilet door again, and shaking it vigorously. "Let me out!" he shouted. Penny was beginning to wonder if she had come to some kind of asylum. Lizzy went to his aid, and tried to open the door. "I can't. It's stuck! Try pulling it! There was a pregnant pause...."Pull it!" shouted Lizzy once more, and then the cistern flushed!

Mary tried to ignore them, by diverting Penny's attention and starting polite conversation. "We are so pleased to meet you."

"No' that. Pull the door!" yelled Lizzy as she tried again to open it. "Oh dear! It's well and truly stuck!"

Hughie, who had endured all this time covered in clothes in the confined space of the cupboard next door, could not resist the opportunity. "No it's no'!" he claimed, as he came out the cupboard, fancy costume and all!

Lizzy, to her credit rescued the situation, as she pounced on him before the others could see. "Get back in there at once!" she whispered as she pushed him back into the cupboard, and he sneezed once more. Lizzy had her handkerchief out again in no time, blew her nose, and returned to the kitchen. Mary was convinced she was catching a cold.

Angus came down the stairs, feeling more comfortable, and Mary introduced him to Penny, with some difficulty. She had to repeat Penny's role three times before it sunk in. He could not believe his ears.

Despite the fact that she was pleasing on the eyes, he could not believe that a female had been appointed as Public Relations Manager. He may have recently experienced changes brought about by the "Swinging Sixties," and the growth of the 'Sex equality' campaign, but even in these days, this was a step too far. He could not fathom what possessed the Company to appoint an English female from London, to market Scotch Whisky! He felt that it would be a case of "Scotch on the Rocks" if they had descended to this. As far as he was concerned, the only good thing that came from London, were...the roads!

Nevertheless, Mary's glare, with which he was quite familiar, made him keep within the bounds of diplomacy, at least for now. After calling her "Miss Lighthouse" then "Miss Whitehorse" by mistake, he finally got her name right, with a little help from his mortified wife. "Penelope Whitehouse?" he contemplated, as he wished he hadn't been so liberal with the whisky earlier. Gradually it began to dawn on him that her name was familiar. "I ken yer mither fine" he confided, recalling that Mary Whitehouse was the self-appointed defender of strict moral standards in Television programmes. "She comes over well on the TV! I agree with everything she says." He lied unconvincingly.

Before he got into deeper water, Mary asked if Penny had been at the funeral. She had to be honest, and explained that she had arrived too late. "I am sorry I missed it. He seemed to be such a popular man."

At this, Lizzy reappeared with a screwdriver, and started surreptitiously attempting to unhinge the toilet door. Despite Lizzy's best endeavours to remain unnoticed, Penny gave her a quizzical look. Lizzy smiled back at her, somewhat embarrassed. Hector's repertoire had now expanded to *The Campbells are coming, Hurrah Hurrah!'*

Mary, trying to divert her attention, continued her conversation with Penny. "Yes. Archie was always the life and soul of the party." "He was the Glendivot Highland Games Champion for years you know" recalled her mother. "He taught Angus here, how to toss the cabers." At this point, Angus couldn't give a toss, as he endeavoured to come to terms with the situation, and struggled to regain his sobriety.

"The cabers? What are cabers?" asked Penny somewhat naively.

"Great Scot woman! Do you no' ken what cabers are?" Angus was amazed at the English girl's ignorance.

"I'm afraid not" admitted Penny.

"They are...muckle great poles!" he explained.

Penny hadn't a clue what he was talking about, and had to pause to absorb what he said.

"Obviously foreign" she assumed. Angus thought for a moment, "Well, I suppose they could be" he surmised.

"What do they do with the Poles?" asked Penny, trying to show some interest.

"They put them between their legs" he explained.

This took Penny completely by surprise. She thought it through, and came to a conclusion. "That could be painful" she observed. Angus was not put off. "Then... they throw them up in the air" he continued, with an extravagant gesture.

"What? Their legs?" replied Penny, not quite understanding.

"No. The poles" said Angus.

"Do they not object?" asked Penny, feeling sorry for the Poles.

"No...They love it!" he maintained.

"Funny. Why do they throw them up in the air?" She wasn't giving up that easily.

"To turn them upside down!" was his explanation.

Now, by this time, Penny was totally mystified. "In their kilts?" she persevered.

"Ay, of course". He wondered, what else would they be wearing?

"How embarrassing" she postulated.

Angus was non-plussed. "What d'you mean?" It was Penny's turn to explain. "For the Poles...wearing kilts!"

"The poles don't wear *anything*!" Angus expounded with a final gesture of impatience. Penny paused, looked at Mary, Mary looked at Mrs Grant, and Mrs Grant looked at Angus with contempt. Lizzy returned to the kitchen.

Hector continued to sing away in the toilet. By this time he had sought solace from the decanter, which he was progressively emptying. His singing was enthusiastic, but his diction was becoming slurred.

Mary decided it was time to take control. "You came by car Miss Whitehouse. How was your journey?" The young lady was relieved to speak to someone who appeared sane, for by now, she was coming to the conclusion that she had landed in a home for the mentally unbalanced. "I'm afraid we ran into some problems...with some sheep....and we got lost in Glenbroom."

Before she could explain further, Angus interrupted "Oh you don't want to get lost in Glenbroom. There's nothing but witches and warlocks there...like Violet Hannah, and her wee poodle....."

"She doesn't have a wee poodle! It's an Alsatian she has!" countered his wife.

"I'm referring te her sister, Rose" replied Angus.

"Ach, she's harmless."

Penny decided she better move on before a domestic row erupted. "We were caught up in traffic for the funeral, and all the hotels were full. We could only get a single room in the Commercial Hotel, in the Main Street. Mary's mouth fell open at the very thought. "Surely not" she said.

"Even Angus wouldn't be seen dead there!" to which Angus added "It's full of drunks and layabouts!"

Mrs Grant was not to be outdone "In that case, maybe he would." she suggested. Lizzy then returned with a large crowbar, and proceeded to attack the door lock.

"I'm glad you got my letter Mr. McDougall" said Penny, continuing to give him the respect he hardly deserved. Angus was about to show his ignorance, when his wife thrust the letter at him. Penny went on. "Yes. In fact, I haven't been able to get any accommodation, and I was wondering. I believe you are hoping to develop Balroonie House into a private hotel, I wondered, if you could spare a bed?"

Mrs Grant had been adjusting her hearing aids by this time, and immediately reacted violently to the mere suggestion. "He is not sharing a bed with anyone....except my Mary!"

"She is asking if we could *spare* a bed mother....not *share* a bed!" explained her daughter.

"Oh my, what have I said?" Mrs Grant was mortified, and full of remorse.

Angus, ever the man for the main chance, couldn't resist the temptation. "It's tempting. That's the best offer I've had for a while." Penny was even more convinced she had come to a home for the bewildered.

"Of course you can stay with us Miss Whitehouse" said Mary reassuringly.

"I have however, a little complication" Penny confessed.

"Oh? What's that?" asked Mary.

"Mr Ponsonby!" replied Penny.

Chapter 10

A NARROW ESCAPE

Meanwhile, Ponsonby had reached his room in the Commercial Hotel, to discover it was a garret bedroom with low sloping ceilings that for some reason, made regular annoying contact with his head. His cranium was already sore with the bumps he had sustained in the car and with the sheep. He surveyed the scene before him.

His creature comforts comprised a hard old-fashioned iron bedstead, a lumpy uncomfortable mattress, a threadbare carpet, wooden surrounds with splintered floorboards, an ancient grimy wash-hand basin with a dripping tap, and a central light-shade with cobwebs, hanging at a jaunty angle. He was sure the bulb was no more than 40 watts. The whole scene made him feel far from jaunty, especially after his arduous incident-packed journey. No wonder the previous lady had left in a hurry.

He was stiff and sore, and felt as if he had gone 15 rounds with the World Boxing Champion, Mohammed Ali. Reluctantly, he started to unpack his holdall, laying his clothes on the bed. However, he couldn't open the drawers in the small dressing table. They were stuck, and as rigid as the toilet door at Balroonie House. He concluded that they had probably not been opened for years.

He sat on the bed for a moment, fatigued and in despair, and began to wonder why he came to Scotland in the first place. He thought of the soaking at Gretna, the contretemps in his underwear with the police sergeant, the stampede of the sheep and getting lost in the backwoods of the Haughs of Cromdale. And now this! One could hardly blame him from wondering if his journey was going to be worth all he had endured.

He would have to have good reasons for persevering, and continuing his eventful journey to this remote region. He did of course have good reasons for persevering. He barely remembered his mother, and had never known his father. All he knew was what his maiden aunt, and to a lesser extent, her sister, had told him. It had been a Wartime romance, and the marriage had taken place in the Morayshire area where his father had been stationed. His one hope was that he had never received official notification that he had been reported missing, presumed dead, so there was still a slight chance he may still be alive.

He had harboured hopes that his father had been a brave Commando, training in the rugged Highlands, where they made killing machines out of raw recruits. All he knew for certain was that his father had served in the Seaforth Highlanders, who still had an active Regimental Headquarters at Fort George on the Moray Firth. He hoped to get access to their records.

He had brought with him the only photographs that his aunt had kept all those years, for this very purpose. No wonder he was prepared to suffer all the hardships of his journey so far.

Meanwhile, he had to come to terms with his current circumstances. He had never experienced a hotel quite like it. It made Fawlty Towers look like The Savoy. He had always been used to at least four star hotels with en suite facilities, on expense accounts, thanks to the taxpayer. This however, was a totally new experience!

He went out to the landing and found a bathroom. There he saw that there was no paper in the toilet roll holder, and a pair of knickers in dirty water in the small washbasin. Surely the 'lady' who had left in a hurry, hadn't gone without her knickers! He gave up. He went out the hotel, if that is what one could call it, and looked for a gentlemen's outfitters, to replenish his wet and soiled clothes.

Having become a Member of Parliament, meant that Rod Ponsonby was naturally quite status conscious. He found it rather bizarre when half the population stopped to stare at the dirty stranger in the soiled clothes, who had come to their village. It was a far cry from wearing his black jacket and striped trousers with which he started out his journey.

The locals could normally smell a stranger from a distance, but in this case, they could also smell the sheep off him. He even heard one lady ask her companion, if he was the new shepherd! No wonder the Under Secretary of State was in quite a state.

After walking the whole way up and down the Main Street without success, he was about to concede defeat, when he crossed the little square, and there, hiding behind the Clock Tower, only a few yards from the hotel, he found the one and only gents' outfitters in Glendivot. There he purchased the only Harris Tweed suit that fitted him in the shop, a shirt, a tie and two pairs of socks.

Suddenly the cumulative effects of the journey and his experiences caught up with him. He found it difficult to think clearly and logically, as was his habit. He came out the shop with his purchases in a parcel and still felt very grubby, so he proceeded to look for somewhere... anywhere...where he could have a wash to freshen up. He was some yards from the shop when he realised his mistake. He should have put on his newly purchased clothes, instead of continuing to wear his grubby ones.

His first thought was to change back in his room at the 'Hotel', but it was then that he came upon the local primary school. The children had been playing joyfully in the playground, but for once, his luck changed. At that moment, the school bell rang, and in a few moments, the little darlings all trooped back into their classrooms, and the playground was empty and quiet once more. The Under Secretary of State, on his first visit to Scotland, had to take his chance while the opportunity was there.

He looked around to see if the coast was clear, made sure there were no stragglers, teachers – or policemen – about, and sneaked into the playground. He reached the children's washrooms in the corner of the playground, and entered. Now bearing in mind these were primary children of no more than 11 years of age, he forgot how low and small their wash-hand basins and toilets were.

First things first, he used one of their toilets, with limited success but at least he felt more relieved. He then proceeded to wash himself at a basin that was less than 3 feet high, without slipping a disc in his back. He didn't even complain at the cold water they used up in the Highlands. 'A hardy lot these Scots,' he thought. There were no towels, so he had to make do, drying himself with his dirty shirt, which he had taken off before he intended making a complete change to his new clothes. He couldn't remember when he last changed his clothes three times in the one day.

He couldn't help smiling to himself as he stripped to his underwear. It reminded him of his encounter with the policeman earlier in the day. It couldn't possibly happen twice in the one day. He reassured himself that the situation was unlikely to be repeated here in Glendivot. The village, he felt sure would only have one bobby, and he was unlikely to be near the primary school, or its washrooms. Nevertheless, as a precaution, he looked out. He could not believe his eyes!

A small stocky lady, in her fifties, had entered the playground, and was walking purposefully towards the washrooms. She was carrying a container, with a selection of toiletries including paper towels, toilet rolls and soaps. She also carried a mop and pail under her arm. She was obviously the cleaner coming to replenish the washroom supplies, and probably going to clean them out while she was at it.

Ponsonby was still in his underpants when he first saw her. Suddenly he had visions of being exposed in the local press. "Under Secretary of State caught in a state... of undress... in children's toilets!" A story like that was bound to reach not only the Local press, but the National press as well! They would have a field day at his expense. He could be denounced on television! How was he going to explain himself to his Minister in Whitehall? He could even imagine awkward questions being raised in the House of Commons! He could see his career going up in smoke!

Having been exposed once already that day, was more than enough. What would the Minister of Tourism in Whitehall make of it? What about The Prime Minister? A potentially glittering Political career would be over before it had hardly begun! He was doomed!...as they say in Scotland.

The lady was no more than ten yards away when he put on his new trousers in record time. He didn't even have time to do his zip, which, being new, was stiff. He could hear her footsteps approaching. As he gathered up his belongings, he could even hear her singing to herself, a jolly Scot's song. She was obviously completely oblivious of the situation she was about to confront.

There was simply no escape for Roderick Ponsonby as she approached the open doorway. In blind panic, he entered one of the cubicles, and closed the door quietly.His consternation was palpable as he discovered there was no lock! Even if his father had been a wartime Commando, behind enemy lines, he surely couldn't have experienced a more nerve-racking situation! Talk about a close shave, he could hear her breathing less than three yards away. He could only hope she couldn't hear *his* breathing. So frightened was he, that he could hardly breathe anyway.

The poor man was almost fainting with the thought of the implications of being discovered. He was pouring with perspiration and shaking like a leaf, as she blithely started to clean the basins and replace the soap and paper towels. It was just a matter of seconds before she would turn to the cubicles to replace the toilet rolls. Ponsonby was in such a state of terror, he could easily have made use of the toilet again, but that was out of the question.

He looked around, and to his enormous relief, he found he was in a cubicle which had a small window. His luck was really turning for it was slightly ajar, for hygienic reasons. Could he open it further without her hearing him? Was the window large enough for him to squeeze through? What was on the other side? Was there a ten foot drop on the outside? Did the local river flow underneath? All these thoughts overwhelmed his scrambled brain within seconds.

He heaved at the window, trying desperately to coincide his efforts with the cleaner rinsing out the sinks from the taps, and singing away to herself. He was convinced she must have heard him, but for once it appeared as if his luck was holding. He only managed to open the window a further 12 to 15 inches when to his relief, it appeared that she had now decided to mop the washroom floor. This gave him some precious added time.

He tried again, but could only move it a couple of inches more. However, he thought it was enough for him to squeeze through. He threw his dirty clothes out the space, followed by the parcel. Then, with some hesitation, he parted company with his brand new tweed jacket, and pushed it through, hoping he would see it again, and in reasonable condition. He was glad that he was slim and fit enough to wriggle through the space. Unfortunately for him, he went through head first, and didn't have time to choose his landing.

On the very moment the cleaner turned the door handle to enter the cubicle, he disappeared from sight in a rather undignified manner, only to land in five foot high nettles, and a rubbish tip with beer bottles, cans and assorted domestic rubbish. He had to be thankful for small mercies, for the drop was a mere six feet, and he had apparently not been seen!

Despite the discomfort of the nettles, and a few more bruises, he dared not move until he was sure that all was well. He was relieved to discover that no bones were broken, although the wound in his hand from the sheep encounter, had started bleeding again, and he had twisted his ankle. It seemed an age before he saw the window being closed above him.

It appeared that the cleaner was none the wiser. To this day, that dear lady does not realise how close she came to being a witness at his trial, and a celebrity on National news!

Ponsonby, somewhat out of character, contemplated saying a prayer. He was not very religious, and his first thought was the 23rd Psalm, '*The Lord is my shepherd....I shall not want.*' But then he thought the better of it. Having had enough of shepherds for one day, he gave up the idea.

He then extricated himself from the nettles, and managed to retrieve his new jacket in reasonable condition. It still had the price-tag on it. However, he could not avoid noticing the pervading smell from the pile of rubbish into which he fell. It was just as well he had kept his old clothes on. He was literally itching to get out of there, and again felt he still needed a bath or a shower, as he made his way back to the hotel.

He tried to remain as inconspicuous as possible as he crept past the Reception Desk, avoiding the attention of the unkempt receptionist, and upstairs to his room, to await the return of Penny. He opened his briefcase, and took out some old sepia photographs, and laid them on the bed. They consisted of a wartime Regimental photograph of the Seaforth Highlanders, and two others of a couple. The gentleman was dressed in Army uniform.

After gazing at them for a moment, he began to feel emotional. He started to wipe a tear from his eye, for these photographs were the real reason he had come to Glendivot. They were the only link he had with his long lost parents.

Chapter 11

PLANS FOR PONSONBY

Penny was watching Lizzy trying to prize open the toilet door with her crowbar. "Mr Ponsonby? And who is Mr. Ponsonby?" Mary asked. "He is the Permanent Under Secretary of State for Tourism" replied Penny, giving him his full title. Mary was astonished at the coincidence! Surely the Secretary of State had not come especially to Scotland just because she had applied for Government help with her modest plans? She had not expected such personal attention from such high authority.

As Penny observed Lizzy wrestling with the stubborn door, she could not resist asking "Is there something wrong?"

"No. Nothing" replied Lizzy hiding the crowbar behind her back. Although not entirely satisfied, she returned to her conversation with Mary, explaining "He is a very influential Member of Parliament who could be of considerable help to us, and I have been able to persuade him to come with me to Glendivot."

"My my" replied Mary, very impressed. "That was very good of you. He did not need to go to all that trouble, just for me."

"He has come to see the Distillery, and the Visitor Centre" explained Penny. "You see I want him to help us with Government Grants, to finance a big new Reception Centre and Gift Shop that I'm planning." The conversation had become like a game of tennis. It was now Mary who was confused.

Penny's plans had implications for Angus as Distillery Manager. "Oh ye are, are ye?" he said suspiciously. Almost as an afterthought, Penny added, "Oh, and...a Museum.... for old exhibits!"

"Ay, ye can put her in it for a start" suggested Angus pointing to Mrs Grant, who was beginning to doze off in front of the fire. Mary was busy thinking how generous it was of Mr. Ponsonby to come all the way to Glendivot to help her. She had not expected such personal attention, and she hardly heard Angus's remark.

Lizzy made to return to the kitchen with the crowbar. Hughie sneezed again from the cupboard, and Lizzy got her handkerchief out once more, and pretended it was she who sneezed. This prompted Mary to remark "I'm sure that girl's getting a cold."

By now, Angus was beginning to come to terms with the situation. "So you are the new Public Relations Manager?" he said.

"That is right" replied Penny, crossing her legs on the low settee. For one brief moment, Angus was in a trance. "I need a drink" he contemplated, as he poured himself one at the cocktail cabinet. "There must be some mistake...." He turned to look at her again. "I mean....You are a woman!" His wife was horrified.

"I can see you are very observant Mr. McDougall" said Penny, flinging her hair back with a flourish, and looking even more feminine than before.

"You're, no' a man" observed Angus.

"Do I look as if I am?" asked Penny posing alluringly on the couch. Angus was non-plussed. He didn't know where to look now. "Well no, no' exactly" he stammered.

"But a woman…in the whisky business! I mean, It's not right."

"And why not?" interrupted Mary.

"Don't tell me you are a male chauvinist Mr. McDougall?" said Penny, taking a risk. Angus turned round sharply from the cocktail cabinet. "Certainly not!" he insisted. Then he paused, and added, almost as an after-thought, "It's just…I cannae stand women!" Mary thought 'Here we go again.'

"Do you drink the cratur?" he asked as he held up his glass.

"Yes, as a matter of fact I do, especially after that long journey. Thank you." Angus relaxed a little. He thought how great it was that sharing a dram often breaks the ice, and works wonders in overcoming tense situations. "That's always something" so he poured her a drink.

"With soda please" she added. 'What a waste' Angus reflected under his breath as he reluctantly added the mixer.

"Do you know there is one thing that women and soda have in common." he expounded, sniffing her mixed drink. "They baith get up ma nose!" and he then gave her the glass.

Penny decided to remain silent, and enjoy her drink... for now. She was not going to rise to his taunting, for she had more subtle methods for winning him over, and she would pick her time.

Lizzy came back again, this time with a set of ladders and a larger screwdriver. She climbed the ladders and proceeded to unhinge the top screws of the toilet door. Penny's curiosity was beginning to get the better of her. "Are you all right there?" she asked Lizzy perched precariously at the top of the ladders. The enterprising maid turned round, and swayed slightly as she almost lost her balance,

"Yes. Yes thank you Miss" she replied, and continued with her unscrewing.

Penny decided to change the subject, and get down to business. She explained that it was very important to impress the Under Secretary of State, which they understood. She also expressed concern that he would not be impressed with the Commercial Hotel, which they also understood. She then asked if by any chance they had another room which they could offer him.

The house was large enough, and Mary, who was so impressed with the trouble he had gone to, to come and deal with her application, had no hesitation. She willingly agreed, "We'll give him The Prince Charlie Room!" Angus, who had never heard of "The Prince Charlie Room" avoided showing his ignorance by keeping his mouth shut, and for once, avoided appearing 'A proper Charlie!'

"There is one other important matter that has to be dealt with" continued Penny, who obviously had something on her mind.

"Oh, and what is that?" asked Mary.

Penny was intrigued again by Lizzy, perched as she was at the top of the ladders. "Excuse me?" she asked. Do you need any help?"

"No Miss, thank you" replied Lizzy.

By now, Hector could be heard "Diddling" (A form of rhythmic gaelic singing to which the ancient Scots used to dance their reels and strathspeys, before the days of Dance Bands) in the toilet. By this time Penny had begun to ponder whether she had landed in the set of 'One flew over the cuckoo's nest' or 'Alice in Wonderland.'

"What, may I ask, is going on?" she asked, her curiosity getting the better of her. Angus explained

"It's just Hector."

"Hector?" she asked, curious as to whom he was referring.

"Ay, Hector!" confirmed Angus. "He's just diddling.... in the toilet!"

'What next?' Penny thought to herself. "I beg your pardon?"

"He's diddling. Do ye no' ken what diddling is?" queried Angus. She stared at the shuddering toilet door which Hector had resumed shaking vigorously, in his efforts to open it.

"I shudder to think" she said.

Mary felt this had gone far enough, and tried to bring back some sanity to the conversation. "Eh, what was this important matter you were referring to, Miss Whitehouse?" She was an expert at changing the subject when Angus got into difficulties.

"We need to appoint a new Chief Guide to replace Mr. McNair....and I need him to look after the Under Secretary of State while he is here." explained Penny.

"Oh you do, do you?" proffered Angus.

Penny was starting to assert herself. "It is of the utmost urgency. I want the new Chief Guide to take Mr. Ponsonby round the Distillery, and show him the ropes."

"What do you think this is...a shipyard?" Angus was beginning to feel his authority being challenged, but Penny ignored his remark.

"Then, after that, he will need to see the Visitor Centre" she continued.

"The Visitor Centre" repeated Angus.

"I want him to go round Balroonie Castle as well....and The Chief Guide can explain its history, its mysteries and intrigues...."

"There's many an intrigue in these parts" said Angus.

The P R Manager was getting into her stride. After all, she had been thinking about this for weeks. "You know what I mean. I want him to get a taste of the old Clan feuds,...ancient battles... stories of pillage and rape...."

"Aye, there's many a rape in....." enjoined Angus.

"Angus!" interjected his mortified wife.

"You see, I'm hoping to develop the Castle as an additional tourist attraction." added Penny, who was now in full flow. 'Oh ye are, are ye?' thought Angus, and without hesitation, he responded with his own suggestion.

"We could put up a mock gallows and hang her ladyship here, for all to see!" referring to Mrs Grant, who was still half asleep by the fire. She gave a grunt. It was almost as if she had heard him. "That is enough" exclaimed Mary, defending her mother yet again.

"It will make a change from her swimmin' up and doon Loch Ness, for the tourists." He was determined to get the last word.

Penny was relieved as she watched Lizzy descend from the top of the ladder, and start to unloosen the lower hinges of the door. It hardly distracted her however, as she turned her thoughts to how best to entertain her guest. She had a list of suggested activities for Mr. Ponsonby.

"Maybe he could go on a shooting party" she continued.

"Up the Carse?" responded Angus with a little more enthusiasm.

"The what?" cried Penny, somewhat taken aback.

"The Carse...of Glen Rhinnes. That's where the grouse are." He looked at his mother-in-law, and added "And I can think of an auld grouse te shoot!"

Penny was not to be diverted as she ignored his disparaging remark. "What about a fishing party?" she enquired with a glint in her eye.

"Nae problem" Angus assured her.

Penny was satisfied, and her eyes returned to Lizzy still wrestling with the door. "Are you sure you don't need help?" she enquired of the maid once more.

"No thank you Miss. It won't be long now." Lizzy rejected her offer again.

Returning to the subject of Mr. Ponsonby, Penny suddenly had a new thought. "Would it be possible to take him to see a Highland Games?" Angus and Mary began to wonder how long The Under Secretary was going to be staying in Glendivot. Before they could react, Penny carried on "Then we could *all* see the Poles, tossing their cabers....with nothing on!"

At that, Angus drew the line. "That's not on...Ye will have te wear clothes" he insisted. Penny said she understood that at Braemar you could have 100 Pipers, to which Angus retorted, "Ay, but ye'll get Glenfiddich too!"

The subject was brought to a conclusion by Mary, who indicated that there were no Highland Games in the area in the foreseeable future, but she suggested a better alternative. "We could take him to the Camanachd Cup Final a week on Saturday Angus." Coming from South East England, Penny had no idea what the 'Camanachd Cup' was all about.

Angus explained it was the equivalent of the FA Cup Final in England, except it was the game of 'Shinty.' This is a particularly fierce form of men's hockey with fewer rules! Almost anything goes, and it is not for the squeamish. Penny thought he was referring to 'Shinto' and couldn't quite believe there was such a Japanese influence in this part of the Country. Either that, or there must have been more Japanese tourists than she had thought!

Mary explained that Glendivot were in the Final this year, a feat they had not achieved for well nigh 40 years, so it would be a grand occasion. "Angus is the Team

Manager" she said with pride. Whereupon Lizzy added, "And Hughie is the Team Captain!"

The Public Relations Manager was once more at a loss. "Hughie? Who on earth is Hughie?" she asked. Mary explained that he was Lizzy's boyfriend, and Lizzy added proudly, "He is the goalkeeper of the shinty team."

"That's marvellous" said Penny, immediately seeing it as an opportunity for product exposure and some publicity.

"Yes, we'd love to come, if I can persuade him to stay on till then" before continuing her probing, "Pardon my curiosity, but what exactly are you trying to do?" she enquired of Lizzy one last time.

"I'm trying to get into the toilet" replied Lizzy thinking 'What a stupid question to ask.'

"You must be desperate! Isn't there an easier way?" asked Penny, becoming even more convinced she was in a retreat for the bewildered, for she certainly was bewildered by this time!

Mary tried to elucidate "She doesn't usually try to get into the toilet that way." Penny felt she should not pursue the matter.

"Whatever turns you on I suppose" and left it at that.

Chapter 12

THE NEW CHIEF GUIDE

Penny then addressed Angus.

"Now you understand, we will need to impress Mr. Ponsonby if we are to receive financial assistance from the Treasury. We have to make it truly memorable." She was not sure if he had understood the importance of the point she was making, so she emphasised,

"It simply must be a visit he will not forget." Angus reassured her "It will be Miss Whitehorse, it will be."

"Whitehouse!" Mary corrected him.

Lizzy appeared to have completed her work, and took the ladders back to the kitchen.

"So, Mr. McDougall...who have you chosen as the new Chief Guide?" asked Penny, lifting and opening her briefcase. Angus was at a loss. He stuttered and stammered incoherently.

Penny was now at her commanding best, as she summed up the situation.

"He has to be... well educated, articulate, and someone who can command the respect of the guides, and the visitors!

We need a cultured man, who knows his whisky, the

history of the area, and one who can organise shooting and fishing parties....and, most important of all... he must be able to impress the Under Secretary of State!"

"Is that all?" responded Angus, playing for time.

"So, whom Mr. McDougall, have you appointed?" demanded the Public Relations Manager, ignoring his stalling.

Lizzy came back and proceeded to remove the door of the toilet, to reveal Hector, sitting there, happy as Larry, with an empty glass in one hand, and an almost empty decanter in the other. He was clearly stoned out of his mind, and diddling merrily 'The Ball of Kirriemuir,' tapping his feet to the rhythm, and conducting an imaginary orchestra.

As he rose unsteadily, he started to dance as best he could, to the rhythm of the tune, quite oblivious to the visitor from London. Meanwhile Angus huffed and puffed, but could not think of an answer.

Penny's patience was on the point of snapping, as she searched for a pen, when Angus suddenly caught sight of his crony coming forward, swaying happily from side to side, like a drunk sailor on the deck of a rolling ship.

"You must have someone in mind" insisted Penny, who was not yet aware of Hector's presence.

"Eh...yes..of course I have..." At that moment he took the plunge. "I've appointed....Dr Hector McPherson!"

His wife let out a shriek and even her mother wakened from her slumber.

"Lord preserve us!" exclaimed the older woman, while her daughter despaired.

"No' Hector?" she muttered, questioning her husband's sanity once more.

Angus had to hold Hector steady as he tried to justify his selection.

"A very esteemed member of our Community" he claimed.

"He looks steamed" said Mrs Grant.

"Stewed if you ask me" added her daughter.

"Well and truly pickled" continued the old lady, not to be outdone.

Angus simply had to defend his decision. "He's better preserved than you, auld yin" he countered.

Penny had found a pen, and taken out a notebook during these exchanges. She still hadn't noticed Hector being propped up by Angus, as he was barely able to stand. "Right....Dr. Hector McPherson" she said slowly, writing down his name "I should like to meet him."

Angus, having committed himself, had no alternative. He took the bull by the horns.

"This...is Dr. Hector McPherson...our new Chief Guide!" Hector barely understood as he asked his pal, "Am I?"

"Hector!...Meet Miss...Lighthouse!"

"Whitehouse!" shouted Mary and Mrs Grant in unison.

Lighthouse or not, it didn't really matter, for Hector was in a fog anyway, as he tried to emerge from his haze, and shake hands with Penny. Firstly, he transferred the decanter from his right hand to his left, only to find the glass in his left hand. After attempting to hold the glass under his arm, then in his crotch between his legs, he thought the better of it, and gave it to Penny to hold in her left hand. They then shook hands.

"This...This is Dr McPherson?" she enquired with incredulity. Hector answered for himself. "It is indeed... indeed it is." he replied. This was the one phrase he had mastered, without stammering.

"Is he really a Doctor?" she asked suspiciously, wafting away the smell of his breath.

"Yes indeed, indeed yes" Hector answered, nodding his head to emphasise the point.

Penny decided to pursue the matter. "What does he know about whisky?" to which Mrs Grant replied "He only knows how to consume it!"

"Yes indeed, indeed yes" agreed Hector, nodding his head vigorously.

Angus took a chance. "Hector is an authority on whisky...sure you are Hector?"

Hector, in his state of inebriation, was to Angus's surprise, momentarily inspired.

Perhaps it was the effect of the amber nectar. He raised the almost empty decanter, poured the remaining whisky into his glass, and declared, "Ahha! Uisge beatha....the water of life!.....Sh-Sh-Shcotland's gift to mankind!" He drank a mouthful in response to his own toast. Penny was intrigued "How that?" she asked.

"It p-p-prolongs youth, and it s-s-slows down ageing" Hector started. Whereupon Angus sought Mrs Grant's opinion, "Sure it does mither?"

The old lady dismissed him with a wave, and he turned to Penny to confirm, "You can see, she doesnae drink much!"

Hector, swaying gently, continued "It d-d-develops digestion. It p-p-prevents p-p-pain, and...it h-h-helps the heart!"

"Don't forget the heart" added Angus, supporting his pal. "Ye cannae survive without the heart!"

Hector went on "It s-s-s-sooths the m-m-mind and it unb-b-b-burdens the brain."

"It loosens it, ye mean" Mary begged to differ. Hector whispered to Angus "How am I doing?"

"Just fine." Angus encouraged him.

"It c-c-c-carries away cares. It raises the s-s-sp-spi-spirits. It c-c-c-cures cuts...and it t-ter-ter-terminates toothache." Hector carried on, trying desperately to keep his balance. "It makes yer teeth fall out!" disagreed Mrs Grant, adjusting her false teeth.

Angus could hardly believe it, but Hector seemed inspired. "It p-p-p-preserves the heid from whirling, the eyes from d-d-dazzling, the t-t-teeth from chichachichattering, and the sh-sh-sh-stomach from sh-shwelling."

"And the feet from smelling!" added Angus, getting into the spirit.

"And the f-f-f-feet....." continued Hector.

"Is that all?" joked Penny, not expecting any more.

"Naw. It stops the g-g-guts from rumbling, the h-h-h-hands from sh-sh-shivering, the veins from c-c-c-crumbling and...the b-ba-ba-bones from breaking!"

"But it doesnae stop you from stammering Hector!" pronounced Angus, shaking his head as if to emphasise the point.

"No, b-b-but I'm working on it!" he replied.

Penny was impressed. "Quite an authority" she observed.

Angus had to grasp the initiative while the going was good. He was convinced Hector could not keep this up a moment longer. "Now Hector, ye might as well try and look the part" he suggested, endeavouring to usher him towards the door.

"Of course, you will need to wear the kilt!" added Penny.

Hector was immediately petrified. "N-n-no me! I am p-p-p-pissed...."

"We know you are" confirmed Angus, putting his arm round his shoulder.

"I'm *p-pissed-passed* wearin' the kilt!" pleaded Hector.

"But you have to be a true Scotsman." said Penny, not realising the implications of her statement.

"I will c-c-catch my death of c-c-c-cold!" cried the Doctor. "Besides, I d-don't have the knees for it!"

"He doesn't have the...." Mrs Grant started. "Mother!" interrupted Mary.

"....for it!" concluded her mother, clearly not impressed.

Angus patted Hector on the back and told him to go over to Mrs McNair's, and ask for a loan of Archie's kilt, even though it would be too big for him. He managed to get his friend out the door, when suddenly Hector, in a moment of unexpected sobriety, stopped and turned to say "I've f-f-f-forgotten my b-b-b-boots!"

"You'd forget your heid if it wasn't screwed on" said Mary unsympathetically. There then began an almighty rush for the cupboard in which poor Hughie was in the early stages of suffocation and dehydration. Mary, Angus and Lizzy made a beeline for it, to recover Hector's boots, and once again, Lizzy won the race...if only just. She began to wonder how long her luck would hold out.

Hughie, on seeing Lizzy groping about him, looking for Hector's boots, complained "What are you doing with your hands? Get me oot of here, I'm dying with the heat!"

"Be quiet" she whispered, picked up the boots and shut the door.

Hector put them on without tying the laces, and they ushered him out the door without further mishap. They all stood and watched him stagger down the driveway, diddling away to himself, looking for all his worth, like Charlie Chaplin.

Penny closed her briefcase, and after thanking Mary and her mother for their hospitality, left to fetch Mr. Ponsonby. She had had a long day.

As she got into her car and drove away, she was being watched closely by two curious spinsters from across the road. They were Violet and Rose Hannah, from Glenbroom.

Chapter 13

GHOSTS FROM THE PAST

They returned to the lounge and Mary remarked that it wasn't often they had Members of Parliament staying with them. They had a lot to do. Lizzy was told to prepare the dining room table for their guests. Mrs Grant went grudgingly to help her, and Mary went upstairs to prepare the bedrooms. Angus shouted after her "Was that you opening my mail again?"

"It was just as well" she replied from the landing, adding in the local 'Doric' accent to which she resorted whenever she scolded her husband, "Whit on earth possessed you to appoint Hector as Chief Guide? A mair gormless loon you couldna find!"

"Whit chance had I? He was the first person that I could think of." explained Angus. "I had to think on my feet."

Talking about thinking on his feet, made him think of his feet. He suddenly realised that he had no shoes on.

"Where's ma slippers?" he shouted.

"They will be in the cupboard where you left them!" Mary shouted from up the stairs.

Lizzy could not avoid hearing the pair of them shouting at each other, even though she was in the dining room, absorbed in finding a solution to the problem of Hughie, still stuck, and sweating in the cupboard.

Mary came down the stairs with bed sheets as Angus made for the cupboard once more.

"I have come to the conclusion you are an ass Angus McDougall! An absolute ass!" she repeated. Angus put his hand on the door and turned to her "Well, if I am, it was you that landed me in it..." whereupon Lizzy came running back into the room, but this time she was too late. Angus opened the cupboard door, concluding "Right up to my a...aah!"

A red-faced, perspiring Hughie stepped out in his Lord Darnley costume, handed Angus his slippers, threw the rest of the clothes on the floor and said "Well in that case, ye can get somebody else te do your donkey work!" and strode out the front door.

Chapter 14

SHOOTING PARTY

A few days later, Glendivot Distillery was a hive of activity. Lorries were parked outside, and workmen were unloading a variety of artefacts for the Museum, and various pieces of equipment for the Audio-Visual Theatre. These were being installed by Penny, who was supervising affairs.

Painters and joiners were busy converting the old Malt Barn they had been using, to host the visitors up till then. New 'Reception' signs were being erected above the door. They were not the only erections Penny was responsible for since she arrived.

Half a dozen very attractive young ladies were being issued with grips containing sexy new uniforms, including tartan mini-skirts and revealing tight-fitting chiffon blouses. This was the early seventies, and mini-skirts had only recently reached the backwoods of Scotland. They were still regarded as a novelty, and looked upon with derision, suspicion, glee or excitement, depending on your point of view. They certainly were going to provide the Distillery workers, who were 95% men, with a point *to* view!

"Hurry along now girls, and get changed" instructed Penny. "And remember I want you all to look your best" as she ushered them to a changing room. "Just remember all you learned in your training programme." Penny was not one to let the grass grow beneath her feet.

She had already arranged to recruit the glamorous guides through an Agency, and had them complete a crash course on the distillation processes as soon as she arrived. All were bi-lingual as a pre-condition of their employment, to ensure that as wide a range of foreign visitors were catered for. This was a step ahead of the competition at the time. They received a basic grounding in marketing techniques, customer relations, bonding with foreign visitors, and selling the range of products.

Meanwhile, Rod Ponsonby, had taken the opportunity to recover from his gruelling journey and his various escapades. He had taken advantage of Penny's offer to make use of her sporty little car, and enjoyed the time available, exploring the beautiful countryside around Speyside. He declined Hector's offer to accompany him.

Angus was uncertain if this was not a blessing, for he could not be sure that his crony would let him down sooner or later. The Under Secretary of State's official assessment tour of the Distillery and its Visitor Centre, was not scheduled until Penny had made more progress with her initiatives.

Ponsonby had never divulged his alternative reason for accompanying her North, and had been surprisingly secretive about where he was going. He was very unforthcoming about where he had been, or what he had been up to, and Penny had to be very discreet in her enquiries. She did discover through her local contacts, and general gossip, that he paid a visit to the local Library, and also spent an afternoon at the Seaforth Highlanders' Regimental Headquarters at Fort George.

She was somewhat intrigued to learn of these choices, but after what the poor man had gone through, Penny felt he deserved a break. She knew he wanted to explore the area, but she was also suspicious that he might be assessing the competition. However, as far as she could ascertain, he had not visited any other distilleries. There were plenty of distilleries in Speyside who would have welcomed Government aid to set up or expand their Visitor Centres.

Their biggest rival was Thomas Hannah, the brother of Violet and Rose Hannah, who had been taking such an interest at the funeral and at Balroonie House a few days earlier. He managed the Glenbroom Distillery in the next village, while his inquisitive sisters ran the local hotel.

Thomas, known to Angus as 'Doubting Thomas,' was always suspicious and jealous of Angus's initiatives at Glendivot, the latest of which appeared to be the expansion and upgrading of their Visitor Centre. Angus claimed he had more brains in his big toe, than Thomas had in the whole of his body. Meanwhile Thomas's sisters were concerned about rumours of Mary's plans to develop Balroonie House into a rival hotel.

Penny always liked to be in control of things, and she could not risk leaving Ponsonby alone for too long. Worse still, if only she knew, it would be unwise and even dangerous to leave him in the hands of 'The new Chief Guide' Hector, for any length of time. Mary and Mrs Grant had also discouraged contact with him, for fear that it could be counter-productive.

She had to give him credit however for dressing up in Archie McNair's kilt and bonnet, even though they were grossly oversized for the Doctor. They made him look like a rather ridiculous Disney character out of a scene from the Hollywood fantasy film "Brigadoon." She would have to arrange for a proper fitting with a local kiltmaker, if his appointment was to become permanent.

However, in the meantime, Penny had much to do, and she had to take advantage of Ponsonby's absences. Although she had no illusions that the new guides had much to learn, and lacked experience, she simply had to get things underway while she had the Under Secretary of State on the premises. It was a race against time. He had to be impressed, and they were part of her armoury, in her battle to win him over!

Sexy billboards were being erected outside at the distillery entrance, the car park and the Reception Centre. They advertised 'The most exciting Whisky Tour in the World!' with poster photographs of the glamorous girls, which would have done a West End Theatre billboard proud, inviting the tourists, and any other interested parties to see round the Distillery. She was raising the stakes in the rather douce whisky industry's Visitor Centres to a whole new level!

Ponsonby arrived as Penny was dealing with a small group of rather dowdy and elderly former guides whose faces were tripping them. They were not a happy bunch. "I am so sorry you have to go ladies and gentlemen. I'm afraid it is a sign of the times. You will get your Redundancy Pay at the office....and thank you for all you have done."

She had even organised that they received an additional ex-gratia payment for 'Services rendered.' This would help to soften the blow, and was arranged in double quick time. They shuffled out of the Malt Barn and crossed to the office, and into retirement.

Ponsonby was dressed in his new tweeds for the shooting party. "Quite a hive of activity" he observed.

"I hope you can see the improvements I'm making. I am trying to make this the best Visitor Centre in the Highlands" she replied. "That is why I need your help." She was never one to miss a chance. "I have the accountants working out the costs for you at present."

Even Ponsonby, with his strong sense of public responsibility, was impressed with her ideas and what she had already achieved. The wheels of progress appeared to turn more slowly in the Civil Service with which he was so familiar.

"I see what you mean" he said continuing to assess the situation, as more equipment arrived, and workmen busied to and fro.

"We will give you an official tour once everything is in place" announced Penny.

He may not yet have committed himself, but if the Government's purse was not yet opened, at least he had taken it out of his pocket!

Hughie drove up in an Estate car. "Well, I'll leave you to it for now. I'm off on this shooting party you organised. So I'll see you later," said Ponsonby, as he got in the car.

"Right... Enjoy yourself....and take care."

"I will" he replied with a cheery wave.

"We don't want any more accidents!" she called after him, and off he went.

They drove up to the moorland of the Carse of Glen Rhinnes, and met the shooting party who were preparing for the day's shoot. There were about a dozen guns with accompanying ghillies and dogs, milling around the Range Rovers parked in a small car park just off the main road.

Although he was employed at the Distillery, Hughie was assigned to act as ghillie to Ponsonby. This was a duty he was called upon to perform from time to time, when VIP guests required entertaining. It made a pleasant change from the daily routine of the Distillery stillhouse. It was a fine afternoon and Roderick Ponsonby was beginning to wind down after his long and arduous journey from London, and his baptism of fire in the school washrooms.

He had been in Glendivot a few days now, and was more relaxed as he began to feel the benefit of the Highland air. Even his cuts and bruises, were healing by now. They walked as a group over the moors towards the birds, and gradually spread out.

He had never done this before, but he soon came to the conclusion that it was a pleasurable way to keep fit. He had now gone three days without any more catastrophes. 'That must be a record' he thought, and likened it to going a whole day at cricket, without losing a wicket. He noted that his ankle was recovering and his hand injury was healing nicely. As for his nettle stings, they were a thing of the past.

It was a long way from London, and he was now well rid of the carbon monoxide emissions, the air pollution and raucous hubbub of the city. He was able to admire the vast expanse of rolling moorland, interspersed with heather and occasional yellow broom, stretching out before him, to the forests of Scots pine and Douglas fir trees in the distant hills.

There were no tubes, trains, taxis, buses or motorways here, to disturb the peace. The only noises to be heard were the gentle ripple of clear flowing water from the streams that were tributaries of the Spey, the distant call of the curlew, and the flutter of birds as they rose from their nesting places among the heather and broom.

It was certainly a healthy lifestyle, and he felt a million miles from the dangers of mob demonstrations, terrorist alerts or being run over by the heavy traffic in the Metropolis of London. He had a stressful job, always in the front line of fire from the public's criticism, and for the first time in years, he felt relaxed, safe and at peace with the world.

Hughie was quite helpful. He was obviously an experienced ghillie and he loaded and unloaded Ponsonby's double-barrelled rifles with calm efficiency. He was also a competent tutor, and gave him useful tips on the art of 'Bagging' birds. Ponsonby didn't need any training in this art when it came to the unfeathered variety. In that situation, their roles could have been reversed.

Gradually, after several unsuccessful attempts, he came to the conclusion that he was better at hockey than he was at shooting on the grouse moor. He wasn't entirely comfortable killing innocent birds and so it didn't worry him that, as time went by, he had not bagged one bird.

"Blast!" he said as he missed for the umpteenth time.

"Hard lines Sir" said Hughie trying to console him for the umpteenth time. "Better luck next time."

"I don't think I'm cut out for this" said Ponsonby, somewhat disappointed.

"Nonsense! You'll get the hang of it." Hughie tried to encourage him as he handed him a reloaded gun.

"Just remember...to aim in front of the bird."

"In front of the bird?" repeated Ponsonby.

"So far, we havnae found any that fly backwards" replied the ghillie.

Ponsonby gave him a wry smile, waited, then aimed and fired. "Missed again" he said.

"Where did you aim that time?" asked Hughie.

Ponsonby pointed to the sky and said "Up there." As he pointed with his right hand, he inadvertently dropped the barrel of the gun with his left, and accidentally shot Hughie in the foot!

"A-a-a-a-r-r-rh! O-o-o-oh! yelled Hughie, as he writhed in agony and hopped about the heather.

"Well your aim is rubbish!" he cried.

"What *have* I done?" uttered the Under Secretary of State.

"O-oo-oh my foot! My poor foot!" shrieked Hughie as others came to his rescue. There was nothing for it. They had to take the poor fellow to the hospital. 'So much for the peace and quiet of the Highlands' thought Ponsonby.

Chapter 15

CHAOS

Hughie's foot was being put in a plaster at the Local Cottage Hospital. He knew the nurse who was attending him, for she was a local girl.

"There you are now" she said as she finished. "No more shooting yourself in the foot."

"I told you, it wisnae me! It was that Englishman that did it!" replied Hughie. She helped him off the trolley.

"Come back again in six weeks...and we'll have it off."

Hughie was taken aback. "But...You never told me you felt that way about me! I've already got a girlfriend" he pleaded. "What will she say?" he asked in all innocence.

"Your plaster Hughie!" the nurse replied with disdain, "Your plaster!" As she walked him to the door, he was in such a state, he remonstrated,

"I'm no' plastered...I'm as sober as a judge!"

The next day at the Distillery, the tourists were already queuing up outside the Visitor Centre. The bush telegraph had got round that this was a tour with a difference. Some of the local unemployed men, many of whom knew the Distillery processes inside out, and had therefore no need to learn, were first in the queue, attracted by the sexy looking guides. Even some local wives, and a selection of straight-laced ladies, had come to satisfy their curiosity.

The Reception Centre was already crowded with visitors mingling with the tradesmen, and the mini-skirted guides were having difficulty keeping control. Even the Japanese tourists were training their cameras on the guides as much as the surroundings.

Keith Crowther who happened to be the reserve goalkeeper for Angus's Glendivot shinty team, was unloading barrels from a lorry. He had heard of Hughie's misfortune, and was quietly looking forward to taking his place in the forthcoming Shinty Cup Final. He gently pushed his load along a ramp towards the warehouse, when suddenly one of the new guides, came round the corner into his view.

She was leading a group of mainly male visitors, and showing them round. The warehouseman had never seen such a vision before. She was quite different from the old guides he was used to ignoring. He could not ignore this beauty. Every few minutes, she was being asked to interrupt her tour, to pose for photographs with the visitors. At this rate, Guided Tours were going to take twice as long!

His attention was diverted, and all thoughts of the Cup Final disappeared, as he lost control of his barrel, full of precious whisky. The barrel rolled off the ramp, with him hanging on for all his worth, and he and the barrel, bounced onto the roadway simultaneously. He split open his jaw, and the barrel sprung open some staves. It rolled past the party, down the hill into the burn where it burst open, and spilled the golden nectar into the flowing waters. No doubt the fish had a ball that day!

Minutes later, a fork-lift driver was carrying a puncheon of whisky on his truck, minding his own business, when he came across another attractive mini-skirted guide who was taking another large party round.

On seeing this apparition, he couldn't take his eyes off her, and didn't look where he was going. He lost control, and the fork-lift truck seemed to accelerate as it disappeared into the duck pond adjacent to the warehouse. They never did know how deep that pond was! The truck was never seen again. The fork-lift driver splashed about among the ducks as they fluttered away, quacking noisily among the chaos.

A short time later, a third glamorous guide had reached the Bottling Hall with her party of interested visitors. They also tried to show some interest in the bottling operation. The bottles were loaded automatically on to a conveyor belt. They travelled along it, to be filled with whisky and then labelled, capped and checked by a team of female operators. At the end of the line two sturdy young men were responsible for packing them into cartons, for shipment abroad. They had to work at a steady pace to keep up with the speed of the line.

The guide's tour took her party past this operation, on an open-grated gantry about six feet high, in order to give them a better view. It also gave the young men a better view of the new guide!

On seeing this vision of loveliness, the two young men stopped to admire her. Gradually the bottles started to pile up, and in no time the whole line went out of control, as the bottles piled up, overflowed and started falling off the end of the line! They smashed on the concrete floor, and the place was soon swimming in whisky. If Penny had wanted to make an impression, she certainly succeeded. The Distillery First-Aiders never had such a busy day!

Chapter 16

ON YOUR BIKE

Mrs Grant was on her exercise bike again. She was wearing track suit bottoms over her print dress, and peddling away with difficulty.

Her daughter came in from the kitchen with a watering can. "Is that you on that contraption again? You will drive yourself to an early grave...I'm telling you" said Mary. Her mother tried to pedal faster.

"It's my age that's telling on me" she admitted breathlessly, while Mary watered the house plants.

"Well, you know what Angus says. "A woman stops talking about her age, when it starts telling on her."

"If I had known I was going to live as long as this, I would have asked you to take better care of me," conceded Mrs Grant.

"I don't know why you do it, really I don't" continued her daughter, as she went out the front door with the watering can, where she started watering some outside plants. Lizzy came in from the kitchen with dishes for the sideboard. Mrs Grant shouted to her daughter, "The Doctor told me I had to lose 30 pounds."

"I'll spend it for you" offered Lizzy, not knowing to whom the old lady was talking.

Suddenly, Mary came rushing back into the house. "You had better get off that contraption if you don't want to be seen by Angus. He's coming up the road." Her mother started huffing and puffing again "Heaven preserve us, from him of all people."

They quickly helped her off the bike, and between the three of them, managed to fold it up and hide it in the cupboard, before he appeared. Suddenly, Mary declared, "You'll need to take off your pants."

"I will not!" retorted her mother, shocked at the very idea. Mary pointed to her track suit bottoms, and while Lizzy held Mrs Grant steady, Mary helped to remove them with considerable difficulty. Mrs Grant was now quite flustered, so she sat down on the couch and put her feet up.

"That reminds me Lizzy" said Mary, I've run out of eggs. I want you to go down to the village and get me a dozen. Come, I'll give you the money" and she took Lizzy into the kitchen. Rather than face Angus, Mrs Grant adjusted the cushions, and pretended to sleep.

A moment later Angus came in, noticing the front door had been left open. 'That's funny' he thought. 'They never leave that open.' It was only then he saw Mrs Grant lying with her mouth open, apparently asleep on the couch. 'And she never keeps hers shut' he said to himself as he gently touched her chin and closed her mouth.

At that Mary appeared, and greeted him "You're back early."

"Is the lunch no' ready?" asked her husband.

"No it's no'. You'll have te wait till I feed our guests." and with that, she returned to the kitchen.

"Again" said Angus, as he sat down at the fire and picked up the paper.

Mrs Grant grunted and Angus looked at her. "These sleeping pills Hector gave me for your mother....must be working now" he called, as his wife returned with cutlery for the sideboard.

"What do you mean?" she asked.

"Well, they've been hopeless up to now."

"How do you come to that conclusion?" asked his wife.

"Every time I give her them at night....she keeps wakening up again in the morning!" he pronounced.

"You have never given her anything in your life" she countered. Not to be outdone, he reacted "Oh yes I have! D'ye no' mind last year, when yer father died....I bought her a plot in the cemetery...." Mary felt that did not count. "And she hasnae had the decency te use it yet!" His wife strode out to the kitchen in disgust, and Angus crept out the front door.

Chapter 17

BAD NEWS

Lizzy came out the back door to go for the eggs. She was approaching the gate when the local postman arrived. "Hello there Lizzy" he greeted her cheerily. "I've got a special delivery for Mrs McDougall. Will you sign for it?"

"Sure" said the maid. "It's probably the one we are expecting from Mr. Knox. I'll give it to her when I get back," and with that, she signed for it, stuffed it in her coat pocket, and walked smartly to the village.

She bought the eggs in the local Spar and came out the shop in somewhat of a hurry, and immediately bumped into Rod Ponsonby! She dropped the eggs and a number were smashed. "Oh, it's you Mr. Ponsonby" she uttered in surprise. "I'm so sorry." Having stayed at Balroonie House for a few days, he now knew the maid.

"My fault Lizzy," he confessed.

Across the road, Violet and Rose Hannah were about to go into the Bank. They only did this when there was no alternative. They were more tight-fisted than Mohammed Ali and Henry Cooper were together. They stopped to witness developments.

Ponsonby offered to buy replacement eggs. After attempting as best they could, to clean up the mess with the help of some local dogs, they re-entered the shop and purchased more eggs...much to the surprise of the shopkeeper, who on seeing Lizzy again, observed "Surely ye havnae eaten them already Lizzy?"

Violet and Rose waited and watched them come out the shop, and walk towards Balroonie House. Not knowing the stranger, their curiosity was aroused, so they decided to follow, at a safe distance. Their Banker could wait.

They had started to hypothesise who this gentleman might be. Gossip was rife. He had now been in Glendivot for almost a week, and was known to be staying at Balroonie House, so he wasn't just passing by. Their first guess was that he was a senior executive of the Company, perhaps a new Board member. They both had very vivid imaginations, but this was a case of their imagination running out of control.

Ponsonby had just recovered from shooting Lizzy's boyfriend in the foot, and had taken him to the local Cottage Hospital. This was the first time he had seen Lizzy since the accident. "Am I right in saying you are Hughie's girl friend?" he asked.

"That's right. He normally works at the Distillery, but I thought he was to take you shooting today?" replied Lizzy, adding proudly, "He's the goalkeeper for the Glendivot shinty team you know."

"Yes" replied Ponsonby, feeling distinctly ill at ease.

"He's playing in the Camanachd Cup Final next Saturday" Lizzy continued, with obvious pride and enthusiasm.

Ponsonby hesitated, "Yes...well, I'm afraid I've got some bad news for you." Lizzy stopped dead in her tracks. This startled the ugly sisters. "He's not....been fired?" she enquired.

"Well, in a kind of a way...yes" was his reply.

"Hughie?" uttered Lizzy in surprise.

Ponsonby continued "I am sorry to have to tell you this, but....I shot him!"

"You what? asked Lizzy incredulously. Violet and her sister noted the body language from a distance. He was obviously giving her bad news. What on earth could it be?

"I shot him.....up the Carse!" he replied. Lizzy's mouth dropped open, her face was in contortions. She thought for a minute.

"Can he no' sit doon noo?" Clearly she was not on his wavelength.

"No, you don't understand. It was in the foot I shot him."

"He'll still be able to go to the toilet then?" she said with relief.

"And... he'll be able to...?" "Yes yes" Rod reassured her. "But he will not...be able to play in the Cup Final I'm afraid." Ponsonby had to be honest.

Lizzy started to weep, and Violet could not keep her thoughts to herself. "What is he doing to that girl?" she pondered. "He is obviously upsetting her."

"He may be, but he's rather dishy isn't he?" replied Rose, who had not given up her search for her Adonis, even though she was a little past her prime. The ugly sisters wondered what was going on between the maid and the stranger.

The fact that this man was clearly upsetting poor Lizzy, convinced Violet that he must be a banker, or maybe even a lawyer. Recently there had been some rationalising of the industry with Distillers amalgamating, so true to their natural negative and pessimistic instincts, they surmised that he might be a merchant banker brought in to negotiate a take-over. Would this affect their brother's Distillery at Glenbroom? This filled them with horror as they did not relish the thought of being subsumed by the Glendivot Distillery.

While the two Distilleries occasionally co-operated in raw material supplies and interchanges of fillings for blends, they had not been without their arguments and disputes over the years. Litigation was threatened from time to time. The nature of the characters involved in these disputes meant that the vast majority were petty and trivial in the extreme. But the lawyers made a good living off their continual arguments.

The Unions also got wise to this rivalry and would play one off against the other. They would inflate the rates of pay being paid by their rivals in order to obtain improved pay offers, and they would fall out over the supply of Company uniforms, the timing of Company holidays, and poaching each other's employees. Accusations of industrial espionage often occurred through gossip and the inter-marriage of employees.

However by far the most irritating problem as far as the Glendivot people were concerned, was that over the years, almost every new initiative they introduced, was immediately copied by the Glenbroom people. Glendivot management were more pro-active, compared to Glenbroom's being more re-active.

It became so obvious that Angus and his team got wise to it, so they started setting traps, either by laying false trails or starting rumours that led the Glenbroom people off on wild goose chases.

For example, they would let it be known that they had negotiated a much more competitive price for their barley from a non-existent farmer in some remote island in Orkney, or that they were spending £1m changing from coal-fired to gas fired stills, when they had no intention of doing so. This they could be sure, would send the Glenbroom management off chasing rainbows, and keep them occupied for months on end.

Other hoaxes were, to divulge that Company cars were going to be offered to all employees who lived more than 20 miles from the Distillery to help them travel in the winter, and to let it be known that they were going to double the size of their cooperage thus panicking the Glenbroom management into thinking they were going to lose half their coopers.

It may not have been very professional, and it was certainly mischievous, but it was great fun to watch the panic, and note the wasted rival management man-hours, put into planning counter measures.

Ponsonby and Lizzy resumed their walk back to Balroonie House. Lizzy told him, it will break Hughie's heart to miss the Camanachd Cup Final. It would also be a massive blow to Angus's dreams of Glendivot bringing home the Cup for the first time. However, to her surprise Ponsonby said he thought he might be able to come up with a solution to the problem. They continued in animated conversation and in due course came to Balroonie Castle, followed discretely at a distance, by the two ugly sisters.

Chapter 18

SKELETON IN THE CUPBOARD

Mary came back into the lounge where her mother was still pretending to sleep. "It's OK mother, he's gone" she said looking out the door, and then closing it.

"The further the better" grumbled her mother as she eased herself into a sitting position.

"He must have changed his mind" speculated Mary.

"Well I hope it's an improvement on the last one!" announced the old lady, sharp as a tack.

Mary was deep in thought as she looked out the window, observing her husband taking something out of his car. "What is he up to now?" she pondered. Then the expression on her face changed from inquisitiveness to one of anxiety.

"Oh no! He's coming back! Go back to sleep mother!"

"Oh no, not again! There is nae rest for the wicked!" and with that, Mrs Grant breathlessly stretched out again on the couch, and shut her eyes!

Mary returned to the kitchen and a moment later. Angus popped his head round the door, paused and entered. This time he was carrying a human skeleton, covered by a raincoat, which he removed. He then spoke to the skeleton! "Right Sammy, come and meet the old battle-axe."

He then placed the skeleton on the couch beside his mother-in-law. Mary called from the kitchen. "Angus! Is that you?"

Her husband spoke again to the skeleton, "You sit there and behave yourself" he said, as he crossed its legs and took an arm.

"Ay, its me!" he called to his wife. "She puts the fear of death in me that woman" he said addressing the skeleton, as he started to tickle his mother-in-law's face with its arm. "Who are you talking to?" enquired his wife.

"Oh, its just....Sammy....Sammy, the ssskel....the stillman!"

"I didn't know you had a stillman called Sammy," shouted Mary from the kitchen.

Mrs Grant could ignore it no longer. She waved it away as if it was a fly, and then opened her eyes. "A-a-arrrh! E-e-eek! Help!" she screamed. "Help!" Mary came rushing in shouting "What have you done?" and squealed when she saw the skeleton.

Mrs Grant appealed to Angus, "Come on! Get it off!"

"Well make up your mind" replied Angus, prolonging her agony.

"What is it anyway?" asked Mary.

"It's Hector's" replied Angus, taking it off the couch. "I didnae know he was dead!" exclaimed his wife in all seriousness. "When did that happen?"

"It's no' Hector" answered Angus, shaking his head, "It belongs to Hector." "It's for Lizzy" he explained.

Mary studied it for a moment, and continued "I know she's desperate for a man...but this is ridiculous!" Mrs

Grant tried to regain her composure. "That girl will be the death of me."

Angus was enjoying their discomfiture. "It's all right. He won't harm you" he tried to reassure them. He then spoke intimately to the skeleton. "Sure you won't Sammy?" At this, he shook its head from side to side.

"You will be good now won't you?" he asked, then nodded its head. "Come and meet the wife" he strode purposefully towards his beloved, holding out the skeleton's hand.

"Not on your life!" said Mary as she took two steps back.

"Well say hello to....." reiterated Angus, turning to Mrs. Grant.

"Don't you dare!" she interrupted, holding up a cushion before he could get near her.

"He'll no' bite ye!" explained Angus, thoroughly enjoying himself.

Mary asked why Lizzy was wanting a skeleton anyway?

"It's for that play she's in. It's for the dungeons of Fotheringay Castle" Angus disclosed.

"It will scare the living daylights out of everybody" replied Mary. Whereupon Mrs Grant wailed "This is no' good for my heart," and proceeded to ask for her pills.

Mary told him to put it away before it did any more damage. She opened the cupboard door, and was about to tell him to put it in, when she saw her mother's exercise bike, and immediately shut the door. "There's no room in there" she explained.

"Don't tell me Hughie McLeod is in there again?" asked her husband.

She ignored him and opened the toilet door and told him to hang it up on a peg behind the door. Angus then spoke to the skeleton as he hung it up. "Ye'll just have to hang in there Sammy. And promise you won't go away now." He nodded its head.

"And, if ye have te use the toilet, remember there's nae lock on that door! We widna want ye te get a fright if somebody opened it!" With that he shook its head, and shut the door.

Chapter 19

CONSPIRACY

Ponsonby and Lizzy had reached Balroonie Castle, and seemed to be deep in intriguing conversation. They certainly looked like an odd couple to the other odd couple Violet and Rose, who were observing their every move.

Ponsonby stopped, looked round, and quite suddenly he took Lizzy's hand and led her up the slope to the Castle, and out of sight! This was quite an unexpected development for Violet, who always suspected the worst on such occasions.

"I can't believe this" she cried. "What on earth are they up to?"

"I can't wait to see" said her timid sister with feverish anticipation.

"Come! Hurry up!" instructed her bossy sibling.

"I'm coming, I'm coming" replied Rose following, hoping she was going to have her education completed.

They scrambled up to the main gateway, crept into the inner courtyard, just in time to see Ponsonby lead Lizzy behind a ruined rampart, and momentarily out of sight. Violet had wild premonitions of what he was going to do to Lizzy. She led Rose to the far end of the courtyard and through a rear archway. Violet knew her way around almost anywhere in Glendivot, but even she had never been in the inner sanctum of the castle before.

Rose was surprised when they came upon the furtive couple hiding behind a wall, generally frequented only by courting couples, just twenty yards away. Fortunately for the two sisters, the couple had not seen them. They were too engrossed in their own affairs. Unfortunately for the ugly sisters they could only see, but not hear what was going on.

Violet had come to the conclusion that Ponsonby was clearly a man of substance since he was being hosted at the manager's house and the elegant young lady who accompanied him was equally impressive. Between the pair of them, they had obviously made things happen at the Distillery. The whole village was talking about the changes being made, and the grapevine was working overtime.

What Violet and Rose could not understand however, was the influence that Lizzy seemed to be having upon this newcomer to the Distillery. Why was he spending so much time with her, and what was so intriguing for them to be conferring so secretly behind the Castle walls? They must have underestimated the maid.

It appeared that Ponsonby was showing her some photographs. 'Surely he wasn't a conveyor of pornographic literature,' thought Violet, as only she would. Certainly Rose would never think such a thing.

"He's real dishy, don't you think?" suggested Rose, as only she would. Violet would never think such a thing!

Little did she know that he was explaining to Lizzy his ulterior motive for coming to Speyside! And he was seeking her help!

Chapter 20

DEEP WATER

The River Fiddich is a pleasant tributary of the world-renowned River Spey. The Spey is one of the longest rivers in Scotland, and its fast flowing water is a haven for artists and fishermen, and a breeding ground for its famous salmon and trout.

Its tributary, The Fiddich however also provides its attractions. It is also a painter's paradise, and it is more peaceful, intimate and not as fast flowing. It has some lovely picnic spots and deep salmon pools, and it meanders through some of the most beautiful scenery in the Highlands. There are a number of private fishing stretches, and the Glendivot Distillery owned one of the prime beats.

On yet another gorgeous sunny day, Penny had finally pinned Hector down to taking Ponsonby on the promised fishing trip. She had now been working on her guest for a few days, and was hopeful of a satisfactory outcome to her appeal for Government assistance. She felt she just had to go one step further to seal the deal. Following his unfortunate experience up the Carse, she decided to take some time off, and join them on this occasion.

After all his earlier travails, she was beginning to develop some affection for Rod Ponsonby, although she still couldn't understand a certain degree of remoteness in his response. At times, she felt he was in a world of his own. She didn't know it, but she was right. Hector had also been having some difficulty keeping control of him, despite being assigned to look after him.

He explained in his stuttering way that Ponsonby would drive off in the car for a couple of hours at a time, but he never explained where he was going. On one occasion, he did disclose he had visited the nearby Gordonstoun School where the Duke of Edinburgh and Prince Charles were educated, but he did not divulge that he had also gone to the District Council Offices in Elgin.

He had not so far offered Penny a satisfactory explanation for these excursions, but she could not afford to interfere too much, and felt compelled to give him his space. Perhaps he had other business to attend to, and if so, that was none of her business. In any case, she was too busy reorganising the Visitor Centre, to give him 100% attention.

Having offered Rod the use of her car, and recognising his obvious enjoyment driving it, she was a little dismayed that he still appeared to be reluctant to commit the Government's money to her projects. She hoped that his forthcoming tour of the revamped Visitor Centre would finally clinch it.

On this sunny afternoon, she was sitting on a tartan rug on the river bank, beside a picnic basket, attending to the various fishing flies required by both Hector and

Ponsonby. A half empty bottle of Chardonnay was by her side.

Hector was diddling away to himself, in the middle of the river a little downstream, like Rod, in a wee world of his own. He had caught one small fish in three hours of fishing. Perhaps the sun was too strong for them. Rod Ponsonby had already tied himself in knots, trying to handle his rod, and getting his line fankled on more than one occasion. Perhaps the Chardonnay was too much for him.

Hector had another dram from his hip flask. Penny noticed that the Chief Guide appeared to be in his comfort zone, at one with nature, and utterly content with life. Perhaps it was because he didn't need to wear the kilt in the middle of the river! More likely, it was the somnolent effect of the whisky. As Rod came nearer the bank, she also felt the Under Secretary of State was looking more relaxed, and beginning to appreciate the tranquil pleasure of a day's fishing on beautiful Speyside.

"I hope you are glad you came to Scotland after all Rod?" she queried. She was now on first name terms with him. That was another step forward in her strategic battle plan. "At least you can see that it doesn't always rain in Scotland" she pointed out, taking full advantage of the excellent spell of weather they had enjoyed, since the thunderstorm at Gretna.

Rod agreed, and for his part, admitted he was also beginning to appreciate the attractions, as he gave her that extra long admiring look, that she could not fail to notice. He could not avoid noticing how beguiling his hostess was looking in this informal setting.

Having already admired her shapely legs on the journey North, he now began to appreciate that she was blessed with a figure to match. She exuded class and elegance as she sat patiently on the bank, waiting for something to happen. Not only was she an intelligent and capable young lady, she was also a charming hostess.

Like the fish in the river, she too, knew how to play him along. "Even though you haven't caught any fish all morning?" she asked. He paused, looked at her straight in the eye, approved of what he saw, and thought to himself, 'You would be quite a catch. Perhaps I should play you along.'

He then declared "There are...other compensations," and watched for her reaction. Penny felt a tingle down the back of her neck, and came to the conclusion she was now starting to make real progress. Rod felt he had more chance of 'hooking' Penny than he would have, landing a fish. Nevertheless, he was determined to prove he would be more successful at fishing, than he had been at shooting. "I'm afraid I am not doing very well, so far" he admitted, as he turned and made his way to midstream, and endeavoured to look as if he was a proficient angler.

Penny tried to reassure him, as she called, "Dr. McPherson isn't doing much better. But at least he seems to be enjoying himself."

Rod watched the Doctor for a few moments. His conscience was troubling him as he reflected, "Yes... enjoying himself a lot more than poor Hughie."

"Poor Hughie. He is devastated not being able to play in the Camanachd Cup Final" she remarked.

"I wonder if Mr. McDougall has a replacement goalkeeper yet?" Rod pondered as he cast his line over his shoulder.

Rod's concentration had lapsed for a few moments, as he thought of Angus's dilemma, while at the same time, he could not take his mind off Penny. Suddenly, Hector called out "Look out Mr. P-P-Ponsonby! I think you have c-c-c-caught something!"

All of a sudden a large salmon leapt out the water, obviously caught in Rod's fly. Not surprisingly, he panicked as he didn't quite know what to do. Hector came as fast as he could, dropping his own rod on the bank and shouting "Wow! Look at the s-s-size of it!"

"My goodness, you've caught a whopper!" shouted Penny, standing up in admiration. 'Wrong one' thought Rod momentarily, under his breath.

"T-t-take it easy now" called Hector as Rod seemed to try and reel it in as fast as he could.

"What do I do" he cried, seeking help, as he reeled the line in frantically.

"S-S-Steady as she goes" replied Hector, stumbling unsteadily along the bank as best he could.

"Bring her in s-s-slowly." Penny was now jumping up and down with excitement, and Rod seemed to be losing his battle for control as he missed his footing in midstream.

"C-C-Careful! K-K-Keep clear of that p-p-p-pool!" shouted Hector, who knew the pool behind Rod was known as "Fishermen's Folly." The wily old Doctor knew every inch of the river. "It's v-v-very deep!" he called.

"I think I'm losing it!" Rod responded as he referred to the salmon, but he also lost his footing once more. Hector assessed the situation from the safety of the bank a few yards away.

"You need a b-b-bigger f-f-f-fly for one that size." At this point, Penny offered one.

By this time the salmon had indeed freed itself, and Rod by his reflex action, got the hook caught in the front of his trousers below his belt and above his wading boots. Not surprisingly, he panicked again, overbalanced into the deep pool, and disappeared for a few moments! Only his floppy hat, gently floating on the surface of the clear cold waters, gave any indication of his whereabouts.

As he reappeared splashing around like a stranded whale, Penny was overcome with mixed emotions. On the one hand she found it very funny to see this slightly pompous Government Minister, experiencing another hapless encounter, and yet on the other hand, she really felt heart sorry for the poor man. She was beginning to lose count of all his trials and tribulations. Surely he must be regretting his decision to come to Scotland, or he was a glutton for punishment, she reflected.

Hector knew better than to go to his rescue. He was too old and too experienced to be a hero. So poor Rod was left to his own devices, and had to make his own way to the bank. Penny wrapped him in the tartan rug, and Hector offered him his empty hip flask!

They packed up the picnic things, loaded the estate car with the fishing gear, and helped Rod into the car, soaked to the skin and freezing cold. "I never thought that water c-c-could be so c-c-cold" he complained with his teeth chattering. He was more used to swimming in the Caribbean than the Cabrach. He was so cold he was now stuttering almost as much as Hector. Penny couldn't help being amused, as she came into the car and sat beside him.

"This is becoming too much of a habit" she observed. Rod was non-plussed, and asked her what she meant.

"You...coming into cars soaking wet!" He wasn't amused.

Hector got into the driver's seat, and noted Penny in the back seat with her arm round Rod, wrapped in the blanket. With a knowing expression, he started the engine. "We'll have you b-back to B-B-B-Balroonie House in no time" he said as he put his foot on the accelerator, and took off down the winding road to Glendivot.

"There is no hurry" said Rod, as he cuddled into Penelope's bosom to keep warm.

Chapter 21

DOOM AND GLOOM

Back at Balroonie House, Mrs Grant was in her favourite seat beside the fire. She was knitting for a change. Mary came down the stairs as Angus arrived home from work, looking depressed. She was carrying some old loose photographs and an old photograph album she had resurrected from the loft.

"Well, what havoc has Miss Whitehouse caused today?" she asked.

His reply surprised her. "None" replied her husband as he sat on the couch. "We sent her on a fishing trip with Hector and her fancy man, to keep her out of mischief... She can't do any damage there."

"He is not her fancy man" insisted Mary disapprovingly, as she sat beside him.

"Well Hughie McLeod doesnae fancy him anyway. Not after being shot in the foot"

"It was an accident" explained Mary.

"A fine time to shoot Hughie...a week before the Cup Final... I've spent all day trying to find a replacement." No wonder Angus was depressed.

"I thought Keith Crowther was your reserve keeper?" enquired Mary.

"No longer, Keith Crowther fell aff a lorry and broke his jaw and dislocated his collar bone!" replied her husband.

"How did he do that?" asked Mrs Grant.

"He fell aff a..........He got distracted by one of these new dolly birds in their mini-skirts!" explained Angus.

"The ones Miss Whitehouse employed?" Mary presumed.

"The same" answered Angus. "Poor boy" thought Mrs Grant. "Is he all right?"

"Naw!... He's got a broken jaw and a dislocated collar bone!" said Angus, somewhat exasperated.

"Silly old fool."

"He'll no' be able to take Hughie's place in the team then." Mary stated the obvious, while opening the album. "Right first time" replied her husband.

Whereupon Mrs Grant pontificated "First it's Hughie, then it's Keith Crowther. I tell you, everything happens in threes. I wonder who it will be next?" implying that it was bound to be her turn.

Angus ignored her, and asked his wife what she was doing with the photograph album.

"I'm looking for Lizzy."

"Ye'll no' find her there" said Angus. "I saw her going doon the village."

Mary then explained that Lizzy had discovered from Mr Ponsonby, that he was looking for his father, to which Angus responded by saying that she wouldn't find him in the album either. "So that's why he has been disappearing so much" he concluded thoughtfully.

Mary stopped at the page with Angus's old Regimental Photograph. On seeing this, Angus objected "Now wait a minute. That Regiment may have been responsible for a lot, but...." He was interrupted by his wife.

"Mr Ponsonby's father was in the Seaforth Highlanders, stationed at Fort George.... That's where you and Hector served during the War. Do you remember?"

"Ay fine, but...Ponsonby? There was never anyone with a name like that in the Seaforths" said Angus dismissing the idea out-of-hand, "Unless he was an officer."

"He told Lizzy his mother was a Hoare" continued Mary, at which her mother was startled and shocked, and dropped her knitting. She pondered what the world was coming to.

"Not that kind of whore mother. Evidently she came from a well known stock-broking family....The Hoare-Grindlings...or something like that. She was evacuated up here during the Second World War...and she met this...Seaforth Highlander...and, in due course they... had... a little Seaforth." explained Mary. "Mr. Ponsonby!" expounded her mother.

Mary had more to say. "He never knew his father. He never returned...after the War." she reflected.

"His mother died when he was a child, and he was brought up by a maiden aunt in Kent."

"How do ye ken that?" asked Angus.

"Lizzy told me."

"Lizzy? How did she find out?" enquired her startled husband.

"Mr Ponsonby told her." replied Mary.

"Lizzy!" said Angus somewhat surprised. "Dizzy Lizzy?" he paused, "She's been busy." His wife continued "He went to Cambridge...read Russian."

"He's no' a Communist is he?" asked Angus, jumping to conclusions.

Mary dismissed the idea, and Angus rose from the couch, and looked out the window, deep in thought. He then turned and asked, "How will he ken his father?"

Mary had the old photographs that Ponsonby had given Lizzy. She went on to explain. "He brought these old photographs with him...of his mother and father during the War. He is trying to trace them from these." Angus felt he needed a seat, so he returned to the couch.

During this conversation, the ugly sisters Violet and Rose, were back in Glendivot walking their huge dog. It was a large fearsome Alsatian, a bit like its owner in fact, and it required considerable exercise. They quite often made a habit of walking it the three miles from Glenbroom.

After her recent encounter with the scheming Ponsonby and Lizzy, Violet had become almost obsessed with finding out what their conspiratorial tryst was all about. She had noted the impact that Ponsonby and Penny had made on the community since arriving. Gossip had it that they were turning the Distillery upside down! Violet and Rose were determined to turn the whole village upside down if necessary, to find out the reason why they were staying so long at Balroonie House. They also wanted to know why Ponsonby was secretly scheming with Lizzy, and the extent of Penny's influence at the Distillery.

It was certainly unusual to have such guests staying at Balroonie House, and they seemed to be responsible for all the new activity around the Distillery Visitor Centre since they arrived. The employees and their families, and indeed the whole village was agog with stories, some of which were true, while others were pure fantasy. There wasn't a healthier grapevine in all of Scotland, than the one in Glendivot, even though it did grow out of control at times.

Violet was not known as 'Doom' for nothing. She always saw the pessimistic side of everything. For her, the whisky glass was always half-empty rather than half-full. Over the years, she had even affected her younger sister Rose, who, after sharing nearly 40 years in the same house, had experienced a remorseless decline in her naturally pleasant personality, to one of utter gloom and despondency. This was so pervading that she had now acquired the nick-name of 'Gloom,' hence 'Doom' and 'Gloom.'

Violet had discussed the matter with her brother the previous evening, and 'Doubting Thomas' contemplated the implications if Ponsonby was, as suggested by his sister, a merchant banker involved in a take-over of Glendivot. The recent spate of acquisitions in the Industry had made him nervous about the fate of his own Distillery, which he had to admit, was vulnerable. 'Doom' was convinced it was a bad omen. Mrs Grant did not have a monopoly of 'Omens' in Glendivot.

But what to make of Penny? She obviously had the power to turn the Visitor Centre upside-down, so she wasn't just his side-kick, or his 'Floozie.' So, was she something more sinister? or dangerous?

But where did Lizzy come into the equation? That was what was so baffling. If he was a merchant banker organising a take-over, he wouldn't be negotiating it with Lizzy.

So, in for a penny (If you'll pardon the pun) in for a pound, Violet had decided to take them on head first. She prepared herself for a full frontal assault. If given the chance, she would have been first to lead the charge on to the beaches of Normandy on D-Day! Rose was carrying a charity collecting can, and Violet had a large bag over her arm. She was fully occupied handling her enormous aggressive dog, which had, as is so often the case, the same expression and nature as its owner.

As they approached the Balroonie House driveway, Violet cleared her mind.

"We will find out once and for all, what is going on" she determined. Rose, trailing in her wake as usual, appealed to her better nature.

"It is really none of our business Violet!" to which came the assertion "Everything...in Glendivot is our business!" There was no answer to that, so they strode up the drive and rang the doorbell.

Inside, Mrs Grant wondered who it could be, and Mary went to the window. The look on her face said it all. "It's Violet and Rose Hannah!" she announced.

"Trouble and strife!" proclaimed her mother.

"Doom and Gloom from Glenbroom!" wailed Angus, as he sank further into the couch.

'What had he done?' he wondered, 'to deserve such fate,' as they arrived on his doorstep.

Mary had a quick look round to ensure that everything in the room was in order, and Angus said, "I hope she hasn't brought that brute of a dog with her this time. I will not have her in this house again!"

"Fouled the carpet...the bitch!" divulged Mrs Grant.

"No she didnae" Angus disagreed. "It was the dug that did it!"

Mary put the photograph album in a drawer and gave instructions not to tell Doom and Gloom what Penny and Ponsonby were doing in Glendivot. The doorbell rang again. "They're just nosey-parkers" added her mother, as she tidied her hair and put her knitting away.

"If they find out we are getting grants for our Visitor Centre, they'll be after the same at Glenbroom" said Angus. "They are always copying our best ideas."

"And don't let on about me asking Mr Ponsonby for money to develop this house into a Boarding House." instructed Mary as she was about to open the door.

"They will no' take kindly to us competing with theirs." perceived her mother, impervious to the fact that her daughter was in fact, copying them.

Mary opened the door, and the sisters were about to enter. Suddenly, the dog started to growl, and then it barked fiercely! For once, Violet was almost caught off balance, as the dog refused to go further.

"Quiet Thumper!.... Be quiet!" she shouted. "Leave them alone!...Thumper!... You don't know who's been touching them!" she cried. Mary who remained inside the house could not see what the dog was doing.

"You will jag your nose!" warned Violet, still addressing the dog.

"What is she doing?" asked Mary. Rose replied "She is...relieving herself...on your roses!" as the dog whined and growled again, clearly not wanting to be disturbed.

That was enough for Angus. "She is what?" he demanded, as he rose from the couch. Rose tried to retrieve the situation. "Don't do that Thumper." Her appeal had as much conviction and authority as a fox appealing to a pack of hounds.

"Thumper? Wait till I thump her!" threatened Angus.

"Come away Thumper, you'll get distemper" warned Violet, whereupon Angus lost *his* temper.

He grabbed the lead from Violet, and was immediately dragged away by the barking mad dog, down the driveway at a fast rate of knots. They all watched for a moment, until Mrs Grant shouted from inside the house,

"Can you not shut that door! I'm getting my death of cold!"

"You had better come in" Mary reluctantly invited the ugly sisters into the house, before looking anxiously at her husband losing his battle with the animal, and then shutting the door behind her, as she shook her head.

Violet was an intimidating and overbearing matriarch. She had a permanent scowl on her face, always wore the same tweed suit, a flat hat with a large hat-pin, and her hair in a severe bun at the back. She had always been a domineering spinster, who took command of almost every situation she encountered. What she needed was a strong man to put her in her place and keep her there.

Rose was no match for her, and over the years had settled for the quiet life, by playing second fiddle to her older sister, at all times.

"Och! What have you done with your hall Mary? It has gone!" enquired Violet, stating the obvious.

Mary conceded that she had made "A wee change" forgetting that the 'Ugly Sisters' had not been over her door for some time. However, there was no way she was going to divulge her longer term plans.

"Well, I can't say I approve" said the opinionated Violet. "Never mind. There is no explaining folk." Mary could not care less what Violet thought of her changes. At that point, Violet turned, and saw Mrs Grant.

"Good day to you Mrs Grant" she greeted her rather formally.

"I see there's a change in the weather. There's a deep depression coming in."

"Ay. It's here already" retorted Mrs Grant who was no slouch herself.

Violet was impervious to the remark and sat on the couch while Rose remained standing. "Have a seat Violet" invited Mary. "You too Rose" and Rose sat down.

"You will have had a cup of tea Violet?" presumed Mrs Grant, hoping for the best.

Violet knew fine that if they accepted a cup of tea, this would guarantee her some valuable time, to ascertain who the visitors were, where they came from, and what they were doing, staying at Balroonie House.

Rose was about to raise her collecting can when her sister replied.

"No. As a matter of fact we haven't. Sure we haven't Rose?"

"No, we came to...." She was interrupted by the dog barking again, and Angus yelling at it. They were clearly having a right ding-dong battle outside.

"I hope you're not collecting for the RSPCA Rose?" speculated Mary, as Angus appeared to howl in agony outside. "Because if so, you have picked a bad day!"

"No. That is next week" responded Violet before her sister could reply.

Rose raised her can again and was about to appeal for a donation, when Angus came bursting in the front door, looking thoroughly dishevelled. His trousers were torn in several places. He had clearly lost the battle with the dog.

"Where did ye put my gun Mary?" he demanded. "That dug is about te meet its maker!" "Don't you dare Angus McDougall" threatened Violet.

By this time Mary had looked out the window, and called out, "Oh look what she's done now! Really Violet, you will have to do something about that dog of yours!"

"There's nothing wrong with her. We just treat her like one of the family." Violet could see no wrong in her pet.

"Ay. I can see the resemblance" observed Angus, looking her up and down.

Mary decided to leave well alone, and hoped that the dog would calm down. She offered to go and put the kettle on, whereupon Violet called after her, "Scones will do Mary! We don't need anything else. Your scones are filling enough!"

'I ken who I'd like te fill in' muttered Angus under his breath.

Rose tried to be sociable, and asked Mrs Grant how she was keeping. Before the old lady could explain that her particular ailment that day was a sore back, Violet interjected, "I've had a terrible headache you know. Haven't I Rose?"

"Terrible" responded her long suffering sister.

"I was just saying..." said Mrs Grant, trying to answer Rose's question, when the older sister carried on "Migraine...from here to here, right across my head."

"You're just one big headache" uttered Angus.

"In fact I've had two migraines today" claimed Violet, who was notorious for boasting that she had more of everything, than anyone else.

Mrs Grant persevered once more, "As I was saying..."

"And this pain..." continued Violet, oblivious and unsympathetic to the old lady's ailments.

"In the neck!" assumed Angus.

"In the ne...yes, as it so happens" Violet was taken by surprise, so Mrs Grant saw her opportunity.

"It's my back that's really been troubling me" she managed to say. Rose showed some sympathy "It's the weather Mrs Grant. It's so changeable. In my opinion..."

"When we want your opinion Rose...we will tell you!" Violet told her, having recovered from Angus's put-down.

Ultimately Rose managed to ask for a donation to the Old Folk's Home in the Village, and after Angus offered his mother-in-law, Mary contributed some coins from her purse, and Lizzy came in with tea and scones.

"Was that no' terrible what happened to Hughie McLeod Mary?" said Violet, starting her probing.

"They say it was that Englishman who shot him...up the Carse!"

"In the foot it was Violet, in the foot!" Rose corrected her.

"Painful, wherever it was" noted her sister. Angus observed that news travels fast.

"And him with a part to play next week" continued Violet.

Angus thought she was referring to Hughie playing in the shinty team, but Violet soon put him right.

"I mean Lord Darnley. He'll no' be able to play Lord Darnley next week" she said. Rose suddenly thought she had a solution. "Not unless we make Lord Darnley have a club foot!" As usual, her suggestion was dismissed by her sister. "Lord Darnley did *not* have a club foot!" A worried looking Lizzy returned to the kitchen.

Mary had forgotten all about Hughie's involvement in the play, as Violet took the Darnley costume out of her large carrier bag.

"When I think of the trouble I've gone to, to make this costume fit Hughie" she complained, as Angus rose to feed the goldfish. He was beginning to feel like a fish out of water.

The two sisters began to explain that they were at their wits end trying to find a man to play the part of Lord Darnley. Angus said he was not at all surprised. They asked Mary if she could think of anyone who could play the part. Violet's view was that there was not a lot to learn, as Lord

Darnley was a weak and spineless character, whereas her sister's view was not surprisingly, rather different.

As far as she was concerned, his role was to make mad passionate love to Mary Queen of Scots. "Control yourself" said Violet.

"We don't know where to turn" said Rose despairingly Even Violet had to admit they were now getting desperate.

"Nae wonder" retorted Angus, chuckling to himself and enjoying their desperation. That was his fatal mistake. If only he had kept his big mouth shut, he might have remained anonymous. Instead, all he had done, was to draw attention to himself.

Suddenly, they all turned to him and cried out together... "Angus!" There was a moment's silence. "You're mad!" uttered Angus, petrified at the mere thought.

"No' Angus?" queried Mrs Grant in disbelief.

"Yes, Angus!" announced Violet. This was a development she had not anticipated, but even she would settle for him in this crisis.

"You'll need to help them out Angus" said his wife, as he opened the front door.

"Aye...Oot the door!" he demanded, and the dog resumed barking.

The ridiculous suggestion put more fear into him, than the dog. Mrs Grant expressed her opinion. "He couldnae make mad passionate love to save himself." Her remark was almost counter-productive.

"Oh I don't know" said Angus shutting the door, and preening himself.

"Come on Angus, we really are stuck" implored Rose. The poor man was cornered, outmanoeuvred and outnumbered. He claimed they were all mad, to which Violet still had a cutting response.

"I suppose we are...if we are down to asking you!" she admitted.

They then set upon him to see if the costume would fit him, despite his protestations, such as "I don't suit green," or "I wouldnae be seen dead in these" and "Besides, I need to go and look for a goalkeeper!" being some of them.

"If we've got no choice, why should you? You'll have to do" insisted Violet, as she loosened his tie.

"Leave me alane" pleaded Angus. "You're no' stripping me in my ain living room!" as Rose went for his jacket.

"Well, if you won't co-operate, what do you expect?" said Violet with no sympathy.

Angus knew in his bones that Doom and Gloom would bring trouble. He shouldn't have come home early. Out of the blue, his wife brought some sanity to his situation.

"Wait a minute" she said, and the ugly sisters hesitated for a moment.

"I tell you what Angus. We will make a deal with you." Angus thought of drowning men clutching at straws.

"If you take Hughie's place as Lord Darnley...I...will get *you* a replacement for your shinty team."

Angus could not believe what he was hearing. What did she know about shinty? He had spent endless hours in the last two days trying to solve the problem created by Hughie's injury. He could not get anyone to take on the task of goalkeeper in the shinty Cup Final. It was a position that was notoriously dangerous, and no one he asked, would risk it. He had even resorted to visions of having to step in himself, despite the fact he hadn't played for 20 years! He was that desperate!

"Now there's an offer you can't refuse" said Violet, resuming stripping him.

"You must be joking?" Angus asked his wife, in a befuddled state.

"No. I am serious" confirmed Mary.

"How will you do that?" he queried.

"Never you mind" replied his wife. He was in no position to bargain.

"You'll no' let me doon?" he checked.

The ugly sisters now went for his trousers.

"If you'll just let these doon" said Violet, trying to pull them off him.

"Leave them alone!" he called out in consternation. "Ye never had a man's breeks off in your life Violet Hannah, and you're no' starting with mine noo!" he screeched.

Mary opened the toilet door, and saved his dignity in the nick of time.

"You go in there and try on Lord Darnley's costume, and we will see if it fits you."

Angus reluctantly took the costume into the toilet, thinking 'Any port in a storm.' Mary poured tea for the sisters, Rose declining sugar because she was 'Sweet enough' while Violet had three spoonfuls.

Mary offered Violet one of her home-made rock cakes. "Take your pick" she said.

"They're no' as hard as that?" countered Violet, who then resumed the interrogation.

"So who are the strangers you have been looking after Mary?"

"Strangers?" repeated Mary pleading ignorance.

"Yes. The girl with the red jacket and the man, who looks like a banker." probed Violet.

"I would bank with him anytime" added Rose.

Mary was at a loss, and procrastinated as long as she could, but her inquisitor would not let go. She was truly one of the bulldog breed. One could be forgiven for thinking that Violet had been trained by the KGB or the Gestapo! "Well, who is he?" she demanded to know.

It was Mrs Grant's turn to come to the rescue. "He's... the Minister!" she proclaimed. Mary, was firstly taken aback, but then somewhat relieved, she latched on. "Yes. He's the Locum, for the summer months" she confirmed.

Violet was speechless for a moment.

"For Glendivot Parish? How did we not know that?" she enquired, turning to her sister.

"Yes. We normally know these things" piped up Rose.

"He doesn't look like a Minister to me" meditated Violet.

"You never can tell these days" agreed Mrs Grant, who was not slow at criticising the new generation of clergy.

"And who is the woman with him?" Violet continued her questioning. Again, Mary stumbled over an explanation, until her mother rescued the situation again. "She is...his wife!" Now, things were getting complicated, especially after she added, "They are on their honeymoon!"

Violet was not convinced. "From what I've heard, she doesn't sound like a Minister's wife...on her honeymoon." Mrs Grant asked her how she would know, as unlike her, Violet had no experience!

At that, there was a frantic commotion outside, and Hector burst in. "Mary, Mary. We've got a c-c-c-crisis on our hands!" He was clearly in an agitated state.

"*You've* got a crisis!" cried Mary, consumed by her own problems. "You are not the only one!"

He then saw the ugly sisters. "Oh, I see what you mean. B-b-but this is just as bad. There's b-b-been another a-accident!" Having heard the commotion, Lizzy came from the kitchen. "What is it this time?" enquired Mary.

"I keep telling you. Everything happens in threes" said her mother.

Before Hector could explain, Penny entered with her arm round a soaking shivering Ponsonby, who was still wrapped up in the tartan rug. Mary motioned to Lizzy to pour him a dram as he was still shaking. "What happened?" she asked.

Hector explained "He f-f-f-fell in the river" and Ponsonby sneezed as they ushered him to the fire.

"How did you come to fall in the river?" asked Mrs Grant innocently, offering him her chair.

"I didn't!" replied Ponsonby. "I came to fish!" clearly distraught at his latest misfortune. Lizzy gave him the glass of whisky.

She then took the picnic basket from Penny and the wet clothes from Hector, and carried them through to the kitchen. Hector disclosed, "It was Mr P-P-Ponsonby's f-f-f-fly that caused the p-p-problem!"

The ladies put their cups down in their saucers with a clatter. He certainly had their attention.

"All of a sudden, this great b-b-big one appeared. It was this s-s-size" he indicated the fish was about three feet long.

They all stared at Ponsonby. "Well, this size" said Hector, reducing his hands gesture to about 18 inches. Penny said she had never seen anything like it, to which Mrs Grant responded, "I could believe that!"

Ponsonby then admitted he lost the fish, and Hector went on to say, "It was no d-d-disgrace. He needed a b-b-bigger f—f-f-fly for one that size!" Penny added she was trying to give him a bigger one, but he "Got all excited".

"I'll bet he did" confirmed that wily old bird Mrs Grant.

Hector explained it had caught in his trousers. "The fish?" asked Mary.

"No, the f-f-f-fly!" exclaimed Hector.

"Where else would his fly be?" Mrs Grant posed the rhetorical question.

"And he fell right over, into the water!" added Penny.

Mary suggested he went upstairs to change into dry clothes, and then realised she had not introduced the young couple to Violet and Rose. "These are our neighbours from Glenbroom, Violet and Rose Hannah. Meet....Mr and Mrs Ponsonby!" Rod and Penny looked at each other, aghast. As he shook hands with Rose,

Rod sneezed without warning, and Rose said "Bless you Minister." He looked quizzically at Mary. "How could this stranger know he was a junior Minister in Her Majesty's Government when he had only just met her?" he thought to himself.

"How are you enjoying your honeymoon?" enquired Violet boldly.

Rod and Penny paused, and looked at each other again. Violet continued to pursue the matter, noting their embarrassment.

"There is no use denying it! We can tell honeymoon couples a mile away!" she pronounced, with all the authority she could muster. Mary ushered them up the stairs before any more damage was done.

Chapter 22

A MIRACLE

They reached the upstairs landing, and were about to go into their separate rooms, when Mary told them to wait. She went into her own bedroom, and a moment later reappeared with a Minister's dog collar. It had belonged to her father.

"I don't have time to explain just now. You will have to trust me. But for now, *you* Mr Ponsonby, are the Minister..."

"I am only a junior Minister," he explained.

"Not that kind of Minister" Mary continued. "I mean, you are our new Parish Minister. And *you* Miss Whitehouse, are his wife...."

"We are what?" they protested.

"And...you are both on your honeymoon".

"Oh that makes a difference" said Ponsonby, as he thought through the implications, and warmed to the idea. Perhaps things were beginning to take a turn for the better at last.

"I might enjoy this trip to Scotland after all!" he said, with a suggestive grin. Mary gave him the dog collar and asked him to wear it, and try and act like a Minister of the cloth. She pleaded with them both to pretend they were on their honeymoon, at least for now, and she would explain everything later. Of all the challenges he had faced so far, Rod felt that this was the most appealing.

Mary turned to go downstairs, and once she was out of earshot, Ponsonby mischievously suggested to Penny that this meant they could now share a room! Penny, was not prepared for that at this stage, but didn't object to a bit of flirtation. It might get her closer to Ponsonby...and the money!

Violet and Rose were somewhat overcome by this new development. Hector nearly put his foot in it, by saying he didn't know they were married, until he was firmly put in his place by Mrs Grant. "Ye ken noo!" she told him, in no uncertain terms.

It was when Hector asked where Angus was, that they all realised he was still in the toilet! Perhaps he had gone to sleep. He was certainly suspiciously quiet. Hector suggested he must have a p-p-p-problem if he had been in the toilet for such a long time, to which Mrs Grant agreed "He has Hector, he has."

As if by telepathy, at that very moment, there was a loud banging on the toilet door and Angus demanded to be let out. Perhaps he would have been better to remain where he was, and hope they would all forget about him. Violet asked if he couldn't open the door, to which Angus responded, "If I could open the door, I wouldn't be asking you to let me out!"

As Mary came back down the stairs, Hector said he knew how Angus felt, as he had been in that situation before. He offered to try and open the door. After much twisting and pulling, he was getting nowhere, so Violet took over, saying "Let me at him."

She took to her task with such vigour, that Mary thought the door was going to come off its hinges again. At that point Hughie the goalkeeper arrived on crutches, and his ankle in plaster. He was carrying his goalkeeper's gear and a shinty stick.

He knocked on the front door, and asked if he could come in as the door was open, only to be put down savagely by a flustered Violet saying "No it's no' ye stupid....*oh that* door?" as she realised he was referring to the front door.

Mrs Grant felt vindicated. "My, it's all happening the day. Here's accident number....I don't know what. I've lost count now."

"I've brought my shinty gear for Keith Crowther. Angus was going to ask him to take my place" said a disappointed Hughie. He was obviously unaware of his replacement's accident.

"He's in the hospital" explained Mrs Grant.

"Angus? Why? What happened?" responded Hughie, to which Rose countered, "No, not Angus. He's in the toilet!"

Mrs Grant enlightened Hughie that it was Keith Crowther who was in the hospital, with "A broken collar bone and a dislocated jaw, or was it a dislocated collar bone and a broken jaw?" Lizzy then came back from the kitchen.

Angus resumed his banging on the door and calling to be let out, and Lizzy offered to get the screwdriver and ladders again. Ponsonby then came down the stairs with his new 'Wife' Penny. He was wearing the dog collar, his original black jacket and striped trousers, and looking for all the world, a Minister.

Mary was surprised and very impressed. She had never seen him dressed like this before, and for one moment, she wondered if he had stolen some of her father's clothes. Even her mother was impressed by his traditional clerical clothing, which would go down well in Presbyterian Glendivot.

Rose asked him if he could help, to which Violet said it would take a miracle to open the door, and for once Rose had the last word. "Well, if that is the case, he is better qualified than any of us!" she asserted.

Penny pointed out the last time this happened, Hector McPherson came out. However Hector assured her that would not happen this time.

Just then, Lizzy came back with the ladders, and screwdriver, but they weren't necessary. Ponsonby rose to the occasion, cleared his throat, and in a sombre ministerial voice, declared "What is it again? Seek...and ye shall find...knock... (and he knocked)...and it shall be opened..."

Slowly the handle of the door turned, and out came Angus, looking somewhat ridiculous in the Lord Darnley costume. He gave them the fright of their lives... as he suddenly threatened them with the skeleton!

Chapter 23

GLENBROOM

Glenbroom is the nearest village to Glendivot on the Cabrach road. It is about three miles away, past the tall imposing Auchindoun Castle, which, because of its tall tower and steep spiral staircase, is fondly known as 'Upandoon Castle.' Glenbroom has a population about half that of its neighbour, and only one Distillery, one hotel and one small church.

The green fertile land which borders the Fiddich River flowing through Glendivot, gives way to the coarser moorland of the Cabrach. It is about 500 feet higher, with few trees, and subsequently, is a windswept landscape. It therefore suffers from a harsher climate, despite its proximity to Glendivot. Often the snow lies in Glenbroom for weeks on end, while Glendivot is clear. Sometimes the village could be shrouded in fog or mist when there is none in its larger neighbour.

Angus and Mary had for once agreed, that the climate in the Cabrach reflected the harsher, coarser personalities of its inhabitants. They both thought they were a dour lot, the folk from Glenbroom, but then Angus and Mary were biased.

For generations, there had been a great rivalry between the two Communities, and it manifested itself in many ways. The inter-village football and shinty matches were battles to behold. No one living in the area would agree to be the referee or linesmen, for it was far too dangerous. Wrong or even doubtful decisions, would invoke the wrath of rival supporters to such an extent, that officials' lives, and those of their families, were threatened.

Now that is saying something, for their brave forefathers had fought bravely at Culloden, Waterloo, the Somme, El Alamein and on D-Day. There came a strong fighting tradition from such a pedigree. They now took it out on each other on the football and shinty fields, rather than the battlefield. Heaven help them if they took up rugby!

Even the genteel ladies' Flower Clubs fought tooth and nail for the prestigious Annual Flower Show Prizes. Long embarrassing silences were conspicuous, when rival ladies refused to speak to one another, after floral exhibits were judged. It was a brave or naive judge indeed, who awarded 1st Prize to someone from Glendivot, over her rival from Glenbroom, at their annual 'Glenbroom in Bloom' Flower Show.

At least the adults had three miles separating them, but the poor children did not have that luxury. They had to attend the joint school. Many a child grew up very quickly as they had to fend for themselves in the playgrounds and school classrooms. Perhaps that is why there were so many upstanding young people in Speyside. It is because they had to stand up for themselves so often at school.

Things really came to a head after Mrs Grant's husband, the Rev. Alasdair Grant died the previous year. This event strained inter-community relations in the area to an unprecedented breaking point.

The Presbytery of Badenoch and Strathspey had in their wisdom, taken the decision to amalgamate the two Parishes of Glendivot and Glenbroom, and appoint one Minister for both congregations.

Now the Protestant congregations in Speyside were very devout people, and took their Christianity very seriously. Their commitment to brotherly love was such that the Presbytery expected the Parishes of Glendivot and Glenbroom to live together in peace and harmony. The problem was, they misjudged their parishioners, who were so devoted to their Church, that they were reluctant to share it with the other congregation.

The poor man who was inducted to the joint charge and assigned to bring these warring Parishes together in joint Christian fellowship, was one Rev. Carmichael McCutcheon, who had served his apprenticeship in the mining community of Cumnock in Ayrshire. Not as a miner, but as a minister.

The Presbytery knew what they were doing, for Cumnock and the neighbouring village of Auchinleck, had a history of notorious rivalry, that would make the Israeli/Palestinian conflict appear like a Women's Guild bun fight. He certainly had his work cut out for himself in this situation.

He had spent so many years knocking folks' heads together in Ayrshire, that his reputation had gone before him. However he was now of such an age, that the experience had affected his personality, and he had acquired a nick-name, prior to being inducted to the Speyside charges. He was known, not as Carmichael McCutcheon, but 'Curmudgeon McCutcheon.'

Although this was a little unfair, it did to some extent reflect his personality. One could hardly blame him, for he had spent over 20 years trying to reconcile the irreconcilable, and as time went on, he became more and more intolerant of those diehards for whom he was expected to act as peacemaker.

He had not expected to find a similar situation in the peaceful Utopia of Speyside, and his patience became very strained, within the first year of his Ministry in what was supposed to be 'God's Country.' He was astute enough to have already assessed the infamous sisters, and to a lesser extent, their brother. Not surprisingly, he had made a point of keeping a safe distance from them. This they assumed, may have been the reason why they had not been informed of the appointment of the new 'Locum Minister.'

Not everybody there was like Violet and Rose. Their reputation was such that they were commonly known collectively as the 'Ugly sisters' and individually as 'Doom' and 'Gloom.' They lived with their brother at the Distillery on the edge of the village, and because it was just beyond the 30mph road sign, the locals claimed 'There is nae room for Doom and Gloom in Glenbroom!' In fact, between the three of them, they had acquired various nick-names from the locals, including 'The Three Craws' and 'The Three Stooges.'

The ugly sisters' brother Thomas Hannah, was the manager of the Glenbroom Distillery. His eyes were a little too close for comfort, and he lacked ambition and imagination. One could be forgiven for thinking that he would not have reached his position, had his father not held the post for 30 years before him. Nepotism was not unknown in the whisky industry.

His physical appearance was not impressive. He was prematurely bald, rather rotund, and his waist coat often showed signs of food stains. Having Violet as an older sister had made him introverted and suspicious by nature. Accordingly, he had a naturally defensive personality. This was hardly surprising, given that he was regularly defending himself from her constant complaints and criticism.

Violet being older, was very much the boss of the family, while his younger sister Rose, was made very aware that she was the 'Afterthought' of the family, or worse still, 'A mistake,' as she was nearly 10 years younger. The only thing that would have been more demeaning for her would be, to have been 'Born on the wrong side of the blanket.' She lived very much in their shadow, and had subsequently developed an inferiority complex.

Thomas was a bachelor, so he shared the Distillery Manager's House with his sisters. At least this meant that he often, though not always, had his meals made for him, and they did come in handy for shopping and the washing of his dirty linen. His sisters were experts at washing other people's dirty linen. Notwithstanding, he had to do his own ironing.

Doom and Gloom had inherited the local hotel next to the Distillery, which had seven rooms for guests, but its furnishings and decor reflected their character, that is, dull and drab. It was hardly inviting, rather cold and dated, and in need of modernisation. The sisters were constantly in dispute with the Hotel and Tourist regulatory Authorities and the Health and Safety Inspectorate. This was unsurprising, for Violet would pick a fight with anyone, and her running battles with them were legendary.

If Penny thought she had difficulty impressing Rod Ponsonby, there was simply no way he would be impressed with Doom and Gloom's efforts at attracting the tourists. Indeed they were only one step up from the Commercial Hotel in Glendivot. As a result, their business was rather sparse, even in mid-season, and they tended to rely on passing trade. Anyone who knew of their reputation would pass by, if they had any sense. Advance bookings were rare, and repeat bookings non-existent.

They depended on the locals who had nothing better to do, using the public bar with its television, one-armed bandit, darts board and pool table. Some joker at the Distillery suggested, the only way to revive their fortunes, would be to install pole-dancers and a night club! The ugly sisters did not understand what he meant. If they had any initiative, they could perhaps have recruited some of the new Glendivot Dolly-birds to dance for them.

Doom and Gloom returned to their house in the evening, shortly after meeting the new 'Locum Minister' at Balroonie House. They sought a meeting with Thomas and were having something to eat when he appeared about half an hour later.

"Where have you been?" demanded Violet, requiring him to justify his absence. She had the temerity to assume he should be at her beck and call whenever she required.

"I was having a bath if you must know." he replied, explaining his delay with commendable patience.

"We have we got news for you!" chipped in Rose, still quite excited at the day's developments.

"We have been to Glendivot" Violet started.

"Do you know what is going on there?"

"No, what?" he replied, trying to sound interested, and wondering what was coming next.

"Well you *should* know. It is your job to know what the opposition are up to. They have recruited a whole lot of mini-skirted guides."

"They haven't" responded her doubting brother.

"They have, I'm telling you. Do you not believe me?"

Before he could respond, she challenged him to ask Rose, but he knew his sister well enough. That would not be necessary. Rose was simply her "Yes" man, as they say.

"You will need to do something about it" she demanded, "Or you will have no visitors to your distillery."

"Where am I going to get mini-skirted guides at this time of night?"

Rose changed the subject as she could see this conversation was as usual, going nowhere. "Did you know that we have a new Locum Minister for the Parish?" she enquired. Her brother again, tried to appear interested.

"No. When did that happen?"

"This afternoon" said Rose.

"It didn't *happen* this afternoon Rose. We just met him this afternoon" Violet corrected her as usual.

"But I saw the Rev. McCutcheon in his car this afternoon." responded her sceptical brother. "He seemed all right to me."

"The new Locum Minister is a bit of 'All right' to me too" said Rose, clearly infatuated by Rod Ponsonby. "But he is on his honeymoon" she added, somewhat crestfallen.

"That's the point. I don't believe a word of it" declared the ever suspicious Violet.

"The way they have been carrying on down there, I just do not believe it...and I intend to prove it!"

There then followed a prolonged discussion as to why the Parish had appointed a new, albeit temporary Minister, without giving them advance notice. Violet and Rose were pillars of the Kirk, and they would expect to be informed, if not consulted, on such developments in advance. There had been no mention of it at the Kirk Session Meetings which Violet attended religiously, every month. This was a great source of gossip, and there was nothing in the area they did not know.

After all, the Rev. McCutcheon had taken the Chief Guide's funeral service barely a week ago. They had no warning that he was going on holiday or was sick, or required a replacement at such short notice, for whatever reason. Worse still, Thomas postulated that McCutcheon was perhaps fed up with the internecine squabbling between the two Parishes, and that he was therefore tendering his resignation?

There were only 57 members in the Glenbroom congregation, so any such developments would quickly become known by all, and the ugly sisters did not relish being last to know. After all, they did have a 'Reputation' to maintain.

The whole issue was further complicated by the strange activities of the new Locum Minister, who had been seen lurking around Balroonie Castle, apparently showing what were thought to be 'pornographic' photographs to Lizzy the maid, at least, according to Violet.

As far as the ugly sisters were concerned, this would be a whole new experience for the poor girl. How could they reconcile this behaviour with that of a new Minister? Also, what about his glamorous bride? What was she doing, taking such a leading role in the new developments at the 'Sexed up' Glendivot Visitor Centre?

A Minister's wife was expected to play an active part in the local community, but hiring Dolly-birds to act as guides and displaying erotic billboards to attract the visitors to the local Distillery, was not the behaviour expected of the Minister's wife, and certainly not when she was supposed to be on her honeymoon! There would be a right good 'Hullaballoo' if she were to suggest placing such sexually explicit billboards outside their church in Glenbroom, just to attract more worshippers.

The situation required calm deliberation, but of course, this did not materialise. An immediate response was demanded of the doubting and sceptical Thomas. The siblings' debate was as usual, both heated and emotional. It became stressful enough for Thomas to survive, only after consuming a couple of large drams, during the discussion. Time was passing, and Violet insisted in going to demand an explanation from the Rev. McCutcheon at the manse there and then.

Thomas argued not unreasonably, that the first course of action should wait until the following day. As that was the Sabbath, he suggested that they all attend the Glenbroom Church service at noon. This followed the first service which was to be held in Glendivot at 10am. At least this would give him his customary Sunday morning long lie.

It would also provide them with the opportunity to ascertain whether the Rev. McCutcheon was still in place, or it would establish whether Mr. Ponsonby had in fact, replaced him. Perhaps the matter would be resolved quite simply in the fullness of time. In any case, after a couple of 'drams' he now felt a little too soporific, to bother going down to confront the good Minister at that late hour.

Violet was not to be deflected. Her brother's presence was not essential, and she would drive anyway. Indeed, no one was indispensible, except herself. She was a graduate of the school of 'If you want something done properly, do it yourself,' and 'The sooner, the better.' She didn't persuade Rose to accompany her. She instructed her!

And so, even although it was approaching Rose's bedtime, she had to put on an extra jumper before venturing out into the cooler night air, to act as batman, aide-de-camps and general dog's body, to Violet.

Little did the unfortunate Rev. Curmudgeon McCutcheon realise what was coming, as he put the finishing touches to his Sunday sermon. Ironically, he had chosen as his text, 'Blessed are the peacemakers' from the Sermon on the Mount. In the peace and tranquillity of his study in the Manse, he was blissfully unaware of the gathering storm about to descend upon him. It was a far cry from his thoughts of being blessed as a 'Peacemaker'.

Chapter 24

COUNCIL OF WAR

After dinner the same night, Mary held a Council of War with Penny, Rod Ponsonby, and Angus. Mrs Grant attended as a kind of 'Special adviser,' partly because it was she who landed them in this mess in the first place, and partly due to her claimed unique experience as the widow of a Minister herself. If she was honest, she was simply being inquisitive, and did not want to be left out.

Mary knew better than anyone that her mother's assertion that the young couple were the 'Locum Minister and his wife, on their honeymoon,' would come back to haunt them, if they did not take emergency action immediately. Angus lost no time in criticising his mother-in-law for landing them in it. The problem now, was how to extricate themselves from the hole in which they now found themselves.

While they had for the moment, wrong-footed the enemy in Violet and Rose, Mary knew fine that the ugly sisters had only beaten a strategic retreat, and were far from defeated. Like Napoleon, they would return. They were sure to regroup...and counter-attack soon!

The question was, what would they do? The 'Council' rightly came to the conclusion that the Hannahs were bound to seek out The Rev. McCutcheon as soon as possible, to find out if there was any truth in the story. They had to get to him first, so they resolved to pay him a visit without further delay.

The deputation from Glendivot comprised of them all, even though it was approaching the time for Mrs Grant to retire for the night. She hadn't experienced excitement like this since her Alasdair had died, so she wasn't going to miss out now. They all squeezed into Angus's car and made their way to the Minister's Manse, with an increasing sense of anticipation.

They did have one advantage over Doom and Gloom, in that although the Rev. McCutcheon covered both villages, he lived in the Manse in Glendivot. The old Manse in Glenbroom had been converted into a pre-school kindergarten. The Glendivot Manse was therefore nearer Balroonie House, being across the Fiddich River, beyond the farm where Lizzy McPhee lived, and up the Kininvie Hill. They reckoned they should reach it before the ugly sisters, whom they knew fine, would be hot-footing it very soon, to check out the story with the Rev. McCutcheon.

It was after 9pm and already getting dark when the deputation passed the farm. Angus was a little surprised to see 'Godzilla of Glendivot,' Mr McPhee's enormous prize Aberdeen Angus bull, standing guard at the gate, next to the hedge which bordered his field. The bull appeared to pay more attention to them than to the cows in the field.

This mighty and majestic animal, Champion of Champions at several Highland Agricultural Shows, was due to defend one of the many titles it had won, in the next few days. As a precaution he would be brought indoors for the night, as he was much too valuable to leave out overnight. Although Angus assumed that Mr. McPhee the Grieve, would bring him in before settling down for the night, he took a mental note to check on their return journey. Meanwhile, Angus had other things on his mind.

The Manse, like most churches in the area, was situated on the highest position above the village, and appropriately 'Nearest to Heaven.' The car had to negotiate a steep and winding one-track road. There was a chill in the clear night air, by the time the deputation arrived, at the door of the Manse.

They were relieved to see there was still a light on, although only one, and a dim one at that. The Rev. 'Curmudgeon McCutcheon' was notorious for being parsimonious, and had by now established a reputation for using the minimum electricity required. As someone who preached the teachings and parables of one who claimed to be 'The Light of the World,' this practice seemed contradictory. Mary rang the doorbell.

He made a habit of going to bed early the night before the Sabbath, particularly when he had two services to conduct the following morning. He did not obtain his sobriquet without just cause. Accordingly, he was not overjoyed to receive such an imposing deputation at this late hour. He was just about to have his bedtime mug of Ovaltine and two ginger snaps, before retiring for a good night's rest.

Somewhat hesitantly and grudgingly, he ushered them into his lounge. It was a room with which Mrs Grant was familiar, having lived there for 30 years. She could not help noticing his choice of furnishings, particularly the new carpet and curtains. Despite these new innovations, she found it rather untidy and it lacked a lady's touch, so she was not impressed.

Being naturally outspoken, she found it quite an effort to keep her tongue between her teeth. It was not like the old days. To add to her discomfort, the temperature was at least 5 degrees lower than she was used to, so like the others, she kept on her coat.

Mary introduced Penny and Rod Ponsonby, and the minister lit the gas fire. However, he noticeably did not offer them anything at this time of night, so it did not take long for Mary to explain their predicament.

He listened to their story half-heartedly to begin with, but gradually, as the story unfolded, the old curmudgeon began to warm to their situation. He had already come across the ugly sisters, and crossed swords with Violet on more than one occasion. Violet had never made life easy for him since coming to the area.

He had learned the hard way, she was a perpetual moaner, and critic par excellence, and Ministers are usually in the direct firing line of such creatures. Rather than 'Love your enemies' or 'Turn the other cheek,' it would give him at least some quiet satisfaction, if not pleasure, to 'Put one over' on the same Violet.

They then devised an elaborate and comprehensive plan to thwart the ugly sisters. The deal they negotiated was that they would all come to the service in Glendivot in the morning. That would at least swell his congregation and the offering takings. Rod Ponsonby would listen and watch intently how the Minister conducted worship. At the end of the service, 'Curmudgeon' McCutcheon would give him the order of service, and his sermon, for Ponsonby to take the service in the little church in Glenbroom at noon.

He would also brief the elderly lady organist, who played at both services, so that she could keep Rod right, while ensuring she would not let the cat out the bag. Fortunately, she was another who did not care for Violet Hannah, and thus would have no compunction in co-operating.

Penny was overwhelmed by the demands being put upon the Under Secretary of State, and his apparent willingness to co-operate without complaint. After the physical trials he had already endured, he was now expected to come to the rescue of all and sundry, by undertaking this intellectual and spiritual challenge. This was certainly not what she had envisaged when she brought him to Scotland.

She knew that Members of Parliament were called upon to undertake all sorts of unusual tasks, but he was again being asked to embark on service well beyond the normal call of duty. Was there no limit to the man's capacity for overcoming adversity? She thought to herself 'Here for once, I have met a Member of Parliament who deserved to be on the New Year's Honours List.' She would not blame him if he demurred.

However, life is full of surprises, and this was just one more, when he decided to accept the challenge without any hint of complaint. 'Truly, here is a man with spirit' she thought. His maiden aunt's strict upbringing in Kent meant that he had attended the English Episcopal Church regularly as a choir boy, and he was reasonably au fait with the etiquette of church worship. The Scottish Presbyterian service was a cakewalk in comparison.

Penny's opinion of him soared as he appeared to relish this new challenge. She had no idea that he was already looking forward to the second half of the deal...namely, the honeymoon! Was this to be his only reward?

The meeting went smoothly enough, until they all realised that the hoax would have to last for as long as the Londoners remained in Glendivot. If they were going to remain in Glendivot in order to attend the Camanachd Cup Final, this would entail maintaining the hoax for a further week.

One church service was one thing, but one week is completely different. An outside observer would be forgiven for thinking that they were getting into deep water and, perhaps even be out of their depth. Ponsonby had already been in deep water. Surely once was enough!

Originally, the Under Secretary had planned to be in Scotland for about a week. He reckoned it would only take a day or so, to assess the Distillery's financial case for assistance. His plan had been to do this once Penny had completed such changes and renovations as she could on her first visit. He also planned to visit one or two other distilleries to compare their Visitor Centres with that of Glendivot.

Between them, Angus and Hector gave him a short-list of the least efficient and the most backward distilleries in the area in order to show Glendivot in the best light. Glenbroom was among these, but Ponsonby, having met the ugly sisters, had yet to pluck up sufficient courage to undertake that visit! He had intended taking the rest of the week doing his own thing, for he did have his ulterior motive for coming to Scotland. While Lizzy and the others now knew what this was, Penny was still blissfully unaware.

Perhaps his search for his father was the reason he had not given up, and returned to London, after all his embarrassing experiences since coming North. Meanwhile Penny was to be fully employed, networking with the local personnel, and establishing the new modernised systems for the up-graded Visitor Centre she had planned, for the Distillery.

They had now been in Glendivot almost a week, and Rod had arranged another appointment at Fort George, this time with the Commanding Officer. He was also keen to accept Angus's unexpected invitation to stay and be his VIP Guest at the Camanachd Cup Final. He felt a responsibility to attend especially since Angus was the Team Manager, and Hector and Hughie and indeed the whole of Glendivot, were so involved. He like them, was becoming caught up in their 'Cup Final Fever.' In addition, he was acutely aware that he was responsible for Hughie McLeod's injury, and felt extremely guilty for landing them with a major problem.

There was nothing for it, he would have to phone the Minister, that is, the Minister of Tourism in London, and tell him he had to take an extra week to undertake 'Additional Ministerial duties.' They were not to know that these were to carry out religious services and associated pastoral duties as part of the Ministry of the Church of Scotland, and nothing to do with the Ministry of Tourism. Unfortunately, this created a whole new set of problems, for the Rev. McCutcheon did not sit around twiddling his thumbs all week.

If Ponsonby was to take his place, he would have to take on all the commitments that the Minister could not cancel or postpone. This required the Rev. McCutcheon to look out his diary for the week, and see what would have to be undertaken by the 'Locum' Minister.

They both sighed a sigh of relief when he found that he had no weddings, baptisms or funerals (So far), but he did have to address the Glenbroom Women's Guild on the Wednesday on the subject of 'Sex Discrimination in a modern Society.' That would be a challenge even for a Government Minister, as the two ugly sisters were sure to be there.

He also had to pay a pastoral visit to the local maternity home, and present a 90th Birthday card and bouquet to a resident, not of the Maternity Home, but in the Old Folk's Home next door, that is, assuming the old lady made it, for there were still 5 days to go. They could get away with postponing the maternity home visit. The ladies there would just have to wait for the returning Rev. McCutcheon. After all, they had waited long enough to be where they were, so they could wait a little longer. However, he had to attend the 90th Birthday Celebration.

Other items in the diary like the parish visitation, visiting the sick and taking a school service could be postponed. All in all, they reckoned that he would have to carry out half-a-dozen assignments, including chairing a meeting of the local Alcoholics Anonymous. 'That should be interesting' he thought, for it was quite impossible to remain 'Anonymous' in a small close-knit community like Glendivot.

The last problem they had to overcome, was how to hide the Rev. McCutcheon from the clutches of Doom and Gloom for the next week. Knowing the sisters' resolve, and their ability to poke their noses into places others would fear to tread, this presented as big a hurdle as Beecher's Brook in the Grand National.

They suggested he took a holiday...in the Algarve! That should be far enough away. But the old 'Curmudgeon' was too miserly to spend his money. Someone suggested a cruise to the Faroe Islands, as that would be 'Refreshing,' and it would 'Clear the air,' before Mrs Grant came up with one of her brainwaves...again!

She suggested that her daughter put him up for the week in Balroonie House. They had one more room available, but it had no en suite facilities. At least not until Mr. Ponsonby gave her the go-ahead with 'Government financial assistance,' Mary was quick to point out.

He would be pretty safe there, and would be on hand to give Rod Ponsonby advice. Mary was confident she could hide him from Doom and Gloom, for she had resolved she would not allow them over her door again. And so the elaborate and complicated plan was concluded.

It took them well over an hour to work out the details, and it was well after 10pm when the deputation left the Manse and returned to their car. The Rev. McCutcheon finally relaxed with his mug of Ovaltine, and looked forward to his 'Week off.'

Chapter 25

LIZZY TO THE RESCUE

There was still no sign of Doom and Gloom when the Balroonie party made their way slowly down the winding road from the Manse. They had made it before the ugly sisters. At least, that was some relief. There was a full moon that night, and the sky remained clear. In fact visibility was better than normal, and as they came to the foot of the hill, they saw two figures at the gate where "Godzilla of Glendivot" had been.

Mrs Grant, as usual, began to panic, as she immediately assumed the worst. "They must be some Highland rustlers, about to make off with the village's prize asset!" she claimed nervously. "Or is it the ugly sisters trying to disrupt Glendivot's efforts to retain their Prize Bull Championship?" she wondered. The big black bull would be worth a fortune on the black market!

Angus brought the car quietly to a halt a short distance away, and he and Rod Ponsonby clambered out. Stealthily, they approached the two shadowy figures, as Mrs Grant, still in the car, conjectured "Surely it's no' Violet and Rose? How dare they!" But there was no sign of Violet's noisy and rickety old Triumph Herald car.

Angus was on the point of accosting them, when he noticed that one of the figures appeared to have a plaster cast on his foot. "Hughie! It's you. What are you doing here at this time of night?" he asked just in time. One more moment, and Hughie would have had another injury, as Angus had remembered the neck-lock grip, he learned in his unarmed combat training at Fort George, during the War.

"I'm taking Lizzy here, home" replied a surprised and innocent Hughie. Sure enough, the second shadowy figure was his girlfriend. "We were just going to bring Godzilla in for the night, as a precaution," she explained, as if she was referring to her pet dog.

Lizzy was a much more confident character when handling livestock in the precincts of her father's farm, than she was as the oppressed maid at Balroonie House. Having spent all her life on the farm, she took such duties as controlling the Prize bull, in her stride. She stood all of 5 feet 2 inches, and weighed in at about 9 stones. The bull would be well over one tonne, and probably about 200 stones! So Ponsonby could not fail to be impressed by her inbred bravery, when she confirmed that she was quite used to this task. Hughie compared it to his mother putting the milk bottles out at night.

They were all disturbed when out of the dark blue of the night, the bull's enormous head reared above the hedge not six feet away, and let out a frightening roar that might even have been heard in Glenbroom. It sounded as if it just had its way with its favourite cow!

Ponsonby jumped out his skin and nearly wet himself, and even Angus was moved to admire the maid's courage. She wasn't as gormless as he thought. Although she only had to walk him 100 yards, and she had a small rope and stick to 'Control' him, he could only admire her sang-froid.

"What are *you* doing here anyway?" she asked. Whereupon between them, Angus and Ponsonby explained the reason for their visit to the Rev. McCutcheon. They explained the complicated plans they had made to pass over his duties to Ponsonby for the week, together with the rehousing of the Minister at Balroonie House.

This painstaking plan had taken about an hour and a half for the six of them to work out. It involved utilising the combined brains of the Distillery top management, the Parish Minister and Her Majesty's Under Secretary of State. And yet Lizzy the maid, was not impressed. She came up with a better and simpler solution in less than a minute.

"Why don't you just put it off for a week?" she suggested. "After all, Mr. Ponsonby will be returning to London next week anyway."

"You will need to explain yourself" said Angus, doubting the maid's ability to solve their problem so simply for them.

"If the Rev. McCutcheon simply announces that, as the Locum Minister was on 'his honeymoon,' he will not be starting his duties, until next week, he kills two birds with the one stone."

"Don't mention killing birds to me" interjected Hughie.

Ponsonby felt ill at ease, and looked for a hole, into which he would gladly disappear. Lizzy continued to display an unexpected confidence and clarity of thought. "On the one hand, it lets everyone know in advance of the appointment, which is what Violet complained about in the first place...and on the other hand, Mr. Ponsonby doesnae have to take on all that work. I am sure he has other things to do. At least he can enjoy his last week... on his honeymoon."

"Sounds good to me" agreed the Secretary of State.

"Not only that" concluded the maid. "It doesnae disturb the Minister's routine, and it won't disturb us at Balroonie House."

Angus was dumbfounded. Ponsonby was impressed. "You seem to have thought of everything." "But who is going to be the 'Locum Minister next week?' asked Angus. "No one" replied Lizzy. "You simply tell them next Sunday that there has been a change of plan. Either the Locum is no longer required or, is no longer available." "How that?" queried Angus. "He will be on his way back to London, with Miss Whitehouse," concluded the maid. "Problem solved."

Rod Ponsonby agreed with some alacrity. He and Angus then returned to the car, did a five-point turn, and sped back to the Manse before the Rev. McCutcheon retired for the night. They spent the short journey explaining to the bewildered ladies, the simplicity of Lizzy's solution. Penny felt a sense of relief for the sake of Rod. She would accept anything that would avoid putting further demands on him.

"Trust a woman to get you out of a mess" summed up Mrs Grant, conveniently forgetting it was she who put them in that mess in the first place.

Chapter 26

APPOINTMENT WITH FEAR

Doom and Gloom drove through Glendivot, on their way to the Manse. The ugly sisters had infamous reputations for a variety of reasons. Everywhere they went and everything they did, seemed to rub people up the wrong way. The locals either loathed them or loved them, in a ratio of about 100 to 1.

Poor Rose would have fared much better, if she hadn't tagged on to her older sister's apron strings so much. People would have respected her, if she stood up for herself more. It wasn't that she was nasty, like her sister. In fact, she was really rather soft-hearted and kindly, if she had been left to her own devices. The trouble was, she was always in Violet's shadow, and Violet cast a long shadow.

One of the reasons for them being inseparable was that Rose didn't drive. She claimed to feel too nervous to take a driving test, and she certainly wouldn't relish the thought of Violet teaching her! She was therefore dependent on Violet driving her everywhere. Thus, the two of them tootled around in Violet's ancient and noisy Triumph Herald car. They had bought it second hand and it should have been a bargain, for it was in hideous two-tone green and orange colours. It probably came from somewhere on the border of Northern Ireland. Nobody else would be seen dead in such a combination of colours.

The other reason they were so noticeable in this car, was the fact that it was excessively noisy. There were at least three reasons for this. Firstly, the exhaust pipe always sounded as if it was exhausted, and anyone who knew anything about cars, would be convinced it had a permanent hole in it. How any hole got there, or who put it there, was anyone's guess. There were a few theories going the rounds, but the dear ladies were none the wiser. The second reason for the car's noisy reputation was that Murdo McMurray, who owned the one and only garage in Glenbroom, was as devious as the Hannahs. Having spent a lifetime in the garage business, he knew all the tricks of the trade.

As he had no competition, he was able to lead them a 'merry' dance. The car may or may not have come from Ireland, but he certainly had the 'Blarney' to talk the hind legs off a donkey. He would confuse the sisters with all sorts of mythical technical jargon, explaining the reasons for the noisy car, and they were none the wiser.

He would refer to combustion combobulators which seized up, interloping copulators that overheated, drooping defibulators that lost power, complicated computerised compression chambers which had corroded, thus causing critical levels of condensation in the condenser. There was no way the cantankerous Violet could contest such and controversial claims. So after castigating him comprehensively, she had no alternative but to conclude either he was constantly contriving to confuse her with contradictory and conflicting claims, or he was clearly not competent!

As a pair of antagonists, they were well matched. Conversely he was never going to confess to such contentious criticism, so they reached a compromise when she conceded that the only way she could continue, was to replace the engine, or the car!

Until this was achieved, he simply adjusted the engine settings, so that Violet could hardly hear herself trying to talk, above the noise of the engine. That was a pretty serious handicap for Violet. He took a mischievous pleasure at shutting her up. When she complained repeatedly, he always replied, "What do you expect from a second hand car from Ireland?"

An added advantage for Murdo was that he could hear her coming, and he more than once took advantage of that advantage, by disappearing without trace out the back of his garage, before she arrived!

Finally, her car's noisy fate was sealed by the fact that Violet's aggressive confrontational instincts manifested themselves in her violent use of the clutch, and the poor gear-box took a terrible pounding. She may have got away with putting her foot down at home, but when it came to doing the same to the car, the clutch was more inclined to complain than Rose or Thomas. The jarring noise of the clutch seizing, could be heard from some distance, as it did once more, on this clear still night.

And so it came to pass, or rather it came to a shuddering noisy halt, on that narrow one-track country road, as the ugly sisters were confronted by Lizzy and Hughie leading their gigantic beast 'Godzilla of Glendivot' towards the farmyard. Again, there was no competition.

The big black bull appeared to take up the whole road, and could hardly be seen in the darkness. It was almost upon them, when the first thing the ugly sisters saw, was the whites of its eyes!...and its teeth only a few feet away! It looked twice its normal size, from the seats of the low-slung Triumph Herald, when the ugly sisters finally became aware of its presence in the headlights of their car. It was so frightening that Violet did not notice Lizzy and Hughie accompanying it.

The poor ugly sisters endured what must have been their 'Tam o' Shanter' experience, as they were scared out of their wits. Violet had no option but to mistreat the brakes, the gearstick and the clutch once more, as she desperately tried to put the car into reverse as fast as she could.

Rose had always been convinced the full moon had an unnerving effect on Violet. Despite the moon's presence, the little winding country road was really quite dark, with no street lighting, and its ditches on both sides made it very dangerous to reverse at full speed. Even the most experienced Rally driver, would have difficulty in manoeuvring in reverse in these circumstances, with the threat of a whacking great Prize bull bearing down on them.

It is difficult to describe the blind panic that overtook the terrified sisters in such a situation. To put it mildly, Rose began to doubt the sanity of her sister and the wisdom of their journey, and for once said so, in no uncertain terms. She screamed at her sister, in a way she never dared to do before. Quite uncharacteristically, she even used some choice language that Violet had never previously experienced.

Violet's face was a picture. In her terror, she poured with unladylike perspiration, as she wrestled unsuccessfully with the offending gears. She must have reached at least 40mph in 3 seconds flat, as she tried to reverse, without swerving from one ditch to another. The jarring noise of her attempted gear changes, together with her revving of the accelerator, was enough to unnerve the calmest of bulls.

The problem became a crisis as the swerving motion of the reversing car meant that the beam of her headlights consequently also swerved from side to side. As these were shining across the face of the bull, one could hardly be surprised to see it starting to become agitated, with steam rising from its snorting nostrils. It was just as well that the car wasn't red!

Lizzy clipped the rope on to the halter. If it wasn't for her competent handling of this magnificent beast, a more serious situation may have arisen. Hughie recognised that between them, they must delay the sisters for a short time, to allow the Balroonie House deputation to complete their business with the Rev. McCutcheon. He need not have bothered. The task was made easier than he had foreseen.

After swerving in reverse across both sides of the road, the noisy car came to rest with its wheels stuck firmly in the ditch, smoke emerging from the exhaust, and the back of the car embedded half way through the hedge. This made it difficult for even an able bodied man to get round the back, and push it out of the ditch, far less one on crutches, and with a plaster cast on his foot!

While Lizzy steered her steer off the road and into her father's yard with consummate skill, the ugly sisters were in such a state of distress, bordering on hysteria, that their first priority now became that of extricating themselves, and their vehicle from the ditch. Any thoughts of continuing up to the Manse to see the Minister ended there and then.

This was a situation Hughie was able to control with relative ease, even with one foot in plaster. It was the first time he ever had the upper hand with the ugly sisters. Lizzy had put Godzilla in his pen, and returned to the scene by the time Violet and Rose had recovered some sense of decorum.

She and her boyfriend could not resist the temptation to have a laugh at Doom and Gloom's expense. Never before had they seen Violet in a situation where she was not in control. Eventually she emerged from the car, somewhat dishevelled and clearly in a state of shock. Her younger sister was not much better. Her emotions had been a mixture of petrified fear, and unprecedented aggression towards her sister.

Lizzy took the initiative, before Violet could recover her dignity. "What are you doing frightening 'God' at this time of night?" she threatened, getting her own back after the chaos that 'Thumper' had caused at Balroonie House.

"I didn't frighten him" pleaded a petrified Violet. "He put the fear of God in me!" Making the most of the situation Lizzy continued "I have got a good mind to report you to the Prevention of Cruelty to Animals people!" and then she added "Godzilla is quite distressed in there."

"I didn't see you Lizzy. It was only the bull I saw" explained Violet, still shaking like a leaf.

"You were lucky he didn't go for you" warned Lizzy, rubbing it in.

She knew while she had the upper hand for now, it was only a matter of time before Violet would regain her composure and return to the offensive.

"What are we to do?" pleaded an almost incoherent Violet. Her normally sharp brain simply wasn't functioning, as she was at a complete loss for inspiration. Lizzy therefore maintained the upper hand, by offering to get her father to bring out his tractor to pull the car out the ditch "Even though he is probably in his bed by now." Making the most of her advantage, she added "But it will cost you a 'Recovery' charge! Double time if he is in his bed!"

Violet was in no position to bargain. The thought of having to walk over three miles home, at this time of night, did not fill her with enthusiasm. The need for assistance undermined any further aggressive intent on her behalf, and they all converged on the farm to seek help from Mr McPhee.

Chapter 27

CHANGE OF PLAN

Meanwhile, the Balroonie deputation had returned to the Manse again, and rang the bell once more. There was still one light on, but it was now upstairs. They had to ring a second time before the Minister came downstairs, switched off the security alarm, and unlocked the two locks of the door. Although this was Speyside, his Ayrshire security precautions never deserted him. He slowly opened it. This time he was in his pyjamas and dressing gown, with a mug of Ovaltine in his hand.

Mary apologised for this second intrusion, and asked if they could come in once more, to explain, and seek his approval of their change of plan. Up till then the old 'Curmudgeon' had managed to keep his grumpy nature under control, but this was the last thing he wanted to hear at this time of night.

He was already looking forward to an unexpected week's holiday, having his meals made for him, and catching up with some reading while staying at Balroonie House. Their original plan had been meticulously worked out and he saw no reason to change it now.

However he was outnumbered, and rather than stand arguing in his dressing gown in the cold night air, he was persuaded to allow them in to hear what they had to say. So once more, the Balroonie House delegation entered the dimly lit lounge. Once more he lit the gas fire, and sat down with his mug of Ovaltine, in his favourite chair to hear what they had to say.

They explained the logic of Lizzy's suggestions, and to be fair to the old cleric, he grudgingly accepted the changed arrangements. He complimented them on devising such a convincing and effective plan, and he had to recognize the merits of its simplicity. It was more honest, although not entirely so, and it avoided the potential hazards of maintaining the ruse for a whole week.

He therefore agreed to announce the appointment of the new 'Locum Minister' at both the services the next day. Rod Ponsonby ensured that he made it clear that the 'Locum' would not be starting until the following week, so that he could complete 'His honeymoon.' He was determined to make the most of it. Penny clasped his hand. She was impressed and touched by Rod's insistence on this point.

After all he had been through, Penny could not possibly object. Certainly, Rod didn't. He was relieved to be spared the ordeal of addressing the Glenbroom Women's Guild on 'Sex Discrimination in a Modern Society' with the ugly sisters in the audience. It was the first time he had asked for anything in return for all he had endured.

Not only had she grown to respect him, she was now beginning to think there was something quite likeable about him. She even felt she might actually enjoy going along with the idea, just for fun! What had started as a serious business trip, was turning into something much more exciting – and romantic!

They all returned to the car and made their way down the hill again. The conversation was quite animated, as they congratulated themselves on the wisdom and simplicity of their solution, even although it was Lizzy's idea, when they came upon a tractor blocking their way. It was endeavouring to pull an old car out of the roadside ditch. There was a huddle of figures watching its progress, two of whom were controlling affairs, while the other two appeared to be shivering in the chill night air, looking on anxiously.

Angus slowed to a halt and wound down his window. "It's you Violet. What a fine clear night for an evening drive, is it not?" Violet's reaction was unprintable, so Angus turned his attention to her younger sister. "You are out late tonight Rose. It must be something important to keep you out of bed at this time of night." Rose could see him far enough, so he turned his attention elsewhere. He then addressed Lizzy and Hughie. "Is there something wrong?" he asked, knowing full well, the answer was obvious. "Have you had a wee accident?" he went on, showing a distinct lack of concern, and trying to stifle his glee.

Violet could stand the taunting no longer. "You can see fine we have had an accident, and it is no thanks to you Angus McDougall." She was gradually returning to her confrontational best. On seeing this, Angus then spoke to Lizzy's father who was on the tractor.

"Well, will you be so kind as to take your tractor and that...that scrapheap into the field, in order that we can pass. I've got a honeymoon couple here, and it's late. And they want to get to their bed!"

Penny and Rod held hands once more.

"Och well in that case, we will not detain you any longer" said the Grieve on the tractor in his broadest Doric accent. Angus knew that he would respond without question, because Mr McPhee, as manager of the farm, was responsible to Angus, as Distillery Manager.

Angus reversed a few yards, while the ugly sisters stood shivering in a huddle. In the confusion, Violet had lost a shoe. The tractor painstakingly towed the car down the road and through the gate, and into the field.

Angus was effusive in his thanks, and the whole Balroonie House deputation showed their appreciation through the open windows of their car, as they waved handkerchiefs and scarves, and shouted cheerily, 'Thank you,' 'Goodbye' and 'Have a nice night,' leaving Doom and Gloom to their fate. Their car ran over Violet's shoe.

It took a half-hour for Hughie and the Grieve to extricate the remains of the hedge jammed in the rear of the car, and make it roadworthy again. By then it was too late for the ugly sisters to call on the Rev. McCutcheon.

After relieving themselves of £20 for the 'Recovery Fee' the ugly sisters made their way cautiously, back to Glenbroom. It was nearly midnight when the tired but happy deputation returned to Balroonie House, and the Rev. McCutcheon finally got to sleep. It was *after* midnight before the unhappy ugly sisters returned to Glenbroom, where their brother was already sound asleep.

Chapter 28

THE LADY IN THE TWEED SUIT

It was a dry but cloudy day when the Glendivot Church was well attended the following morning, thanks partly to the Balroonie House deputation, and the fact that the rumours of a handsome new 'Locum' had spread round the village.

The Rev. McCutcheon preached his sermon on "Blessed are the Peacemakers" with some last minute adjustments, and more passion than usual. Rod Ponsonby wore his black jacket and striped trousers, together with the Rev. Alasdair Grant's 'Dog collar.' He looked very convincing when he stood up and took a bow, after he was introduced as the new 'Locum' who would be taking up his duties the following week. The congregation was suitably impressed.

The Rev. McCutcheon even excelled himself by announcing to all and sundry, that this would only be 'After he had completed his honeymoon,' to which there were a few suggestive murmurings round the church, and finally a ripple of applause. Penny however, kept a very low profile, for she knew that unlike Rod, she would have to return on her own, to Glendivot from time to time, to carry out her Public Relations duties.

After the service, she made a hasty retreat, as Rod was surrounded by a number of well-wishers, who appreciated him taking time off his honeymoon, to attend the service. He impressed the locals and had made a good start.

Despite their late night, Doom and Gloom attended the mid-day service in Glenbroom, looking rather the worse for wear. Even Thomas attended, feeling refreshed, having enjoyed his undisturbed long lie. Violet was limping, and appeared pale and tired, and Rose had a runny nose. She thought she had caught a cold.

The Minister announced the appointment of the 'Locum,' and there was no need for Rod Ponsonby to attend. So the ugly sisters and their brother had their answer. Mrs Grant had been right all along, and everything appeared in order. Despite this, Violet was sceptical as usual, and remained to be convinced. She never entirely trusted the Rev McCutcheon, the new Minister from Ayrshire. After all, he was a long way from completing his 8 years apprenticeship, before being accepted as one of them. Even the Minister was not exempt from this tradition!

She had felt that it was time her brother Thomas, should do more to investigate what Rod Ponsonby and Penelope Whitehouse were up to. So far, she had made all the running, but was none the wiser.

In the afternoon she cornered her brother, and after what she and her sister had endured the previous night with Godzilla the bull, she made it clear that it was his turn to play his part. During the sermon, she had worked out a 'Plan B' to find out the truth about the strange activities at the Glendivot distillery, once and for all. Rose with the runny nose, chose her bed, to which she retired, with a 'hot toddy' and a hot water bottle.

In Balroonie House, Angus had to forego his Sunday afternoon 'Forty winks'. Instead, he was sent upstairs to learn his words for the part of Lord Darnley, while Mrs Grant went to her bed for her Sunday afternoon 'nap.'

Mary contacted her proposed substitute goalkeeper, and obtained his agreement to take Hughie's place. She then phoned Fergus McTavish, the Assistant Manager of the shinty team, to confirm the arrangement, as agreed in her deal with Angus. She swore him to secrecy from everyone including Angus, as to the identity of her replacement, as it was to be his surprise 'Birthday Present.'

Fergus was so relieved to have the problem solved, that he would do anything she asked. They also agreed the new goalkeeper would attend the two final training sessions, which happened to coincide with the Drama Club's rehearsals that week.

Hughie and Lizzy went to collect Keith Crowther from the hospital. He had been kept in overnight due to some signs of concussion, although he was known to act at times as if he suffered from concussion permanently. "The things some people will do to avoid playing in goal for the shinty team" observed Lizzy on their way there.

Hector had a day off, and read 'The Art and Craft of Whisky Distillation.' He was taking his role of 'Chief Guide' very seriously, so he had to learn how it was made! Up till then, he only knew how to consume it!

Meanwhile Penny and Rod went off to have a look at some of the other distilleries in the area, taking advantage of the Sabbath when no one was around. They then carried on to the ancient battlefield of Culloden where they found their love for each other had deepened, on the very site where there was no love was lost between the Hanoverian and Jacobite armies in 1746.

Their new relationship may not have been quite that of a couple on their 'Honeymoon,' but they had unquestionably enjoyed their afternoon together, and were clearly happy and at ease in each other's company. The first buds of romance were flowering. No longer were they acting out a close relationship for the benefit of others. It is a fine line which is inexplicable, but they had now genuinely fallen in love, and the feelings they felt for each other, meant they could really start enjoying their 'Honeymoon.'

They continued to sample the delights of the Moray Firth coast in their little red sports car, and by the time they returned in the evening, their relationship had changed dramatically. Gone was the formal business relationship with which they came.

After leaving Thomas in no doubt that he had not pulled his weight, Violet finally dragged him out of his complacency, and persuaded him that the time had come for him to find out what was going on at Glendivot. She finally broke his resistance by suggesting he take part in one of the new Glendivot Tours which Penny appeared to have 'Sexed up.' This would certainly "Broaden his education," she asserted.

He was not very keen at first, but when Rose added her tuppence worth, by promising him that if the billboards were to be believed, it would be an experience he would never forget. He finally gave in, admitting, "At least it will make a change."

By spying in this way, he would see for himself, the latest developments in the Glendivot Distillery, plus whatever innovations had been introduced for the visitors. He could then compare them with his own rather unimaginative efforts. He would also be able to enquire quite naturally what Mr and Mrs Ponsonby were doing at the Distillery.

The only problem was, he would be instantly recognised by the Glendivot employees and management. His distinctive bald pate was an immediate 'Give away,' and as a Distillery Manager in his own right, he was well known in the area.

However, the ever resourceful Violet was not to be beaten. She was not the wardrobe mistress of the Drama Club for nothing. Having access to all their stage costumes and accessories, had its advantages. If she could turn a Pumpkin into a Golden Stage-Coach, she could transform her brother into a kind of Mrs Doubtfire.

The following day, she disguised her brother in women's clothes, and gave him one of the Club's wigs, so that he was quite unrecognisable. She rather cleverly chose a discreet tweed suit and plain blouse for him, with a simple pearl necklace. This would allow him to wear flat brogue shoes which she had in the wardrobe department.

Unfortunately, they were at least a size too small for him, but they saved him the embarrassment and difficulty of wearing high heeled ladies shoes.

He wouldn't have to wear them for too long, as the tours only lasted about an hour. When he complained she reminded him of the torment she and Rose had suffered the previous night. So it wasn't too much to ask him to 'Suffer' the shoes that length of time. Rose gave him one of her handbags, and put a purse, a lady's compact, a lace handkerchief and a bottle of perfume in it. Through this straightforward disguise, he would be quite undistinguishable among the tourists.

So, before he could change his mind, they had him dressed, and he even allowed Rose to put some perfume and a little make-up on him. He was beginning to get carried away by their ruse. Her sister wouldn't know how to do that, for she never wore either. Violet then drove him down to Glendivot, in her noisy little car. She dropped him off at the end of the road, leading to the Visitor Centre. That was her big mistake.

Across the road, Balroonie House overlooked the entrance to the Distillery, and Lizzy was making the bed in one of the front bedrooms at that time.. It was the noise of the Triumph Herald that attracted her attention, as it stuttered to a halt, and so she went to the window. She was just in time to see this auburn haired lady alight from the car, and wave goodbye to the redoubtable Violet Hannah, who set off, jamming the gearbox in the process as usual.

Now Violet was careful not to stop too near the Visitor centre, in case she was recognised. However, she forgot that she might be seen by someone on the other side of the road, in the much nearer Balroonie House.

Lizzy watched the tweed-suited lady walk down towards the Visitor Centre, and couldn't help noticing that she appeared to have a rather manly gait. Either that, or her shoes were hurting her! Her curiosity was aroused, not so much by that however, but by the fact that the lady was dropped off by the infamous Violet, their arch rival. Why was Violet helping someone to visit the Glendivot Distillery, and who was the lady in the tweed suit?

Lizzy decided to take the matter into her own hands. Her confidence had grown since her previous contretemps with Violet and the bull. She didn't have time to stop and explain it to Mary, who was dusting the lounge, or the lady could have disappeared and it would be too late. She ran down the stairs and unusually for her, out the front door.

When she reached the Reception Centre for Visitors, the lady in the tweed suit was unobtrusively looking at the photographs on the wall, and waiting to be allocated to one of the large parties being prepared for the tour.

It was then that Lizzy recognised the suit. She was sure that it was one that the Drama Club had used in one of last year's Community Festival plays. She tried to remember which actress wore it. She was having difficulty because of the auburn wig. Whoever wore the suit, did not have auburn hair.

Then she remembered, it was the now pregnant leading lady for whom she was standing in, playing the part of Mary Queen of Scots! That lady was due to give birth any day now, and she was definitely blonde! This lady Lizzy was following was not blonde, and definitely *not pregnant!*

It was however, the wig that gave it away. Lizzy recognised it from the Drama Club, as she had herself worn it on one occasion, when she had a walk-on part in a One Act play some years ago.

By this time big Flora McGuffie the Chief Receptionist and some of the staff had recognised Lizzy, and started to welcome her to their new Reception Centre. They were all quite excited by the revolutionary changes that had been initiated by Penny. The maid was deflected for a moment, and she lost sight of the lady in the tweed suit, in the general confusion of visitors arriving for their tours.

She was about to explain her dilemma to Flora when Penny walked in. Lizzy immediately grabbed hold of her, and then divulged to them both why she was there. She just had time to complete her story when a party which included the lady in the tweed suit, started to leave the Visitor Centre for their tour. "Leave this to me" said Flora who was experienced in handling awkward situations with visitors.

Now Flora was not called 'Big Flora' for nothing. She stood almost 6 feet tall and was well proportioned in every way, for her height, as they say. She was about 40 years of age and had been a policewoman in the Strathclyde Police Force. There, she met a policeman whom she married, and who in due course applied, and was accepted for, a post in Glendivot. He was now the village policeman who didn't turn up at the school where Ponsonby had his cathartic experience a few days before.

Coming from Glasgow, she was a woman of the world, and was well able to handle any situation. Penny, being new and still feeling her way, was happy to leave this to her. Flora went outside, and was relieved to find the party had not gone far. They were only a few yards away, as the new dolly-bird guide was giving them a well-rehearsed introduction to the tour.

Flora, who was an imposing figure, even to the new guides, whispered in the guide's ear, and then took aside the lady in the tweed suit. "Good morning madam" she said, out of ear shot of the tour group. She then proceeded to explain, that each day it was their custom to select one person to be their VIP Visitor of the day.

"Congratulations to you Madam. It is my pleasure to nominate you as our 'VIP Visitor' for today." The lady in the tweed suit suspected nothing, and was impressed. She simply thought 'Here is a new initiative that we don't have in Glenbroom. What a good idea.'

"If you will just step this way, we will take you to the VIP Reception Room to have your photograph taken, and sign the Visitors' Book" said Flora, as she guided her prey to the Reception Centre.

The lady in the tweed suit had heard of the reputation of the 'VIP Reception' but never been in it, so she accepted the invitation with genuine interest and anticipation. This was indeed progress beyond her expectations. How lucky she was to be ushered into Glenbroom's main rival's inner sanctum, within a few minutes of arriving. Even Violet would be impressed. The idea of a photograph did not worry her, for she felt confident that her disguise was convincing.

The 'VIP Reception' was a large high-ceilinged room with wooden rafters. It acted as a combined lounge and dining room, and was ideal for entertaining VIP Parties of up to 20 people. It was beautifully furnished and used occasionally by the Company's Board of Directors, for Board Meetings, lunches, dinners, presentations and for doing business deals with important customers. It also provided an excellent venue for entertaining VIP guests.

It had a large feature fireplace with a warm log fire burning, above which a 'Monarch of the Glen' painting hung. This was complemented by several original paintings of previous Chairmen. There was also a large well-stocked cocktail cabinet, with a lit display unit, filled with very rare and valuable whiskies.

The lady in the tweed suit was inspired by the general ambiance, and readily agreed to Flora's request for her to sign 'The Visitors' Book.'

She was almost caught on the hop when she started to sign her signature as 'Thomas' but at the last moment added 3 letters to make it 'Thomasina Tweedie.' She probably arrived at this surname because she was so self-conscious of her tweed suit.

Flora had by then, poured her a particularly large dram of their 'Finest 15 year-old malt,' and as she offered it, suggested a toast, to welcome her guest, and to celebrate

'An unforgettable VIP visit to Glendivot.' This was a truism if ever there was one! Flora joined her guest in the toast, with her customary apple juice.

She then lifted the telephone, keeping her finger on the button, as she dialled and asked "Hello, is that you Jessie? Could you arrange for the official photographer to come to the VIP Room please? Yes, as soon as possible. Thanks" and with that, she replaced the receiver. As Chief Receptionist, she was an expert in innocent small-talk, and enquired if the lady was a 'Miss or Mrs?' Thomas was caught unprepared, and before he could think it through, he said 'Mrs.' Flora didn't question it at this stage, even though she had already noted the lady did not have any rings on her 'Wedding' finger.

She simply plied her with drink to soften her up, while subjecting her to a barrage of increasingly awkward questions. She aimed to upset the lady's composure, while assessing who she was, and what she was doing at Glendivot.

"Are you on holiday? Where do you come from? Where is your husband? Is your family with you? How long have you got? What do you do for a living? Are you in the whisky business? Why did you come? Do you like our whisky?" etc etc. The last few questions were enough to make the poor woman choke.

The more she subjected the lady in the tweed suit to examination, the more the lady needed time to think. She played for time by drinking repeatedly from her glass. The more she drank, the more befuddled she became.

Flora's investigative police experience in Glasgow was invaluable, and she began to revel in the cut and thrust of the interrogation. "Tweedie?" she asked. "Where does that name come from?" Thomas was caught out, for he had no idea. Most wives would be expected to know where their husband's family came from. "I believe it's from Berwick on Tweed" he blurted out as he ensured that his tweed skirt covered his knees. It was the first thing that came to his mind.

Flora continued to ask more and more searching questions, while constantly weighing her up. Slowly but surely, she was luring the lady into her trap. She hadn't realised how much she missed this aspect of her police work in Glasgow. Her performance could be likened to that of a Spanish Matador, preparing for the 'Kill.'

She became aware that the lady's mannerisms appeared rather 'Butch.' For example, she didn't sit like a lady. Thomas was no actor. This made her notice the lady's rather unnatural falsetto voice. This in turn, led her to observe the texture of her facial skin. Her face was the only skin to be seen apart from her hands, which she had already noted, were unusually strong for a lady.

Each piece of the jigsaw was fitting into place, when Flora went round behind the settee upon which the tweed-suited lady was sitting. She then paid particular attention to her hair. Flora thought it was unnatural and rather coarse. Could it possibly be a wig?

She then made a decision, lifted the phone again, dialled 'O' and simply said "Bring the car to Reception." Thomas was not quite beaten yet.

"The car?" he enquired. "I thought you were going to show me the Distillery."

"Yes I am" replied Flora. "We will start with the cooperage at the far end, and work our way back from there." 'Doubting' Thomas was now becoming suspicious.

"As a VIP Visitor, we spare no expense. The cooperage is about a mile away, and the other visitors have to walk, but we make it as easy as we can for VIP Guests" explained Flora.

"We will take you in the car and make our way back through the malt barns, mashouse, stillhouse, warehouses and bottling hall on foot." This explanation seemed more reasonable to Thomas, who thought of his tight fitting shoes. He finished off his drink, when the car arrived.

It was Penny who came in to tell Flora of the car's arrival. She was just in time to encounter the ex-policewoman from Glasgow, thump the lady in the tweed suit over the head with a log she had taken from the spare bucket of logs, behind the settee. The lady in the tweed suit slumped on the settee, and Flora immediately pulled off the wig. "Just as I thought" she said coldly. "This is Thomas Hannah from Glenbroom."

Penny was flabbergasted. "Violet's brother?" she asked.

"The same" replied Flora with a satisfied look on her face. It took Penny some moments before she could come to terms with the situation. She wondered if she was really in the Highlands of Scotland? People don't go around hitting others over the head with logs! Men don't dress up as women! Or do they? She could expect to meet transvestites in Soho, but not here in the Highlands! But then she thought, 'The nearest they got to that, was when they wear kilts.'

"Don't worry" said Flora, seeing Penny's reaction. "I've only stunned him, so that we can get him in the car," as she clouted him once more to make sure he was out for the count! Thereupon, the pair of them dragged Thomas out to the car, barely conscious. Flora got into the driver's seat, and told Penny to get in the back with the moaning, wigless, semi-conscious Thomas. "If he gets obstreperous, just gie him another clout with the log," said Flora to a shaking, disbelieving Penny.

A few moments later, as they were driving out of the Distillery grounds, he began to regain his wits and mumbled, "That whisky... has got a hell of a kick in it! It's enough to... knock you out." Poor Penny was forced to apply the 'Coup de Grace' albeit reluctantly.

Flora drove them out of Glendivot and up the Kininvie Hill, past the manse, and on to the moorland beyond. Gradually Thomas regained consciousness again, and as Flora stopped the car in a lay-by, he said "That was strong stuff you gave me. What was it?" Flora was prepared for him as she helped him out the car. "15 Year-old Glendivot, Single Malt, Export strength." Then she rubbed it in. "You don't make whisky like that in Glenbroom, do you?"

With that, she waved the wig in his face, shoved him into the roadside ditch, and returned to the car. Before he could react, she drove off. He was left there, sitting in the ditch, barely knowing where he was, wearing ladies clothing, minus the wig, and rubbing his sore bald head.

He felt a swelling, and wondered how it got there, and his rear end was embarrassingly wet!

Flora kept the wig as evidence, while Penny tried to recover from the experience. "What have you done, leaving him there, in that condition? How will he get back?" she asked, showing some compassion for the poor man.

"He is only three miles from Glendivot and another three miles from Glenbroom! It will do him the world of good" replied the ex policewoman. "The fresh air will clear his head...and at least he has got a good pair of walking shoes!"

"What was he doing taking a tour round Glendivot, dressed as a lady?" asked Penny.

"Your guess is as good as mine. His nose was probably bothering him" was all Flora could say.

"Now it's his head" responded Penny, referring to his bruise. "I thought nothing happened up here in the Highlands. Things like that don't even happen in the City of London."

"You no doubt live a sheltered life down there" suggested Flora.

Thomas was like all Distillery Managers in the area. He held a position of high esteem and social respectability. He was a 'well-kent' face, and he now had a decision to make. He certainly could not go back to the Distillery road-end and wait for Violet to pick him up as arranged. Should he walk home by the most direct route? If so, this would take him straight through the busy main street of Glendivot. If he chose that way, he would have an awful lot of explaining to do.

As it was, he could not think of a plausible explanation, and if he did, no one would believe him! It would take him all day to explain to all those Glendivot inhabitants who were sure to stop him, and ask what he was up to. He would be the laughing stock of the community, dressed as he was, and with no hair!

Mobile phones were very rare in this part of the world, in the early seventies, and Thomas did not have one. He could not contact Violet, who was supposed to collect him at noon. She was going to have a long wait for him. Too bad. By now he had no sympathy for his sister. That probably made two of them. Violet had an awful lot to answer for, getting him into this predicament. He resolved to seek his revenge, if and when he got home.

One option was to take off the tweed suit, and the blouse, and get rid of the ladies' stockings (For Violet had not yet succumbed to tights) and jog home as an athlete, in his boxer shorts! While this was tempting, he reckoned that he was not fit enough to run more than 100 yards, far less 6 or 7 miles. He therefore reluctantly came to the conclusion that he would have to keep out of everyone's sight, and take the long way home.

This involved traversing round the boundary of Mr McPhee's farm, keeping out of Godzilla the bull's way, crossing the main road, climbing up the hill on the other side of the Glen, into the woods above the golf course, and back across the River near 'Upandoon Castle.'

He calculated this would be about 10 to 12 miles, and considering it was up hill and down dale, through woods and rough terrain, and across water, all the while keeping out of sight, he would be lucky if he was home by tea time.

Chapter 29

WELCOME HOME

O n the short journey back to the Distillery, Penny began to worry about the ramifications of Flora's action. Not knowing her background, and being all too aware of Thomas Hannah's ugly sisters' tenacity, she feared she may be charged with 'Grievous Bodily Harm' by the local police. "No way" said Flora reassuringly. "My husband is the policeman...and Thomas Hannah knows it."

"He dare not prefer charges for if he did, I would accuse him of sexual assault. It would be his word against mine. And what would they make of him being in our Distillery, dressed as a woman?"

"He wouldn't be able to look the judge, or his employees in the face." Flora seemed to be in total command of the situation.

Lizzy had returned to her duties at Balroonie House when the two ladies came back to the Distillery in the car. She appraised Mary and her mother of events so far. They couldn't wait for the next instalment. Flora resumed her duties, and Penny reported the incident to Angus in his office. "Serves him right" was the Distillery Manager's response. "He has no business coming round my Distillery without permission. It's industrial espionage. He is just trying to find out what is going on."

Penny came to the conclusion that Flora and Angus knew what they were doing, so she left it at that.

She continued working until lunchtime, supervising the changes that she had planned in the Visitor Centre, and making phone calls to suppliers of equipment. She then made her way back to Balroonie House for a snack lunch.

As she approached the main road, she noticed the ugly green and orange coloured Triumph Herald car, with Violet sitting impatiently in the driver's seat. It was with some pleasure, that Penny gave her an innocently cheerful wave, as she passed. There was no response from Violet.

Penny knew she was going to have a long wait, and couldn't help having a quiet chuckle to herself as she felt herself becoming more involved in the local rivalry. She decided to let Doom sit there indefinitely, quite oblivious to the trials and tribulations being endured by her brother.

Meanwhile Violet's brother was in a cold sweat worrying about meeting anyone who might recognise him, and accuse him of being a transvestite. He was at a complete loss as to how to explain away his situation, should the need arise. He was still confused and his mind was in a daze.

However, he successfully circumvented the farm, and dodged the traffic as he crossed the main road, and made for the field beyond. He was still dizzy as he extricated himself from the barbed wire fence, only after tearing his tweed skirt, and shuddering at the thought of Violet's reaction. Having tried to put this to the back of his mind, he then surveyed the journey ahead of him.

He had to cross the open field used by McPhee's cows for grazing, before climbing the hill beyond, and seeking the shelter of the woods beyond. His feet were aching already.

In Glendivot, Violet was still in her car at the road-end, looking thoroughly bored, when Penny, having had her snack lunch, returned to the Distillery in the afternoon. Again, she made a point of waving to her adversary, as she passed. Violet again, did not respond. 'She looks as if she already knows what has happened to her brother,' thought Penny. 'That could only explain her continuing frigid expression of Doom and Gloom.'

Violet was beginning to regret her decision to wait so long, while her brother was beginning to regret his decision to walk so far.

Thomas found the going tougher than he expected. It was becoming unbearable in his ill fitting brogues. He now felt the blisters in his feet. However, he could not remove his shoes, given the underfoot conditions.

Ironically, it was then he heard the noise from above, as he spotted the Mountain Rescue helicopter appearing overhead. It was either on its way to a search and rescue mission, or it was undertaking a training exercise. Suddenly, in his bemused state, the thought came to him that the Pilot might be searching for him! Had he been reported missing already? Could Flora possibly have the decency to call them out to rescue him? 'Rather unlikely' he thought. He always had a great admiration for the Mountain Rescue teams, but didn't think they were so efficient as to be on his trail so soon.

However, given his predicament, Thomas did not fancy being rescued in his lady's clothes, with all the attendant publicity, and explaining to do. He therefore chose to keep a low profile and make for cover as best he could. He was in an open field clearly to be seen, and the nearest woods were at least half a mile away...uphill! The only cover he could see close at hand, was a cattle feeding trough in the centre of the field, about a hundred yards away.

This is where the herds of cattle daily congregated to be fed or watered, and as such, the area round it was constantly trampled upon. In due course, it inevitably became a morass of filthy, slushy, smelly mud. However, in his predicament, he simply had no choice. He made an undignified beeline for it in his ladies' clothes.

Not being used to such vigorous exercise for over thirty years, and still not fully recovered from being knocked out, he lost his balance in the slime. Rather like a New York Yankee baseball player sliding in to base for a home run, he went flat on his face as he slithered in the slimy mud, and came to an undignified halt under the trough. He may have been grateful for the protection it provided, as he lay prostrate in the mud underneath, and listened to the drone of the aircraft above. At least he could console himself that the filthy mud also provided excellent camouflage. The only exception to this was his still clean bald head. He very quickly solved this problem by covering his head and face with the slimy mud. His camouflage was complete, as was his discomfort and misery.

Thomas was by now quite unrecognisable from the squalid mushy sludge upon which he was lying. Thus, he pondered, was it worth the discomfort, if the helicopter wasn't searching for him after all?

He lay there for what seemed an eternity, in his saturated tweed suit, which was now quite filthy, sodden wet and clinging to his body. He was grateful that at least, he did not have to share the trough with the herd of cows. Until then, they had been blissfully grazing in the field, and paying no attention to the intruder. However, they now became aware that he had apparently commandeered their feeding trough. They did not approve of this, so they gradually, but menacingly, moved towards him.

Obviously it was time to go, and he despaired a little as he experienced the mixed emotions of regret on the one hand, and relief on the other, as he watched the helicopter disappear over the hills in the direction of the Cairngorm mountains. Clearly the pilot was oblivious to his plight, and he did not appear even remotely interested!

'Surely things could only get better' thought Thomas, as he gathered himself together, and resumed his wet, uncomfortable overland trek. He was now such a sight that he almost didn't care if he was seen, for no one could identify him without close scrutiny.

When he reached the woods above the golf course, he was bitten alive by the biggest clegs he had ever encountered, and hordes of ferocious midges. It didn't help that he was covered in mud, or that his head was uncovered, thus giving him no protection in that area. Indeed he thought they thrived on the smell of the 'Glaur.' He hadn't realised that these blood sucking, man-eating insects got up women's skirts, and it was of little consolation that this would be the only time he had to suffer them in that area of his anatomy.

However, he had to remain in the infested woods, for there were people playing on the golf course, some of whom he knew, as he recognised they were from his own village of Glenbroom. So, he journeyed on, cursing the helicopter, and the insects as he went, making slow progress, as he trudged through the sickening thickening forest.

Back in Glendivot, Violet continued to display remarkable uncharacteristic patience, as she sat in the relative comfort of her uncomfortable little car. She remained there stoically until well into the afternoon, before finally giving up, and returning to Rose with her runny nose, in the sanctuary of her bedroom in Glenbroom.

Ultimately their brother emerged from the woods, negotiating his way through the ferns, and jagged yellow broom, while trying to avoid the nettles and thistles that were so prevalent in this part of the country. His mud spattered body was now soaking in perspiration, to augment his sodden tweed suit and drenched backside. He was relieved to see no sign of the helicopter that had caused so much of his discomfort.

He came upon the upper reaches of the Fiddich River, where he sought a suitable crossing. Thomas Hannah was not a fit man even for his age, and was worn out by this time. He sat down for a well earned rest, within sight of 'Upandoon Castle', and then surveyed his Glenbroom home in the far distance.

Having been born and bred in the area, he recalled as a boy, adventuring to the Castle, and playing up and down not only the Castle, but also the adjacent river. He had no bother crossing it then. As a teenager, he could jump from stone to stone, and cross it in several places without getting wet. He even used to practise his long jump over the river, when preparing for the school sports, and pretending he was competing in the Olympic Games. It was a different kettle of fish (sic) now that he was in his fifties.

As he sat there, he could see a number of tourists looking round the castle. He could hear their happy carefree voices in the distance, as they enjoyed exploring round the ancient keep. A few were on the highest ramparts, some with binoculars, enjoying the view, having climbed 'up' and not yet 'doon.' This restricted his search for a suitable crossing, if he was to avoid being seen. Ultimately, he chose a crossing point that would have been no problem in his younger days.

He decided he could not get any wetter than he was by now. Just as one gets older, hills appear higher and steeper, and whisky glasses seem smaller, so this river seemed deeper and wider than he remembered it as a boy. He was still having problems with his balance, ever since his encounter with the log, but there was no alternative. He hitched up his skirt to embarrassing levels, and ultimately succeeded in crossing, but not before falling in the river a couple of times.

He was past caring by this time, and he had the consolation of getting rid of some of the mud that was still clinging to him. What was more sobering, was the reminder of how freezing cold were the waters of the river's upper reaches, even in summertime.

It was in this condition that he finally staggered back across the moorland towards his house in Glenbroom. Suddenly he panicked, for it was only then he realised that he did not have a key. He had expected to be picked up, and run home by Violet.

Thomas's house was on the site, next door to his Distillery, and while it is not a labour intensive industry, there is always someone about. He could not afford to be seen standing outside his front door, in his present state. To add to his woe, his feet had developed really nasty blisters, and were killing him. He was thoroughly exhausted, and bitten alive, and he was at the end of his tether.

He had only just survived a most arduous and nerve-racking experience, and never thought he would live to see the day that he would be glad to see Violet, as he rang the doorbell. Surely she would be at home before him.

As he stood there petrified with the fear of being discovered, particularly by his own staff, a group of local schoolchildren appeared out of the blue, from one of the warehouses. They had been on a field day trip, and a guide had shown them round the Distillery. She waved them off with a cheery 'Goodbye' and to Thomas's relief, turned, and retraced her steps into the warehouse.

Thomas thought he was going to have a heart attack, as he cowered down behind the low hedge of his small garden, to avoid being seen by the schoolchildren as they approached him. It was an agonising wait, until his sister answered the door.

The children were stunned into uncustomary silence. They simply did not know how to react. Their emotions ranged from surprise to horror and fear, and then to laughter, all in quick succession. Some of the more sensitive ones expressed sympathy when they came upon what appeared to be a character out of a horror movie. But sympathy was the last thing the Distillery Manager got from Violet, when she ultimately opened the door.

To her horror, he crawled in to the house on his hands and knees, as the children watched in amazement. If he expected sympathy from Violet, he was to be sadly disappointed. She was more concerned about him not returning to the car as arranged, and wasting her time! She then complained about him dirtying the carpets of the house in his bedraggled state. As if that wasn't enough she then went on to accuse him of ruining her good brogue shoes and stockings, not to mention the soaking, and now utterly filthy unrecognisable torn tweed suit, that she had bought in Jenners, the most expensive shop in Edinburgh, albeit over 10 years ago!

She dismissed his counter-claim that the shoes had ruined his feet! The shoes could be replaced, but not his feet! "Where is your wig?" she demanded, changing the subject. "What have you done with it?" going on to bemoan how much it cost. She didn't even notice the bruises on his head, which were now quite obvious, or if she did, she made no mention of them. Doom subjected him to a dressing down (sic) for keeping her waiting at the Glendivot Distillery, and he told her in no uncertain terms, what he thought of her dressing him up, and throwing him into the lions' den.

The pair of them went at it hammer and tongs, each blaming the other, for their stupid ideas. It became so heated that Rose wondered what the commotion was, and had to rise from her bed, and try and pacify them, with her usual lack of success.

There was no doubt about it, the Glenlivet team were winning the battle of wills.

Chapter 30

REHEARSALS

Mary ensured that Angus turned up well prepared for the Drama Club's rehearsals on the Tuesday and Thursday evenings. She ignored his protestations that he should be attending his beloved shinty team's final training sessions, at this vital stage in their preparations for the Cup Final.

He had checked, by telephoning Fergus McTavish, his Assistant Manager, that she had indeed solved his goalkeeping problem, and carried out her part of the bargain. Mary, for her part, insisted he had made a deal. His word was his bond, and bonded he would be.

Mrs Grant had supported her daughter, by taking Angus through his lines as he attempted to act like Lord Darnley. To put it mildly, this was quite a challenge for him, as he had not acted since he played the part of an angel in the school Nativity Play nearly 50 years ago! The effeminate, vain and arrogant Lord Darnley could not have been more unlike him. His mother-in-law read the part of Mary Queen of Scots, and found this equally challenging, as she was no more like the adventurous lusty young Queen, of whom she disapproved.

These practise sessions presented son-in-law and mother-in-law with ample opportunity for friction, argument and criticism. They certainly did nothing to ease their already fraught relationship. So life that week in Balroonie House, was not dull. They also kept his mind off the new goalkeeper whose identity, Mary refused to divulge. This played havoc on her husband's nerves, which were by now testing his patience as never before. He was completely perplexed by her calm confidence, and he had to finally rely on blind faith, that she would come up trumps when it really mattered. As the Camanachd Cup Final coincided with his birthday, all she would say was "You will find out soon enough. It will be a nice surprise birthday present for you."

Angus's fraught sessions with his mother-in-law were nothing compared to the embarrassment the wretched man had to endure at the more public Drama Club rehearsals. Distillery Managers in Speyside enjoyed exalted positions within their communities. The dignity of their role commanded respect from their workforce and their families, whether they deserved it or not. People looked to them for leadership and example, so their position in local society was only one below the Landed Gentry, and was at least, on a par with the local Minister and Doctor.

It was hardly surprising therefore, that Angus found it very humbling to play the caddish, foppish boyfriend and husband, opposite his normally subservient housemaid Lizzy McPhee, as she put her heart and soul into playing the part of his wife, not Mary McDougall this time, but Mary Queen of Scots!

The ridiculous emerald green costume with the ill-fitting tights did nothing to help. The production was less than a fortnight away, and as the opening night drew nearer, the Producer insisted on the cast wearing their costumes in order to help them get into 'Character.' That was the last thing Angus needed, on the week of the Camanachd Cup Final.

Between rehearsing with his mother-in-law at home, and his housemaid at the Drama Club, he did not know whether he was coming or going. He was learning fast that thespians were an eccentric breed. His wife Mary, supported by Mrs Grant and Lizzy, made sure he was last to leave for home at the end of the rehearsals. This was to ensure there was no chance of him going on to his shinty team training sessions which were taking place along the road, at the same time. Despite the long summer evenings, these sessions were well over by the time he was released from his rehearsals ordeal. In any case, the team were probably propping up the bar in the Commercial Hotel by the time Angus returned home quite exhausted, to Balroonie House.

In any case, Mary had made it abundantly clear to Fergus McTavish, that the whole team and the back room staff were sworn to secrecy on the identity of the replacement goalkeeper. Otherwise she would simply withdraw him without notice. She unquestionably had them over the proverbial 'Barrel!' This added in no small measure to her husband's frustrations.

Despite her set-backs, Violet turned up for the rehearsals, as determined as ever, and fussed about the cast with the costumes in her customary fashion. She revelled in the responsibility bestowed upon her as Wardrobe Mistress. If truth be told, no one else would take on this thankless task. However, on these occasions, she was sufficiently chastened, to concentrate on these duties, rather than her usual habit of interfering in everything and anything else, much to the irritation of the Producer, and everyone involved.

The fact that Angus had been pressurised into saving the day, by taking on the role of Lord Darnley, had certainly been a sobering experience, even if it was a great relief to her. She had to admit that, although, not to anyone else.

Angus's embarrassment was tempered to some extent by the fact that he was able to warn Violet that her brother's subterfuge was a serious matter, which he had not forgotten. He kept her in her place by telling her he would be taking legal advice. That added to her sobriety, and was enough to keep her at bay for a while.

Having been made aware that her brother had been unfrocked at the Glendivot Distillery, had a profound effect on Violet. How long that would last however, was another matter. Rose's concentration was stretched to the limits in her capacity as prompt for the play, because she was kept busy as Angus struggled with his lines, in his amateurish efforts to conquer the role.

Mary invited Penny to take a little time off her work, and her 'Honeymoon,' by inviting her to these evening rehearsals at the Drama Club. Penny's first reaction was that the whole visit to Scotland had provided more than enough 'Drama' for her liking. However, Mary insisted in making her feel welcomed by offering her genuine 'Highland Hospitality', and Rod Ponsonby did not appear to object. It gave Penny the opportunity to meet some of the Distillery employees in a social capacity, and it also added to her knowledge of Scottish culture and history, as she observed yet another tragedy being performed!

During the tea-break, Penny felt she had to build bridges, and asked Violet whether her brother had recovered. She remained concerned about his bruised head, never mind his bruised ego. "There's nothing wrong with him" replied Doom, completely contradicting what she said of him, on his return from his experience at Glendivot.

As far as his bruised head was concerned, Violet had no idea what Penny was talking about, so she decided not to pursue the matter. The Public Relations Manager did not want to land in hot water again. She was also relieved by the lack of any accusations or threats against Flora, the redoubtable Chief Receptionist.

By the end of the second week, Penny completed her outstanding work at the Distillery. By that time, she had installed and trained the new guides, learned the basics of the distillation processes herself, modernised and upgraded the Reception Centre, ordered equipment for the audio-visual theatre and arranged for plans to be prepared for an enlarged Gift Shop. She had co-operated with the accountants to work out costings, and made progress in establishing the Museum. However, the new Restaurant would have to come later, assuming she obtained her Government finance.

She had achieved a great deal, and was ready to escort Rod on his 'Official' tour of her new facilities. She felt confident that the money from the Government would be forthcoming. The fact that their relationship had developed into a genuine romance, helped considerably. That was a bonus she had not anticipated.

Rod had even gone several days without mishap, so things were looking up on all fronts. They both now looked forward to being VIP Guests, as excitement grew to fever pitch in the lead up to the Cup Final.

Chapter 31

THE CUP FINAL

The Camanachd Cup Final is a great social occasion in the Highlands of Scotland. It is the equivalent of the FA Cup Final at Wembley or the Super Bowl in the United States. It is like Royal Ascot...without the clothes! They wear clothes all right. It's just they wear clothes suitable for the occasion and the weather, rather than the camera!

It is the climax of months of fierce physical combat where teams from every town and village worth their salt, compete in a series of knock-out shinty matches, for the honour of reaching the pinnacle of their sport. However, "Sport" is perhaps, not the right word for it.

The game of shinty is a modernised form of tribal or clan warfare in which old scores are settled, and the combatants wield fearsome hockey sticks at a hard ball, and at their opponents. The objective is to force the projectile, which at speed, resembles a cannon ball, through a set of goalposts, bravely defended by the opposing team's last line of defence...their goalkeeper!

It is a coarser version of the more refined game of hockey, played by their cousins in the South. The field is bigger, the weapons are bigger, the ball goes farther, and the players are tougher. Anything goes as there are hardly any rules. Such rules that they do have, allow for the sticks, unlike in hockey, to be wielded above head height. Many a good shinty player can hit a golf ball out of sight. As a result, the injuries are more numerous, and more serious.

Accordingly, when some players lose their heads, they often swing their sticks above them like claymores, and when this happens, their opponents are likely to lose *their* heads!

The person who is most vulnerable, being on the receiving end of swirling sticks and hurling balls is the poor goalkeeper, whose protection is nothing like the protective padding normally associated with the more sophisticated hockey goalkeepers in the South.

Their only concession to safety might involve the occasional use of a helmet and/or face mask, to reduce the danger of head injuries. Perhaps they might wear a pair of shin-guards. Very rarely, a shinty goalkeeper who may feel vulnerable for whatever reason, may also wear protection over a particularly vulnerable part of his anatomy, but that is generally only if his wife or girl-friend insists! It is a brave man indeed who takes on this role.

On this occasion, the Cup Final was being played in Inverness, the Capital of the Highlands. It was a grand affair with pipe bands, kilted majorettes, television coverage, and the red and blue colours of the rival teams were prominent everywhere. It was a great family occasion, attracting several thousand spectators.

They organised a parachuting display from the local RAF base, which caused much excitement, due to the strong gusty northerly wind. One of the parachutists landed on the roof of the stand. He finished up hanging on to one of the flag poles, until he had to be rescued, rather red faced, by the local Fire Brigade. Another landed in one of the goals and got tangled up in the net. It took some time to extricate him from both the net and his parachute, as it swirled about out of control, in the wind. A third landed in the River Ness nearby, and the last one received an enthusiastic, if somewhat sarcastic cheer, as he landed on the pitch!

In the last few days, Angus, who had been beavering away, learning his lines for the play, had missed the last two training sessions, and had attended the rehearsals as agreed. Violet and Mary, in a strange and unlikely alliance, had ensured that he kept his side of the bargain, in fear of his life.

Fergus McTavish, the Assistant Manager, who also doubled as coach, had done a good job during these sessions. If truth be told, he was probably more competent than Angus, but he wasn't the Distillery Manager! At this stage of the Competition, everyone was highly motivated, so Angus's presence at training was not essential.

His absence however presented Mary with the opportunity of introducing her mystery goalkeeper, without any interference or debate from her husband. In addition to the Tuesday and Thursday training sessions, she and the coach arranged for him to have some extra practice with the forwards, who benefitted from the additional shooting practice. The new goalkeeper took full advantage of these sessions to hone his own skills. It appeared that her substitute had been well received by the players in the team, and to everyone's surprise, including Mary's, he showed himself to be a worthy stand-in.

Rod Ponsonby had more important things to consider. He intimated to all at Balroonie House that he had an appointment with the Regimental Commander of the Seaforth Highlanders, at their Headquarters in Fort George on the day of the Cup Final. The old Seaforths' Barracks were considering opening their premises and Museum to the public, and were also applying for financial assistance from the Government. He was required to make an assessment, and prepare a report for his Minister. He therefore regretted he would be unable to attend the match.

They were all deeply disappointed, after all he had done for them. Considering all the poor fellow had endured since leaving London, if anyone deserved to enjoy the game, he did. Penny was especially disappointed that he would not be able to join her as a VIP Guest. This was to be the highlight of her first visit to the Distillery. Nevertheless, she reconciled herself that the Seaforth Highlanders were also seeking help from Rod in his official capacity. Her new boyfriend was obviously a man of some importance and influence.

However, the occasion was not without its share of last minute drama for the Glendivot team. They had arrived, stripped, held their team talk and even completed their warm up, and still their replacement goalkeeper had not turned up! Both individually and collectively, the team's concerns mounted, as they went through their pre-match exercises. Angus's already taught nerves were stretched beyond breaking point as it was, given that it was the biggest sporting occasion of his life! This was not the time to upset the players further.

He had sent Hector off on a wild goose chase to find the culprit. The stammering excitable Doctor in his panic, ran up and down the stand, pleading in his faltering way, had anybody seen his goalkeeper? The situation became so critical, that he even went into the opposing team's dressing room, to check if they had an extra keeper, just in case his last-minute replacement had inadvertently gone into the wrong dressing room!

As the minutes ticked by towards kick-off time, Angus had now become a nervous wreck, as he searched high and low for a goalkeeper he did not even know!

"Where the hell is he?" he demanded of Fergus who was now the target of his wrath. At least Fergus would recognise the person they were looking for.

"I haven't a clue" replied the equally panic-stricken coach.

"We have searched everywhere, and we are running out of time. I have even checked the toilets, and he is nowhere to be seen." By this time, Angus could well have used the toilets himself, but he had no time for that now.

"He surely can't have got lost" he pondered. He then rushed up the stairs from the dressing rooms to the main stand, and accosted an innocent looking young policeman, who was stewarding some late arriving supporters to their seats. "Have you seen my goalkeeper? He is not in the dressing room." "No, sorry. I can't help you." replied the officer, resuming his duties.

Whereupon Angus collared one of the Camanachd Cup Committee Officials who was about to take his seat in the Directors' Box. "Excuse me. I have lost my goalkeeper. Have you seen him at all?"

"No, I am sorry. I can't help you." replied the surprised Official, thinking 'How would I know his goalkeeper, even if he did turn up?'

"Can you hold the game up until we find him?" pleaded a desperate Angus, who was now perspiring profusely.

"No way. You will have to play your reserve keeper." was the Official's unsympathetic response.

"But he *is* my reserve! In fact he is my reserve's reserve!"

"That is your problem" was the unhelpful reply.

Having hit that proverbial 'Brick Wall,' Angus wiped the perspiration from his brow. He then had an inspiration. He would tackle his last hope. After clambering over three rows of spectators, disturbing all and sundry, spilling their pop corn and beer, and hurting his shins. He finally reached his wife Mary, who was sitting taking in the atmosphere, with her mother.

"What have you done with my goalkeeper?" he demanded.

"What are you talking about?" responded Mary, noting her husband's agitated consternation.

"My goalkeeper! You promised me a goalkeeper! Where is he?"

"Is he not with the team?" asked his wife, trying to keep calm.

"No he is not with the team! I wouldn't be here asking you, if he was with the team!" shouted her almost hysterical husband. By this time he was attracting the unwanted attention of those around them, as the Announcer started to read out the teams over the tannoy.

"I have no idea where he is" said Mary, not exactly truthfully.

"You made a bargain with me Mary McDougall. You promised me a goalkeeper!" The spectators around them paid more attention as Angus threatened her.

"I will see you later!" he said menacingly. With that, he turned on his heels and returned to the dressing room.

As he reached the foot of the stairs, two St. Andrews Ambulance ladies were attending to a prostrate Hector McPherson in the narrow corridor. His frantic search had all been too much for him. He felt faint and was being forced to take a drink of water! That was the last thing Hector needed at this time. It was also the last thing Angus needed.

The opposing team were now coming out of their dressing room, and stumbling over Hector and the ladies, as they made their way to the tunnel. The medics were trying to reassure Angus that his crony would be OK, when Fergus came rushing out of the dressing room, and bumped into Angus, who then went sprawling over Hector and the St. Andrews ladies on the floor! The situation became a chaotic shambles in the confined space of the corridor, as several of the shinty players, whose minds were on the upcoming game, fell over them, thus creating something of a collapsed rugby scrum, in a mass of heaving bodies! By this time, the poor Ambulance Ladies were in need of medical assistance themselves.

"It's all right Angus, we've found him!" shouted Fergus as they tried to extricate themselves from the melee of medics and players. It was some consolation that he was already changed into his sports gear when he arrived. He was even wearing Hughie's protective face mask and helmet. As far as one could see, that was the only protection he was wearing! He apologised for being late, but everyone was so glad to see him, that no questions were asked, and he was listed in the programme as 'A N OTHER.'

Angus was greatly relieved as he met his new goalkeeper for the first time, albeit briefly, even if it was in the overcrowded noisy tunnel. He shook his hand, thanked him for standing in, and wished him 'Good luck,' before leading out the team. The most important game in the history of Glenlivet was about to commence.

Mary and her mother were joined in the stand by Hughie and Lizzy. They were all adorned with the red and white colours of the Glendivot team. Even Hughie's white plaster cast was painted in the red and white stripes of his team's colours. Mary breathed a sigh of relief when she saw that the goalkeeper had arrived after all.

Violet and Rose sat a few rows back, more soberly dressed.

Doom looked as if she was at another funeral, and Gloom looked in amazement at the scene before her. She had obviously led a rather sheltered life, and the action on the pitch, together with the language and behaviour of the rival supporters, was a whole new educational experience for her. It was not for the faint-hearted, and she had to cover her ears and close her eyes when it became too distressing.

Penny was there, looking radiant as an honoured guest, wearing a red and white rosette and scarf. Naturally she missed Rod's company, but she sat beside Hughie, who explained the finer points of the game to her.

As it progressed, Angus strutted about the touchline cajoling his team to greater efforts, becoming redder in the face as the match went on. Even his wife was reduced to expressing her concern about his blood pressure. Hector recovered enough to take his role as 'Water carrier' very seriously. He kept a special bottle of 'c-c-coloured' water for himself, in the hope that it would control his blood pressure.

The game proved to be a brutally ferocious encounter with no quarter given. The Glendivot supporters roared their team on with great gusto, while an unimpressed Violet watched dourly, constantly criticising the players of both teams for either fouling or diving. When she wasn't doing that, she was criticising them for their lack of skill or courage, or both.

However she reserved most of her vitriol for the poor referee whose decisions were never correct! She even claimed to be an authority on this sport, although she had never attended a game in her life! One wondered how she could possibly be enjoying herself! Rose meanwhile covered her eyes at most of the action.

Half-time came with the score goalless. What was emerging was the fact that the opposition had a big muscular and intimidating centre forward who was obviously their star player. He was noted as their top scorer, and fired in shot after shot at the Glendivot goalkeeper who was proving to be an outstanding last line of defence. He made a number of breathtaking saves, despite being injured on more than one occasion, and he kept his team in the game.

The second half continued much the same, and it became a dual between the two, to see who would emerge the victor. Naturally it was a case of attacker versus defender, and by the nature of things, the poor goalkeeper was on the receiving end of a growing number of hair-raising shots. It was only a matter of time before he was badly injured, or he would concede a goal.

Three times the trainer had to come on to attend to his various injuries. Hector tired himself out, running on to the pitch several times to give the goalkeeper water to sustain him. Ultimately, he had to utilise the services of a ball-boy to help him carry water to the players. In the end, the poor goalkeeper's injuries were so debilitating, Hector resorted to offering him some of his 'coloured water' to revive him. That seemed to do the trick.

The unknown keeper gradually won the hearts of the Glendivot supporters, and the admiration of the neutrals. Even Hughie admitted that he could not have done better. He had to admire his replacement's bravery and skill.

As the game drew to its conclusion, he had clearly emerged as 'Man of the Match.' After one more outstanding save at the feet of the centre forward, his forwards broke away and scored an unlikely goal. There were only two minutes left! Could it be that the little village of Glendivot could actually win the prestigious Cup?

No one in their right mind really thought they had a chance that morning, but now they were on the cusp of victory, and permanent fame! The opposition put on all their substitutes, in one last desperate attempt to wrest the Cup from the hands of the underdogs. Again, a long searching pass from midfield found the charging centre forward. He shrugged off his markers and closed in on goal like an Olympic sprinter, swinging his stick as if he was William Wallace wielding his famous sword at the Battle of Stirling Bridge!

The Glendivot keeper, despite his injuries, in true 'Braveheart' fashion, rushed out and dived at his feet, just as the centre unleashed his driving shot. It appeared to hit the keeper flush on the face, and dented his protective mask. The shot was deflected and the ball flew harmlessly past the post.

Unfortunately the centre forward's momentum was such that he fell on top of the keeper who went down awkwardly, and stayed down. It appeared that he may have broken his leg. With that, the referee blew for full time...and Glendivot had won the Trophy! The crowd went crazy!

Chapter 32

MAN OF THE MATCH

Immediately, the Glendivot supporters swarmed on to the pitch to congratulate their heroes. Everyone went berserk and in the confusion, the goalkeeper disappeared under a host of bodies. It was the last thing he needed, or wanted. The Inverness Provost presented the Trophy to the winning Captain, who was then interviewed by the TV people.

The team then did a lap of honour along with a delirious Angus their Manager, Fergus McTavish and a puffing and blowing Hector. However, they were without their goalkeeper, who was still on the ground. He was surrounded by hysterical supporters, who were preventing another group of St. Andrews Ambulance Medical Assistants from getting anywhere near him.

The Glendivot team and their reserves returned to the dressing room, and were congratulating one another, when one of the Officials came in to announce that A N OTHER had been named as 'Man of the Match!' The trouble was, they didn't know his name! He had wanted to remain anonymous, and at the final training sessions, had simply asked his team mates to call him 'Hughie Two' as a mark of respect for Hughie, who had been denied his life's ambition to play in the Cup Final! It was only then that they realised that he wasn't with them!

Angus rushed out, quickly followed by a breathless Hector, to see if he was still on the pitch. In their excitement, they had forgotten all about him. Fortunately, he wasn't difficult to find. He was being carried on a stretcher by the St. Andrews Ambulance crew, who had rescued him from the pile of bodies who had celebrated the victory on top of him. If he hadn't injuries before this, he certainly had them now!

Angus and Hector escorted him to the ambulance, where the Camanachd Cup Officials finally caught up with them, to present their 'Man of the Match' Trophy. He was in no fit state to be interviewed by the TV crew or local media.

They then went with him in the ambulance, and persuaded the driver to take him straight to the Glendivot Cottage Hospital, rather than to the larger Raigmore Infirmary in Inverness. Their reasoning, which was even more flawed by then, was that he would be greeted as a hero of Glendivot, and be treated quicker, and with more personal care. It never crossed their minds at that time, that anyone likely to have the skills required to treat his injuries, would be at the match in Inverness!

Meanwhile Mary, Mrs. Grant, Lizzy and Hughie made their way back to the car park in a state of euphoria. This was unprecedented in their lifetimes, and they were determined to make the most of it. They were still jumping up and down in their excitement when Mary asked Violet "Will you be coming to the 'Hoolie' in the

Glendivot village hall tonight?" "Not me," was the reply. Doom would not be seen dead on such joyous 'over the top' occasions. Rose, who was by then caught up in the general elation, said she would come, until she was put in her place once more by Violet.

They were about to part company, when Violet informed them that she and her sister would be following them back to Balroonie House...to pick up their Charity collecting can, which Rose had left, the day their dog caused so much havoc. Mary tried to put them off, as they had enough of the killjoys' company for one day, but Violet insisted as it was 'On their way home to Glenbroom in any case.'

Violet was determined to make one last attempt to ascertain the purpose of the Glendivot visitors from London. She made this decision when she was consumed with jealousy, on seeing Penny given VIP Status during the game. The collecting can provided her with the excuse.

Chapter 33

LOCAL HERO

On the way home, Mary observed that "It doesn't take two of them to pick up a can." Her mother lamented that she would have to double her doze of medicines, if she had to put up with Violet a moment longer. They were no sooner in the house celebrating their unexpected victory, when sure as fate, the ugly sisters arrived behind them, having pushed their little Triumph Herald to the limit.

Hughie was still on a high when he greeted Violet, and lifted her clean off her feet, twirling her round and round until she was dizzy, and in the process, he hurt his foot.

"We arra Champions! We arra Champions! Eh Violet?" he declared, ignoring the pain. "What did you think of that then?"

"Put me down!" shouted Violet, clearly distressed at being manhandled. Bodily contact with the opposite sex was something she had never previously experienced. Her response was therefore as warm as the iceberg that sunk the Titanic.

"Bet ye didn't expect that, eh?" he continued to taunt her. He put her down, and they all enjoyed watching her stagger about like a Saturday night drunk, until she adjusted her hat and recovered her balance and composure.

While Mrs Grant searched for her pills, Lizzy could not contain herself any longer. "Was that no' something else?" she exclaimed. "What a finish! Exciting is no' the word for it!"

"Can that girl not come back down to earth?" asked Violet, holding on to a chair. Lizzy ignored her and carried on "I was so excited, I nearly...I nearly...well...oh you will have to excuse me..." whereupon she made a beeline for the toilet.

Even Mrs Grant was overcome with all the excitement... She found her pills, and was about to pour herself some water from the water jug on the sideboard, when she changed her mind, and poured herself a dram of whisky instead, to help her swallow them. "For medicinal reasons" she commented, trying to justify herself.

Hughie then returned to the outstanding contribution of the goalkeeper who replaced him. "That was a rare goalie you got. I would not have believed it if I hadnae seen it with my ain eyes" he said to Mary.

"Ay, he did us proud" she replied modestly.

It was then that Doom struck like a rapier. "Who was he anyway?" she demanded to know. Gloom suggested "Whoever he was, he was our... "Local hero."

"Are you not going to tell us who he was Mary?" Clearly Violet was not going to let this go.

Hughie could see that Mary was reluctant to tell her, so carried on regardless. "See that save he made...in the last minute!" he eulogised.

"I'm sayin', who was he Mary?" continued Violet, stamping her foot on the carpet.

"It was out of this World!" declared Hughie, keeping her at bay.

"And it knocked *him* clean out of this World!" proclaimed Mrs Grant.

"It was just as well he was wearing a face mask." Rose chipped in, remarking on how brave he was.

Violet was ready to recommence the inquisition, when the toilet flushed, and Lizzy came out. "How did you manage that Lizzy?" asked Mary, just as Violet was about to resume the inquisition.

"It was quite easy" replied the maid in all innocence, "My mammy taught me."

"I mean, opening the door" explained Mary. Hughie who was still dreaming of the goalkeeper's exploits, reflected "It was magic! Sheer magic!" Lizzy who was on a different wave-length, disagreed.

"No it wasnae. I just turned the handle, like that" as she demonstrated the twisting action with her hand.

Chapter 34

STRETCHER CASE

Angus and Hughie found the Cottage Hospital in Glendivot virtually deserted. Almost all the staff had been to the game, and only a skeleton staff remained. There was no one competent to deal with the full extent of the keeper's injuries, particularly a suspected broken leg. However, they did manage to dress his wounds, and put his leg in makeshift splints.

Rather than wait for the returning medical staff, as they would probably be in no fit state to help, the two cronies decided to bring him back to Balroonie House in the ambulance, to recover. By hook or by crook, they wanted to present him as 'Man of the Match' at the Glendivot 'Hoolie,' that was to take place that evening, and there was no way they wanted him detained overnight in the hospital.

They staggered up the driveway and in the front door, carrying the stretcher with the goalkeeper holding his 'Man of the Match' Trophy and The Camanachd Cup, with its red and white garlands. Someone had placed a bottle of Glendivot's finest Malt in the Cup, and by this time Hector's back was about breaking. When he complained, he got little sympathy. Angus said he was lucky, compared to his hero, the keeper... "For his leg *is* broken!"

They got a round of applause as they put the stretcher down in the middle of the lounge, and everybody gathered round. Hector was bent over, and could not straighten up, even when Angus man-handled him, and then slapped him on the back. Angus was not to be beaten as Hector remained doubled up, moaning away, and looking for sympathy. He lifted the bottle of whisky from the Camanachd Cup, removed the top and placed the bottle under Hector's nose. Hector sniffed the aroma and slowly straightened up as Angus lifted the bottle higher and higher. His 'Broken' back was cured!

Angus, as host, then suggested celebration drinks, and Hughie and Lizzy helped him dispense them. Hector sat down for he needed a rest. Rose knelt down to sympathise with the injured hero. "How are you poor thing?" she asked as she placed herself close to him.

"I feel dizzy" replied Hector, whereupon Rose, in her innocence, said to the goalkeeper,

"You know, I could swear your lips didn't move!"

Then Violet told her to take 'His thing' off. Rose was confused by what she meant. "His face mask!" explained her sister. "He can hardly breathe in that." Rose was relieved, and between them, the ladies slowly removed the 'Man of the Match's' headgear. At that very moment, Penny came rushing in the front door, in quite a state.

She had been separated from the party in the stand at the end of the game. After all the hullaballoo at the end of the match, the crowd was ecstatic and running about in all directions. Ultimately Penny, looking in vain for the Balroonie House contingent, made her way to her little red sports car in the car park. There, she found it surrounded by admiring youths and a few old stagers interested in vintage sports cars.

Penny, who was a very attractive young lady, had made sure she was looking her best as a VIP Guest. Therefore, when the locals saw that she was the owner of the car, began to assume that she was some kind of celebrity. Someone suggested she was a film star and others said they were sure they had seen her on TV. Some thought she was a model, and they became as interested in her as they were in the model of car. A few even asked her for her autograph.

She was therefore delayed in leaving the sports stadium, and she was obviously unable to follow Mary and the others on the drive back to Glendivot, for they were long gone. It was hardly surprising that she took a wrong turning, and found herself lost again, somewhere between Culloden and Elgin. This explained her late arrival.

"I'm sorry I'm late. I got lost...again" she explained, before turning, and noticing the goalkeeper on the stretcher. Only then did she recognise it was Rod Ponsonby!

"What the...? What are you doing here?" she asked, barely believing her eyes.

"I thought you were at Fort George". She could hardly recognise him with all his injuries, and she couldn't understand why he was in his shinty gear.

"We c-c-carried him" said Hector. It d-d-damn-near killed me.

"All the way from Inverness?" she asked.

"No, no, f-f-f-from the ambulance" he replied.

"But, I don't understand. I thought you were seeing the Army Commander at Fort George this afternoon?"

"He would have been safer in the Army!" remarked Mrs Grant. Penny had now put two and two together.

"So, it was you...who played in goal..." They all nodded.

"And it was you who won the Cup for Glendivot?" They all agreed, and nodded approvingly, while Rod, clearly still in pain, nodded modestly.

"Yes indeed, indeed it was" announced the slightly inebriated Hector. He had finished the bottle of 'Coloured water' by the end of the match.

"How marvellous!" she exclaimed proudly.

"Yes indeed, indeed yes."

"And you weren't at Fort George after all?" she concluded.

"No indeed, indeed no" repeated the Doctor.

"So you must have been training with the team each night when we were at the Drama Club rehearsals?" Rod nodded again.

"Yes indeed, indeed yes." continued Hector.

Penny was sorely tempted to tell Hector to 'Shut up' by this time. However, she chose to pay more attention to Rod. "I wondered where you had disappeared to." She knelt down on the floor beside him, taking over the caring duties from Rose, and cradled him in her arms. "Can you not do something to help him Dr McPherson?" she asked. "I'm ill just l-looking at him" was the only response she got, as Hector wiped his brow.

On seeing the state of Ponsonby's facial injuries, Violet was moved to say "Talk about turning the other cheek? That's a terrible face!" This prompted Angus to say "Look who's talking...Yours is no' so bonnie either!" Violet could not resist one of her most ferocious scowls.

Mary told Lizzy to fetch the First Aid Box and a bowl of water. As the maid went into the kitchen and took off her coat, she discovered the letter that the postman had asked her to give to Mrs McDougall. She had forgotten all about it.

Meanwhile Penny was all apologetic to Rod who had suffered one indignity after another, since agreeing to come with her to Scotland. Surely this was the last straw. She was now quite overcome with remorse, and said to him "When I brought you to Scotland, I never dreamt you would end up like this."

Violet's heart jumped! At last she might learn what they were up to, and why they were there.

"Yes, why did you bring him to Scotland Mrs Ponsonby?" she asked abruptly.

"They're on their honeymoon Violet" explained Rose, as if Violet was stupid. Penny, who by this time, had other things on her mind, let her guard slip, and asked the sisters what made them think they were married?

This was the cue for Angus, ably supported by Mary, to effusively offer drinks all round, making a particular fuss of Violet and Rose in doing so.

"It's not often we offer you a drink Violet" he said, as he poured her one.

"But this is a special occasion." Even Mrs Grant helped to divert Violet's attention. In the interests of family solidarity, she was even prepared to imbibe more than was good for her.

"I think I will force myself to have one this time" she conceded, as she accepted a glass from Hughie. "After all, it's not every year we win the Camanachd Cup!"

"*You* didnae win the Camanachd Cup!" Violet corrected her as if spoiling for another fight.

She was further diverted by Lizzy coming back with the bowl of water and First Aid Box, which she gave to Penny to administer First Aid to her hero. The maid hid the letter behind her back, at least for the moment.

By now everyone except poor Rod Ponsonby had a drink in their hands. Even Lizzy was allowed to have one on this unique occasion. Angus proposed a toast.... to "Glendivot...the best team in Scotland!" They all rose with enthusiasm, including Hector with some difficulty. "I'll d-drink to that" he said.

"I thought you would" countered Mrs Grant. Then they all sat down, and Lizzy placed the letter behind a cushion.

Doom returned to the attack. "As we were saying Mrs Ponsonby, did you say...?" She was interrupted by Hector this time, despite his condition and his stammer. He stood up again, lifted his glass, and proposed, "A toast... To G-G-Glendivot! May it make amorous women g-g-g-glamorous, and g-g-g-glamorous women amorous!"

They all rose again, Violet with reluctance, muttering under her breath. Her sister was more enthusiastic "I'll drink to that" she said as she consumed a large mouthful.

"I thought you would" said Mrs Grant as they all sat down.

"As I was saying, before I was so rudely interrupted" continued Violet. Ignoring her, Angus enquired of Hector "Are ye not asking a bit much of the cratur?" Hector paused, and after a long gaze at the ugly sisters, replied,

"Yes indeed, indeed yes. M-M-Maybe you are right."

Lizzy was gaining confidence, and it was her turn to stop Violet in her tracks.

"I would like to propose a toast...To oor goalie...who saved us the day!" Rose added profoundly, that it wasn't surprising as "It was his job, for after all, he *is*... the Minister!"

They all rose once more and as they toasted him, they suddenly realised he was the only one present, who did not have a drink! He probably needed it more, and certainly deserved it more than the lot of them put together! They all sat down again.

"You don't have a drink Mr. Ponsonby" said Angus, as he poured him one from the bottle. "You deserve Glendivot's finest after that display, and that big Centre Forward breaking your leg too."

"He may have broken your leg Mr. Ponsonby" interjected Mrs. Grant, "But you broke his heart! It will take him much longer to recover from that." By this time everybody was beginning to feel the effects of their celebrations.

Angus gave Rod a particularly large dram, "To make up for lost time" and thanked him for making them all so happy. Violet told him to 'Speak for himself,' for she was not a 'Happy bunny' as she had not yet solved her problem.

She was about to return to her inquisition, when Mary took command of the situation. She announced, "And talking of being happy Angus, I wish to propose a toast."

"Not another!" protested Violet.

"You do?" asked her husband somewhat surprised, for Mary was not in the habit of proposing toasts.

"Yes, to you Angus! We all wish you a Happy Birthday!"

With all the excitement of the Cup Final, Angus, like many men of his age, had completely forgotten about his Birthday. They all rose and toasted him with various degrees of enthusiasm. Mary went on to say "I hope you approved of my Birthday present to you" as she pointed to Rod Ponsonby.

"You could not have done better" replied her husband, as he pecked her on the cheek in a rare display of affection.

"I could not have asked for more."

Rose was not used to indulging in the demon drink, and was now becoming quite uninhibited. "May you have happy memories of your honeymoon Mr Ponsonby" she proposed, as she raised her glass to have another toast. By now they all took a little longer to rise. Nevertheless they all staggered to their feet and joined her, with the exception of Penny who was applying First Aid to the Under Secretary of State. They then all sat down again.

Penny whispered "You will not forget this trip in a hurry Rod," as Rose stood, swaying gently from side to side, continued in her sozzled state "I should like to oppose....propose another toast!...To marriage!" she declared convincingly.

"Awe be quiet and sit down!" commanded Violet in a thundering voice.

"We will be at it all day at this rate!" Some of them drank her toast, while others were glad of the rest. Rose was confident enough to object, until Doom told her to "Sit!" as if she was talking to Thumper.

Chapter 35

THE LETTER

Hughie thought it was a stroke of genius to get Rod Ponsonby to take his place. He asked Mary how she knew he could play so well. She and Rod had been very successful in keeping their secret. Penny was also coming to terms with the situation. "Now I know why he kept disappearing, but wasn't he marvellous?" she said proudly. Violet remarked with suspicion and a large dose of sarcasm, that for a Minister, he had some surprising talents. Mary agreed that he had 'Saved' them in more ways than one.

Hughie could not control his curiosity, "Where did he learn to play like that?" he asked. Mary explained that they learned he had gone to Cambridge where he won a "Blue." Rose, who was now quite drunk, added "And he got all black and blue playing for Glendivot!"

"But they don't play shinty at Cambridge?" questioned Violet.

"No, but he won it playing at Hockey! As a goalkeeper! He was even an Olympic trialist!" Mary explained it was very similar. Penny now showed genuine affection. "Isn't he brave" she said as she stroked his forehead.

Rose thought it was very clever of Mary working that out. However, Mary put her right by surprisingly informing her, that "It wasn't me! All the credit goes to Lizzy!" who by this time had finished her glass of whisky. She was now turning it upside down, trying to squeeze the last drop out of it, and licking her finger as well.

Everyone was surprised at Lizzy finding this out from Ponsonby, except Violet, who then remembered the pair of them conspiring at Balroonie Castle. "And I for one would like to find out more about Mr Ponsonby" said the matriarch from Glenbroom, while they all looked at a now dizzy Lizzy, as she accepted a second glass of whisky from Angus.

"You could have fooled me" said Hughie, who despite being her boyfriend, used to feel she was a bit glaikit and gormless. He remembered the first time he asked to see her home after one of the village dances, she showed him a photograph of it! Angus added that she would come back from these dances, complaining of sexual harassment... the lack of it!

Lizzy was now as drunk as Rose, and as they watched her, Angus resolved she would have to go back to her old job. On being asked what that was by Penny, Hector replied on his behalf, "She was a f-f-f-Pheasant plucker!" There was a moment's silence.

"I'm glad you got that right" said Angus. Hector expanded "She was a f-f-f-pheasant plucker, for the F-F-F-Findochty f-f-farmers!" Angus added, "That's right. She left...because she couldnae stand the *foul* smell!" and immediately offered Hector another dram as they both enjoyed the joke.

Lizzy was now turning her amorous attentions towards Hughie who claimed she must have had too much to drink. This prompted a ready response from her. "Esschuse me...I've only had one glass...the trouble is...he keeps feeling...filling it up!" she said, referring to Angus.

Rod was clearly suffering as he groaned in agony, and Penny returned the bowl of water to Mary. Mrs Grant, who had also lost her inhibitions by this time, remarked that he will be glad to get back to the peace and quiet of London.

"London? Is *that* where he came from?" questioned Violet, quick as a flash. Now she was making some progress. "I knew it. I knew it all along."

However, before she could pursue it, Angus stated the obvious, "I bet ye never expected to help us in this way, eh Mr. Ponsonby?"

"Help you? enquired Violet. "What do you mean, help you?"

"I thought he was here on his honeymoon" observed Rose, as ever the romanticist.

"No he's no'" interjected Lizzy, who by then was stoned out her mind. "He's here to give us lots and lots of money!"

Mary, in shock, tumbled the bowl of water over poor Ponsonby, who let out a yell. 'What more humiliation could her poor Rod be expected to endure?' thought Penny as she endeavoured to dry him. Angus remonstrated with his wife "Go easy. He has been nearly drowned once already!" "Twice!" interjected Rod, recalling his soakings at Gretna and the River Fiddich. Mary apologised profusely, as she helped Penny.

"What's all this about money?" demanded Doom, homing in on her prey. Angus made one last valiant effort to explain. "It's for...the church organ fund!" he reasoned as he turned to his wife, "Ye ken how your father was always lookin' for money for his organ?" His mother-in-law interrupted him despite her inebriated state, claiming in a rather superior manner, "They were never stuck for money when *my* husband was the Minister!"

Ponsonby by now, was at the end of his tether and had enough. "You are all wrong!" he announced. "I didn't come here for any of these reasons!"

All of a sudden, there was a pregnant pause. You could have heard a pin drop. Despite their various states of inebriation, they all sobered up for a moment, and waited for what was coming.

"I thought you came because I asked you Rod?" Penny appealed to him. Rod took a deep breath and tried to ignore his pain.

"Don't worry Penny, you will get your Government Finance for the Visitor Centre." Penny showed her appreciation by kissing him warmly on the lips. The ugly sisters were stunned into silence for once. Everyone waited for his next pronouncement.

"I didn't come here as 'Locum' Minister," he continued, as Mary and her mother exchanged audible gasps. "I didn't even come to win the Camanachd Cup!"

Angus, Hector and Hughie choked in their whiskies.

"Well what *did* you come for?" demanded Violet impatiently.

"You wondered why I disappeared from time to time. Well, I wasn't only training with the shinty team. You remember my trips to the local libraries, Elgin District Council Offices and Fort George? Well, I came..." He swallowed hard. "I came...to find...my father!"

There was a breathtaking silence. Before any of the others could react, it was Lizzy who was first to respond. "And we have found your father Mr. Ponsonby!"

Rose blurted out, "And I thought Mr. Ponsonby was the Minister," to which Hector responded by announcing with great authority, "If he was the M-M-M-Minister, then his f-f-f-father... is in heaven!"

"That's right" said Rose reacting enthusiastically "Our Father, which art in heaven, hallowed be thy....."

"Awe shut your mouth!" ordered her exasperated sister.

Ponsonby then asked "Did you say you have found my father?"

Lizzy nodded conspicuously, as Mary opened the drawer and brought out the photograph album, which contained the loose photos that he had given to Lizzy.

"We have indeed Mr Ponsonby" announced Mary, bending down to show him the album.

"You remember how you told Lizzy at Balroonie Castle, that your father served in the Seaforth Highlanders during the War?"

"That's where we s-s-s-served Angus" proclaimed an interested and inebriated Hector.

"Maybe we'll k-k-ken him."

"That's what I'm afraid of Hector" replied his crony.

"You will ken him all right" said Mrs Grant, nodding knowingly.

Mary showed Ponsonby the Regimental Photo and compared it with his own. She pointed out his father, and the resemblance to the photos with his mother, and proclaimed "See there is your mother and father...and look...there is your father in the Regiment...standing next to... his crony." She paused as he looked at Angus and Hector. "You can't mistake him, can you?"

"Is that really my father?" he asked.

"Yes. Look, here is a more recent photo we have."

Ponsonby scanned it carefully while she claimed there was no doubt. He then stared up at Angus and Hector. He hesitated for a moment, then stretched out his arms and greeted his father. "Father!" he called, as Hector rose slowly from his chair, and gracefully fainted!

"I might have known!" said the all-knowing unsympathetic Violet, while Angus took out a handkerchief, and wiped his fevered brow. Ponsonby and Penny looked at the photos, while the ladies gathered round the prostrate figure of Hector.

Mrs Grant was the first to panic as usual, ordering them to loosen his tie, and telling everybody else not to panic! Gloom thought he was going to die, but Doom told her not to be so daft, "as that is the last thing he would do!" Mary told Lizzy to bring a cushion to place under Hector's head, and Rose asked if she could give him the kiss of life. "Do you want to be the death of him?" responded Violet. "Please" pleaded her sister.

Penny was now having a more intimate conversation with Rod Ponsonby. "Is that really the reason you came North with me Rod? I thought you were trying to help us with Government Grants." Ponsonby apologised for disappointing her, but reassured her that not only had he found his father, he had found something much more meaningful and precious, namely her.

The ever alert Violet, even after a few whiskies, had composed herself sufficiently to ask "What is this about Government Grants?"

"Oh dear, what have I said?" Penny was full of remorse. Violet went on, "Since *he* fell in the river, I knew there was something fishy going on."

Lizzy had lifted the cushion and found the letter behind it. She gave the cushion to Mary, to put under Hector's head, and kept the letter behind her back. "Does this mean you won't be able to develop the Boarding House Mary?" enquired her befuddled mother, getting them into deeper water yet again.

"Now what is this about a Boarding House?" Violet, as proprietrix of the nearby Glenbroom Hotel, was on the warpath again.

Mary fretted that she wouldn't even be able to employ Lizzy, while her mother complained this was too much for her heart, and staggered about looking for her pills.

"Don't worry Mary, I will see that you will be all right" said Rod reassuringly.

"So you're not a Minister after all?" Violet concluded.

"Not quite, I'm just an Under Secretary of State" replied Ponsonby. For the first time in her life, Violet seemed impressed.

"And look at the state he's in now" remarked the ever observant Mrs. Grant.

Rose turned her attention to Penny, still on the floor beside Rod, and enquired "I thought you were here on your honeymoon?"

"I am afraid not" replied Penny.

This prompted the ever hopeful Rose to pursue the matter. "Does this mean you are not his wife after all?" Penny shook her head. The expression on Rose's face changed into a lecherous grin, as she came to a conclusion.

"Does that mean he is still single?" as she pointed to Ponsonby, who interrupted her before she got any ideas.

"You are right. We are not here on our honeymoon" he stated, as Penny shook her head. "Although we will be when we come back, after we are married" he amplified, taking Penny's hand. She could hardly believe her ears.

Lizzy said "Excuse me?" but no one paid any attention, except Violet, who told her to be quiet. She then proceeded to ask Mary what she had been up to. "What are those Government Grants for?" she demanded to know. Hughie who was on his hands and knees looking after a gradually recovering Hector, then announced,

"I think he is coming too."

"Where are we going to now?" asked a totally confused Lizzy.

"I mean, I think he's coming round".

At that, the Doctor sat up and responded, "Whose round? I'll have a Double Scotch...on the Rocks!"

Lizzy tried to gain their attention again. "Esschuse me!" she cried, without success. Violet told her not to interrupt. Rod asked his father if he was all right, to which Hector replied that he was not feeling well and had a ringing in his ears. At that, Mrs Grant responded, that he was as sound as a bell. She concluded there was nothing wrong with him, as Hughie, despite his plaster cast, and Angus, helped the former Doctor to a chair.

Lizzy tried to attract attention once again. "Essschuse mee!" she called out.

"What is it now Lizzy?" asked Mary, realizing that the maid had something to say.

"This letter!" said Lizzy.

"What about it?" replied her boss.

"It's for you-hoo."

She was told by Mary, to never mind that now for "We have a crisis on our hands."

"I'll say you have" agreed Violet. Mrs Grant, who had been attending Hector, now needed a seat, and Hector followed her example by making his way unsteadily to the toilet.

Despite the lack of encouragement, Lizzy persevered and said, "This letter. It came a few days ago, after the phone call." This reminded her boyfriend Hughie, as he recalled, "Oh yes, when we were rehearsing? The one from Mr. Knox, from Littlewoods?"

"Aye. I had forgotten all about it."

"Don't tell me it's from the pools Lizzy?" asked the judgemental Violet.

There was a prolonged silence, as the maid looked embarrassed. "Well?" pursued the impatient Matriarch. "You told me not to tell you" replied the timorous maid. Mary took the letter.

"Lord have mercy on us" cried an incredulous Mrs Grant. "Surely you don't do the pools Mary?" Before her daughter could reply, Rose intimated "That...is gambling." Mary grabbed the letter from Lizzy, as Doom warned her, to be sure her sins would find her out...and her "A daughter of the manse too!"

The news of the letter from Littlewoods caused considerable interest from Angus, and noticeable disgust from Mrs Grant.

"Your father will be turning in his grave!" declared Mrs Grant, once more looking for her pills.

"Where are my pills?" she asked as she rose with great care, to look for them.

Angus poured another glass and gave it to Lizzy, but she already had a glass in her other hand. Lizzy thought it was very generous of Angus to give her another, and had difficulty deciding which to drink first.

As she searched unsteadily for her medicine, Mrs Grant continued "When I think of all these years when we brought you up in the fear of the Lord, and to walk in the straight and narrow..." as she staggered from side to side, "...if only *I* could."

Lizzy was about to drink from the glass, when Angus indicated that it was for Mrs Grant, as he passed her the pills. The maid then ultimately succeeded in passing the glass and the pills to the old lady as they both swayed to and fro, trying to make contact. Mrs Grant took a pill and swallowed it with a generous dram, and continued her diatribe. "We always told you gambling was a sin Mary" as she hiccupped. "Here, that's good whisky" she observed, taking a second pill accompanied by another substantial mouthful.

Mary had opened the letter, but had not read the contents as she listened to her mother. Angus took it from her, and by this time Mrs Grant was in full flow. "This is too much for me...not the whisky mind you...it has been one damn dram....one thing after another." She hiccupped again.

"All these accidents!...I suppose Hector will say this one was an accident!" She pointed to Ponsonby and had another drink.

"Yes indeed, indeed yes" agreed Angus, mimicking his crony.

"I used to think everything happened in threes, but now, I've lost count of everything that's gone wrong" She hiccupped again. "And if you now tell me Mary...that you have been doing the pills...the pools..." she emptied the glass, "Well, that is more than I can shtand!" As she staggered, she concluded "Sho I shall shit – - sit!" and she did.

Her daughter tried to explain "I only did it to get money for the Boarding House." Mary's admission was too much. Mrs Grant tried to rise from her chair saying, "Well I am fleeing...leaving. I am not staying a moment longer in this house of sin...this den of antiquity." She felt dizzy and slumped back in her chair, complaining of a sore head. Mary told her to stay where she was, while Angus said "Let her go if she wants."

Rose, who was half-cut herself, announced "*She*...has had too much to drink," but Mrs Grant defended herself,

"I am not under the affluence of incahol as some tinkle peep I am!"

"She *is* drunk!" asserted Rose.

Such an assertion brought the old lady to her feet once more, "I tell you, I am *not* draff as hunk as you might drink! I heel so fellish, I feel so...I don't know who is mee...and the drunker I stand here, the longer I get!" She was quite overcome with emotion, and with that, she swayed and slowly but surely, made for the cupboard to put on her coat.

Violet, who had been uncharacteristically stunned into silence, then pronounced "She has had one over the eight if you ask me!"

It had taken Angus longer than usual to absorb the contents of the letter, and he read it twice to make sure. He started jumping round the room, "And you have won, one over the eight too Mary! he announced excitedly. "You have won Eight hundred and Ninety Thousand Pounds!"

He swept his wife off her feet and swung her round in exultation. Doom and Gloom were speechless... once again. One looked doomed and the other looked gloomy. They could not believe their ears. Mrs Grant, who was on the point of reaching the cupboard, turned immediately, and said soberly, "On second thoughts...I will stay!"

The toilet cistern flushed and Hector, who had been in this situation before, tried to open the door. Lizzy and Hughie returned to the kitchen for the screwdriver and ladders, while Violet asked Mary what she was going to do with all that money? "Let me out!" shouted Hector.

"I shall get rid of that toilet for a start!" replied Mary. "I shall install a reception desk and then I shall modernise the kitchen, install en suite facilities in all the bedrooms... and...I shall build an extension, to make it the best Boarding House in the area!"

"Are you really serious? A Boarding House?" said Violet taken aback.

"Like ours?" added Rose.

"No" replied Mary, and the ugly sisters breathed a sigh of relief.

"Far Better!" intimated Mary with authority.

"Let me out!" called the frustrated Hector once again. Rose offered to go to his aid, while her older sister complained "But you can't do that Mary. We have always had the best Boarding House in the area."

"For four generations" added her sister as she tried to open the door.

"It's time for a change then!" responded Mary with an air of finality.

Rose opened the toilet door and Hector came out more than a little relieved. Without warning, Rose grabbed him, and dragged him back into the toilet with her, and slammed the door shut!

Mary, for once had the upper hand over her neighbour from Glenbroom, and was determined to get her own back. She then expounded all her ideas for an extension to the front of the house, new carpets and furnishings etc. until even Violet could take it no longer. She picked up the collecting can for which she came, and stomped out the front door in high dudgeon.

Meanwhile Rod Ponsonby and Penny were in quiet conversation on their own. Rod suggested that Mary wouldn't need him now, whereupon Penny made it abundantly clear that *she* did.

"And not just for the money for developing the Visitor Centre!" she said, stroking his brow.

"Poor Rod. When I think of all that you have gone through since coming to Scotland. How could I not love you?"

"Do you really mean that?" asked Rod, warming to her again.

"Of course I do."

She then reminded him of his two soakings at Gretna and Fisherman's Folly, nearly being arrested for indecent exposure, being trampled over by a flock of sheep, shooting Hughie in the foot and now all these injuries at the Camanachd Cup Final, she couldn't help feeling sorry for him. It was time he had someone to look after him. He had come through them all, and more, and had persevered through thick and thin, without complaint, and had helped Glendivot win the Cup, so what more could she ask? He even offered to marry her.

She then put her arms round his neck and gently kissed him. He was just relieved that she had not mentioned his narrow escape with the school cleaner in the washrooms. As for landing in the nettles, that was just the sting in the tail (tale). The bruised head caused by his encounter with the car windscreen and the cut hand inflicted by the charging flock of sheep were mere details. There was simply no question. He admitted he needed someone to take care of him!

"I wouldn't have changed a thing" he whispered as they kissed again.

"Really?" replied Penny, slightly surprised. "Wouldn't you?"

"Have you forgotten already?" he smiled. "We are... supposed to be on our honeymoon!"

They smiled at each other as their foreheads met, and they embraced once more. Lizzy and Hughie returned with the ladders and screwdriver, when suddenly there was a loud scream from the toilet. The door opened without difficulty, and Hector came out faster than he went in. He had clearly sobered up, and was chased out the front door by Rose. "Help! Get her off me!"" he yelled. He had obviously lost his stammer.

Angus wakened Mrs Grant, who had dozed off again. He waived the Littlewoods cheque at her and announced "Look Grannie! Now we can afford to put you in the Old Folk's Home!" The old lady, disgusted, rose and went for her coat in the cupboard.

"I am leaving. Where is my coat?" she asked as she opened the door. It was then, the poor dear was frightened out her wits, by the sight of the skeleton hanging behind the door! Angus gave her the coat, and chased her out the front door, with the skeleton.

Chapter 36

THE 'HOOLIE'

That evening the Glendivot Community Hall was bedecked in the red and white colours of their victorious shinty team. Banners were strewn across the hall acclaiming the team, both individually and collectively. Team and individual players' photographs covered the walls. A full blown Ceilidh was in full swing. Everybody and anybody from Glendivot and the surrounding area was there.

The place was a heaving mass of humanity, celebrating as they had never celebrated before. There was even an overflow party taking place in the car park outside, as mercifully, many of the supporters had sensibly left their cars at home. They could not get into the hall. This was the first time their team had won the Camanachd Cup, and they were not going to forget the occasion!

The inhabitants of this epicentre of the whisky industry knew how to party, and this was the party to end all parties. It would go down in history, and every second person had a camera to record it for posterity. The local press were there, and even a reporter from the local radio station came to interview those who were sober enough to be coherent. He had his work cut out.

All the local distilleries were falling over themselves to sponsor the event with their own unique products, while all the participants were falling over themselves, enjoying their hospitality. Some of the worst cases no doubt ended in the hospital.

The finest Scottish Dance Band in the area was in full swing, and all and sundry were giving it everything in 'The Dashing White Sergeant.' As the dance progressed, any pretence at elegance went out the window, and by the end, couples were legless, either through over-enthusiasm or over-indulgence.

The Camanachd Cup was displayed prominently on a dias in the centre of the stage, and at the appropriate time it was filled with the local 'cratur.' The whole team, their reserves and backroom staff, rejoiced by passing it from one to another, each consuming its contents with great enthusiasm.

The local girls had a ball flinging themselves at the players in adulation, and fawning over their own particular favourites. The players responded with alacrity, and passion, making the most of their moment of triumph. No doubt some boys became men that night. It didn't matter if they were married or not. Not at least until later!

The ladies of the village excelled themselves with the excellent purvey they provided. They were experienced enough to know how to fill the stomachs with pastas and pizzas for the celebrants, in order to absorb at least some of the alcohol consumed. Otherwise the night was bound to end up in one unholy punch-up, particularly if it was infiltrated by too many neighbours from Glenbroom!

Penny had taken Rod to the local Cottage Hospital to get patched up, while the rest of Balroonie House naturally attended, including Angus, Mary and her mother. He and his mother-in-law had made their peace in the euphoria of the occasion. Lizzy and Hughie took every opportunity to dance the night away, until Hughie had to give up, due to complaints from other dancers, who didn't appreciate their feet being trodden on by his heavy plaster cast.

In actual fact, he was quite relieved, for he would otherwise have had to retire due to sheer fatigue, after dragging his plaster cast round the dance floor for as long as he could. Scottish Country Dances are designed for the light of foot, and energetic at the best of times.

Lizzy, who was in a state of exuberant intoxication, then danced with everybody she could get her hands on, until she too, didn't know whether she was coming or going in the 'Eightsome Reel' and 'Strip the Willow.' She too, became so exhausted that she finished up in a corner, canoodling with her boyfriend, and sympathising with his affliction. She had a great time.

Hector was in his element going round everyone, toasting the team without stammering for the first time in his life, handing out cigars and boasting "I am a father!" His friends could not believe it, and wondered what he had been up to since he retired. He was quite oblivious to the remarks and accusations to which he was subjected. Someone suggested they started a 'Book' on who was the mother, while he didn't give a.... he didn't care, as the effects of the alcohol gradually overcame him.

He very quickly sobered up when to his utter amazement, Rose Hannah appeared through the crowd, searching for him! Clearly, she had escaped the shackles of her sister, and had persuaded Thomas to run her to the 'Hoolie', to join the celebrations, and to find Hector. She wasn't fussy. As far as she was concerned, he was about the only eligible bachelor left in the village, and beggars can't be choosers!

Thomas agreed to help her, on two conditions. One was that he would not be expected to appear himself, for he had not got over his experience as the 'Lady in the tweed suit.' The second was that on no account would she tell Violet that he had anything to do with it.

If Doom found out that Rose had 'Escaped' even for this one special night, he demanded to be exonerated from any culpability. Rose had reached the stage that now was the time to strike out for freedom, so, with a 'Braveheart', she accepted his conditions, and put a couple of sleeping pills in Violet's coffee after dinner. Doom was accordingly none the wiser, as she slept it off in her favourite chair.

The highlight of the evening came when Penny joined the party with Rod Ponsonby on crutches, which they had borrowed from the Cottage Hospital. In case anyone was unaware, or in no fit state to understand, Angus stopped proceedings, and announced to everyone that Rod was their 'Man of the Match', and they all formed a circle round him, and sang "For he's a jolly good fellow."

Rod thanked everyone for their support, and intimated how much he had enjoyed his visit to Scotland, despite all his trials and tribulations, suffering and pain. Penny had wanted it to be an 'Unforgettable' visit, and it certainly was. If he hadn't come and endured all his experiences, he would never have fallen in love! He would never forget that. He then announced their intention to be married.

By this time, even those who had been partying outside, squeezed into the over-crowded hall. They joined the circle round the young couple, who persuaded Angus and Mary to join them, as the whole assembly launched into another chorus of:

"For they are jolly good fellows,
For they are jolly good fellows,
For they are jolly good fellows;
And so say all of us,
And so say all of us,
And so say all of us
For they are jolly good fellows
For they are jolly good fellows,
For they are jolly good fellows,
And so say all of us."

During the singing, Angus was moved to tears. He even showed some magnanimity towards Mary, his long suffering wife. He put his arm round her shoulder, and thanked her for the best Birthday present he could ever have imagined. He even gave her a very public, gentle loving and appreciative kiss!

There was a round of raucous applause, and Rod limped forward once more. He thanked everyone, and announced that he and Penny would be returning to London in the morning, but they would return to

Glendivot on their 'Proper' honeymoon! He then asked his father to join him, and led them all in a rousing chorus of:

"We're no' awa' te bide awa'.
We're no' awa' te leave ye,
We're no' awa' te bide awa',
We'll aye come back and see ye."

THE END

POSTSCRIPT:
I hope you enjoyed the book. If you did, may I suggest that it would make an ideal Christmas or Birthday present, perhaps with a miniature or more of the amber nectar to go with it.

Roy McCormick

Scotch on the Rocks is available from

www.ypdbooks.com

or email enqs@yps-publishing.co.uk

or by post to York Publishing Services
64 Hallfield Road, Layerthorpe, York, YO31 7ZQ
Tel: 01904 431213